HIGHLANDER'S CLAIM

Called by a Highlander Book Nine

MARIAH STONE

Stone
Publishing

GET A FREE MARIAH STONE BOOK!

Join Mariah's mailing list to be the first to know of new releases, free books, special prices, and other author giveaways.

freehistoricalromancebooks.com

ALSO BY MARIAH STONE

MARIAH'S TIME TRAVEL ROMANCE SERIES

- CALLED BY A HIGHLANDER
- CALLED BY A VIKING
- CALLED BY A PIRATE
- FATED

~

MARIAH'S REGENCY ROMANCE SERIES

- DUKES AND SECRETS

~

VIEW ALL OF MARIAH'S BOOKS IN READING ORDER

Scan the QR code for the complete list of Mariah's ebooks, paperbacks, and audiobooks in reading order.

"Doubt thou the stars are fire; Doubt that the sun doth move; Doubt truth to be a liar; But never doubt I love."
    —W. Shakespeare

PROLOGUE

"Aulay, dinna fash. God willing, she will pull through," came his brother Èoin's voice, and Aulay MacDonald looked up from his cup of *uisge*.

Èoin sat by his side at the long table, the fires of the braziers playing against his deep wrinkles, his grief-stricken eyes hiding in the shadows. Around the table, Aulay's six closest warriors sat, everyone's hands curled around cups of uisge.

Beathan, one of his closest friends, was among them. His mouth curved in a smile under his short, dark beard. He laid a supporting palm on Aulay's shoulder and squeezed. "God always has a plan."

The great hall of Dunyvaig Castle with its high cathedral ceilings was quiet and dark. Flickering firelight from the braziers cast feral shadows upon the tapestries of the MacDonald crest that hung on two long walls, six on each side. A dozen red fists holding a dozen crosses didn't fill Aulay's chest with pride as it did most days.

They seemed to judge him. He shouldn't be here, they said.

He should be up on the next floor, in his bedchamber where his wife may be dying in labor.

And there was not a bloody thing he could do about it.

Burning wood crackled. The whisper of the waves came from the slit windows, bringing the salty scent of the sea and algae. Through that quiet, the disturbance of what was going on above assailed his ears...the shuffling of the feet, his wife's agonized moans, and the worried voices of the midwives.

Aulay did his best to shut them out. He could not help Leitis, no matter how much he wanted to.

And yet, he needed to do something useful. He was a man of action, the laird of his clan, and simply sitting and waiting for Leitis to give birth was torture. This was her seventh. She had survived six previous stillbirths and miscarriages.

But Bhatair, the clan's physician, and the midwives had never been as worried as they were now.

So, he needed to be useful. He needed to do something that would bring hope. Plan Colum's rescue with his clansmen.

The place at his right hand was empty. It was Colum's—Èoin's oldest son and the closest Aulay had to an heir.

Aulay brought the cup to his mouth and threw the uisge back into his throat. The alcohol burned in a fiery kick.

"We find Colum," he said through a hoarse throat, meeting Èoin's dark gaze. "Losing him was like losing my own son..." He suppressed the sick, sinking feeling of an impending disaster in his gut. "I dinna ken yet how, but we will. We send out the spies. We quietly ask the common folk. We lie and pay gold and do everything that we can."

Èoin nodded. "Thank ye, brother."

Aulay stared into the brazier. "What do we ken?" he asked to distract himself.

"We ken he was taken by the Earl of Pembroke," said Seoras, Colum's younger brother. "He gathered all the surviving wounded."

"Aye," said Èoin, looking at his younger son with something

like reverence. "We're lucky he wasna killed like so many. And I am so glad ye're still alive."

"We all are," said Aulay.

A long, loud female moan from upstairs made him shudder. The men all glanced at him with worry. His fist curled around his cup, and he squeezed it to stop himself from jumping up and hurrying up the stairs to her.

He shouldn't be jealous of his brother, who had two sons and a daughter. While Aulay had dug six wee graves for his six dead bairns, Èoin had never had to do that.

In his forty-four years of life, all Aulay had wanted was a family. He'd worked hard to build a strong clan and keep it together. He was not a young man anymore. He wanted to leave a legacy behind. Perhaps, today his heir would finally be born.

Or he'd lose the bairn and the love of his life forever.

"Uncle!" his twelve-year-old niece, Anna, called. She had completely changed in the two moons since meeting her father, Robert the Bruce, for the first time. Gone was the girl who ran with the village children and shepherds. Now she was like Laoghaire, Èoin's daughter. A small noble lady in the making. Her hair was done in two pretty buns, one on each side of her face. The dress she wore was clean and new. Her face and hands didn't bear any signs of dirt or dust.

He jumped up.

"Come!" Anna urged. "She's close."

The hall went completely still. Everyone here had lived with Aulay through the six devastating pregnancies. The six wee funerals that followed.

Could this be the one time that Aulay would hear his bairn cry, would feel the wee fist squeezing his finger?

His brother rose. "Go, Aulay." He squeezed his shoulder. "'Tis going to be all right."

"God bless, Uncle," Seoras said and clapped him on the back.

Beathan and the rest of them murmured their words of support. Encouragement. As Aulay marched with long strides out of the hall, he knew everyone wanted them to have a healthy baby.

He flew up the flight of stairs like the wind. His gut twisted in anticipation, in premonition as he opened the door to their bedchamber.

His stomach dropped. Dressed only in her undertunic, Leitis crouched over their bed, supported by a midwife on each side, as Bhatair pressed on her round stomach. Leitis half screamed and half roared. Dark hair misted her face like wet seaweed. She was pale, so pale. Blood bloomed on her undertunic below her large belly.

Aulay was rooted to the spot. The room reeked of an iron tang...it was all that blood. He remembered the day they met before the priest in front of the church for their wedding. He'd been a young man of twenty-four, and hopeful for a good match, which his father had arranged. And he'd been lightning struck by her beauty, by the unyielding pride in her eyes.

A few days into their marriage, he knew this woman had been made to be his wife...as he'd been born to be her husband and protector.

But in the years that followed, every time he'd raised a wee cross over the wee grave of one of his bairns, part of his soul had been buried with them. And now, twenty years later, the love of his life may be dying. Twenty Christmases together... Twenty summers... Countless mornings he'd woken up to her... The woman he'd thought he'd raise his children with. The woman he'd thought he'd die next to.

Only, he wasn't going to.

Because she may be gone tonight.

"Aaaaaaaargh..." Her pained cry tore his own gut apart.

"Dinna push, lass!" yelled Bhatair. "Dinna push!"

"I canna stop..." Her cry was feral, like a wild lynx out of control. "My body...aaaarghhh...my body must!"

"Try nae to, lass," said the midwife to her right. "Breathe through it."

Leitis locked her eyes with Aulay's. He thought that through the pain and agony of the birth, the feral animal in her had retreated, and for a few moments, his wife was back. His Leitis who could laugh like no one else. His Leitis who had built an orphanage in the clan. His Leitis who breathed one breath with him.

"Ye can do it, lass," he said as he walked to her and took her hand in his. "Ye can. Breathe."

She nodded and took a long breath with him. He breathed one breath with her once again.

"Good, Leitis," Bhatair said. "Turn over. I'm going to try to turn the bairn again. Ye're opened up. Its buttocks are at yer entrance. Can ye hold on and nae push for a wee bit longer?"

She never took her eyes from Aulay's. Hope bloomed in his chest as he knew it bloomed in hers. "Aye," she said. "I can."

Aulay helped her climb onto the bed and she sat reclining against the pillows. They breathed together as Bhatair pressed on her round stomach and twisted it. He saw it happen, the moment she snapped. The moment breathing wasn't enough, and the pain took over. The tranquility of the bubble around them tore. Her face wrinkled in a grimace of pain, she opened her mouth and screamed.

Aulay's very bones hurt from the sound. Her mouth opened wide, black and round. Then her scream strained, as though she was tensing once again. Then blood gushed down her thighs, spreading across the sheets of the bed and soaking through her white undertunic like fire consuming kindling.

"Dinna push! Dinna push!"

The rest was a blur. Aulay wished he would remember the last few minutes of his wife's life. The last few minutes of her breathing, of her eyes being able to see him. Of her skin being warm to the touch, her mouth moving. Of knowing she was still here, with him.

But it all sank into a haze, a fog.

When he could think again, cold morning light poured from

the slit windows of the bedchamber onto her grayish, unmoving body in his arms.

The first thing he became aware of was the quiet. That scream of hers that hurt his ears and tore his soul apart was no more.

Then he wished for the scream to return. He'd do anything to hear her make a single sound.

Because the body in his arms was cold. Heavy. Silent.

As the cries of seagulls and the whisper of the sea reached his ears again through the slit windows, he felt numb. He wondered why he wasn't hurting.

Somewhere through those moments he couldn't remember, the moment his wife's soul had left her body, his soul must have left, too.

And perhaps, even though he sat upright and held her and felt alive, he really wasn't.

Perhaps, together with Leitis and his seventh child, he had died.

Only, he didn't know it yet.

One thing he did know was that he would never love again.

CHAPTER 1

IRISH SEA near Isle of Achleith, Scotland, July 2022

DR. JENNIFER FOSTER SPREAD HER RIGHT ARM INTO THE SPACE beyond the charter boat. As seawater sprinkled all over her face and her bright, salad-green and lemon-yellow dress with purple flowers, she squealed.

Her girlfriends, sitting by her side at the end of the boat, squealed with her. They all held plastic champagne glasses.

"Shh," said Natalie drunkenly, "your champagne is sticking out."

Natalie made a movement to shove the dark-green neck of the bottle back into Amanda's purse, but her hand slipped, and she giggled. So did Jenny, Kyla, and Amanda.

"I don't think MacGrumpy over there will tell MacBoss," said Amanda, then drank the rest of her champagne from the glass in one gulp and took the bottle back out from her purse. "Not for the tip we're going to give him."

While Amanda poured more bubbly into her glass, the boat jumped on the waves, and she poured half of her serving onto the deck. Jenny raised her glass.

"Here's to us," Jenny toasted. "Four strong, independent women in their prime! We have our careers, our money, and can eat our cake, too!"

"Yeah!" echoed her girlfriends, clinking their four glasses together.

Amanda added over the edge of her glass, "And to the sexy Scottish guys I've been banging for a week... And Jenny has not!"

Jenny flashed a glare at her best friend but said nothing. She threw back the drink and the bubbles tickled her throat. "I also did not get divorced recently."

"Not recently," said Kyla as she tucked her shining, dark hair behind her ear. "You did three years ago, and you still haven't slept with anybody."

Jenny scoffed. "Pfff. Like it's a bad thing."

"Excuse me!" cried Amanda as she struggled to keep her blond hair out of her eyes. "Sweetie, I love you, but you sound a little judgmental."

Natalie looked between them. She was sporting gorgeous designer sunglasses and a bright-red sundress that was striking against her dark skin. After a week away from her two kids, with more hours to sleep and time to breathe, she looked fresh and full of energy. "Girls, don't fight. I know what'll help!" She took the bottle of champagne from Amanda's hand. "This!"

As she poured more champagne, emptying the bottle, Jenny glanced at her and at Kyla. "I always wanted what Kyla and Natalie have. Kids. Family. And yet, I'm thirty-nine, and..."

She trailed off, unable to say the words. The brilliant blue sky —so rare for Scotland—and the sapphire seawater hurt her eyes. Tightness in her throat didn't let any words out.

What she wanted to say was, she was thirty-nine and her time was running out. She had had three unsuccessful IVF rounds with a sperm donor in the past two years. The IVF failed to implant because of her endometriosis, no doubt, an incredibly painful condition she had lived with her whole life. Her periods had been agony. She had learned to manage it and live with it, but the worst thing was that her chance of getting pregnant and carrying her own child in a natural way was very small.

Her last chance to have her own baby was in fourteen days. The fertility clinic was booked a year in advance, and that was the only time slot they had for her to start the hormone treatment to extract her last viable eggs and freeze them.

She couldn't even think about sleeping with anyone...

"*And*," Amanda continued for her after a long pause, "you're one of the most sought-after private pediatric doctors in New York City, together with me, your partner. You and I have a thriving practice, help a lot of kids get well, and...excuse me for bragging, but we're not exactly hurting for money."

"Amanda!" said Natalie.

"Oh, come on," said Kyla. "It's not like they're using the kids. They deserve their success. It's you and I who are stuck at home wiping snotty noses and chasing after preschoolers."

Jenny smiled. "I want to chase after preschoolers," she said to Natalie and Kyla.

Her life felt incomplete without a child of her own. Something big and sweet was missing, and that emptiness was like a giant hole in her soul that sucked and ached.

"But you don't want to give up your clinic, do you?" asked Natalie. "Amanda and you have been building it for ten years."

Jenny gave out an uncomfortable laugh. Suddenly, it was all becoming too serious and too much to the point. Through the roar of the boat's engine and the noise of the waves crashing against its sides, the voice of her ex-husband was trying to break through in her mind. *Deep down, deep, deep down, men want to take care of women and women want to be taken care of. If only you worked less and spent more time with me...if only we'd started a family earlier...*

And he had started on a family—only, without Jenny. He had a two-year-old daughter now and his new wife was a stay-at-home mom. Exactly how he wanted his relationship to be.

And Jenny...Jenny had zero little girls, only a handful of eggs left, one empty apartment, and a terrifying, sinking feeling in the pit of her stomach that she was too late. That she'd never have her own baby to hold and to adore, to inhale that dear, sweet baby smell.

That Tom had been right. That it was all her fault. All of it. Had she given in and let him take charge and sold her part of the clinic to Amanda, she could have spent more time with him. He wouldn't have cheated on her. They'd still be together. Had she started trying to get pregnant at thirty-two, like he'd suggested, she'd have her own little girl or boy to love and to spoil. A little girl or boy with Jenny's naturally pale red hair and Tom's green eyes.

"And I admire you so much," said Kyla. "You and Amanda achieved what I have dreamed of but didn't dare. And yet the four of us went to the same medical school."

Jenny sighed. "I'm the one envious of what you have," she said. "All of you have kids. Even if your marriage didn't work out, Amanda, you still have a son. And you, Natalie and Kyla, you have happy families. It's most likely too late for me."

"Don't say that," Kyla said. "Women get pregnant in their late thirties and early forties all the time. Cameron Diaz had a baby at forty-seven. Naomi Campbell gave birth at fifty."

The boat jumped over a wave and Jenny's chin rattled. "Yes, but—"

Amanda linked her arm through Jenny's. "Here's what we'll do." She pointed at the sea. "The moment we step on that Irish coast, we go to a pub. And this time, you will come."

"I came to the pubs in Scotland."

"Yeah, right. I mean, this time, you will flirt with hot Irish men, and you'll have lots of sex with them—yes, *multiple* them— and if you get knocked up...well...oops."

The ladies giggled. "Amanda, don't be silly," said Natalie. "She won't get knocked up by an Irish guy."

"Because she should get knocked up by one of those High-landers back in Scotland..." said Kyla over the glass of champagne.

They all laughed. It seemed Jenny was the only one who didn't feel the humor.

"Oh yeah," Amanda said. "As someone who's tried the local cuisine multiple times...and tasted multiple dishes, if you get my meaning...I can highly recommend it."

"We can even extend our holiday!" cried Natalie, raising her glass. "Yes, we have one week left, but we can just return to Scotland for a few more days..."

"Actually, we can't," said Jenny. "I have an appointment in two weeks to start the hormone treatment for egg extraction."

The smiles on the girls' faces fell. "Really? Has it come to that?" Kyla asked.

"Yeah. I only have ten more eggs left, and this is my last chance to have my own baby. And I'd still need to use a surrogate."

They were all silent, looking at her with pity.

"Come on," Jenny forced out with a smile. "Cheer up. Enough about me. We are celebrating Amanda's divorce. Even if it's not in warm and sunny Hawaii."

"That's the spirit!" cheered Natalie.

Amanda rolled her eyes. "I picked Scotland and Ireland because I wanted 'real men' who will take charge and call me 'lass' and make me forget everything. And let me tell you, Highlanders do exactly that."

Jenny giggled. "Oh yeah? I'll stick with Hawaii, where men are gentler and take care of you."

"Oh, believe me, Scottish men can take care of you very well." Amanda winked.

The roar of the ferry motor huffed and puffed. The boat jerked to a halt. Then started again. Then the roar turned to a weak droning and the boat stopped. As they rocked gently on the waves and the vibration of the motor that she had felt for the past hour died down, Jenny had the disorienting feeling of the floor moving under her feet.

There was nothing but open sea all around them, except for a small island with a lighthouse that rose above the water about five hundred feet away. The island was rocky, with an oval top, like a giant head sticking out of the sea. It must be about three hundred feet high and five hundred feet long. Typical for Scottish landscapes, green and yellow moss covered the steep slopes.

"What's going on?" muttered Amanda.

The motor started again, and the boat moved but then died. Then again. This repeated six or seven more times before the captain's door opened and the boatswain stepped onto the deck. He was a man in his sixties, with a balding head of gray hair and a short, gray beard over a sullen, deeply wrinkled face.

"Tough luck, lasses," he grumbled. "Captain says the motor may have died. We will have to dock at Achleith and wait for a coast guard rescue boat from Islay. I doubt ye make it to Ireland today. While the captain waits, I will take ye to Achleith so that ye dinna fall overboard from yer drinking. There's an ancient ruin with an interesting rock that people on Islay believe is a home of the faeries."

"Sounds good," Jenny said and then looked at her girlfriends. "Does that sound like a celebration to you?"

"Sure," said Natalie and stretched her arms out. "I'll take any adventure before I have to go back to my happy, boring reality."

"If we go back to Islay," said Amanda, "Jenny's having sex with some Highlanders."

Jenny giggled and shook her head.

The boatswain went back into the captain's cabin and with more whirs and low droning and stopping of the motor, he directed the boat towards the island.

When they finally stopped close to the island, Jenny realized there weren't even any trees or bushes. Just green moss and cliffs and the lighthouse. The boatswain helped them into the dinghy and rowed them to the gravelly beach.

Once they stood on the firm ground, Jenny regretted her choice of flip-flops and the thin, floaty satin dress with patterns of bright, spring-green leaves and—a tribute to Scotland—violet flowers. Even in July the wind was cool, and it flapped her skirt around, leaving her short legs covered in goose bumps. She could feel every pebble and rock through the soles of her flip-flops. The four of them took selfies all together with the boat anchored several dozen feet away and the island looming over them like a giant cork head. She realized she'd forgotten her purse, which held her phone, back on the boat and felt strangely naked without it.

"Well," Amanda said as she took another bottle of champagne out of her bottomless designer purse, "the mood is kind of a bummer. It's an adventure, girls! Come on, let's keep the party going."

Jenny woo-hooed, and, despite the odd looks from her girlfriends, they were good sports and echoed her as Amanda popped the cork and poured champagne into four plastic glasses.

"To celebration!" cried Jenny as the four of them brought their glasses together high up in the air and drank.

Giggling, they made their way up the steep slope. The damn flip-flops slipped, and her feet threatened to slide out of them.

The top of the island was round and covered with moss and grass. The old lighthouse stood on the north side. Its white paint was chipped, and cracks ran between the brown bricks. Based on the broken glass of the lantern panes, it was probably not even functioning.

It was all so breathtakingly beautiful, the piece of land she stood on tiny compared to the vast sky and the endless sea. And her best friends were right by her side.

"I'm so thankful for you, girls," she said. "And am so glad we're on this adventure together."

With her head spinning, Jenny hugged Amanda and Natalie by their waists. Amanda hooked her arm around Kyla's shoulders and the four of them stood and breathed and looked at the sea around them. Seagulls squawked and wheeled over their heads.

"To many more adventures!" Natalie raised her glass.

"Hear! Hear!" the three of them echoed.

"Even if no one comes and we die here!" announced Amanda. "We'd die together."

They laughed.

"Look, there's that faerie rock that MacGrumpy talked about," said Jenny, looking in the direction of the lighthouse.

When they turned to the rock, a strong wind blew in their faces, bringing the scents of sea and grass and lavender—which was strange as she hadn't seen any lavender on the island.

It was a large, flat boulder sunken into the ground. Around it, Jenny could see other stones protruding from the earth, probably the remnants of some sort of an ancient tower. The rock itself had carvings that Jenny thought could be a river or something...it was hard to concentrate. What she found most interesting was the handprint.

"Oh, look!" said Jenny. "Someone is giving us a high five through that rock!"

They giggled. Jenny stepped closer to the rock and sank to her knees. Amanda followed her and gave a high five to the hand. Natalie giggled and did the same.

"I could almost feel someone high-fiving me back," she said. "Thanks, man."

"Or woman," said Kyla and high-fived the hand, too.

"Oh look, let's go to the other side of the island," Amanda said. "Maybe there's more stony body parts we can high-five."

The girls walked away, but Jenny still wanted to give her own high five. When she put her hand over the rock, the carvings started to glow, and she stopped.

"Cool..." she mumbled, narrowing her eyes to try to see better. "What is that?" She looked over her shoulder. "Hey, girls! Come back! Am I super drunk, or is the rock glowing?"

"It's you, hon!" cried Amanda without turning back. "You're glowing! Because you're beautiful!"

Jenny shook her head with a smile. The scent of lavender and grass became stronger. She looked around. A seagull sat ten feet away from her, watching her glass of champagne with a ferocious curiosity.

"Hey there, little guy. Are you seeing this glowing, too?" she asked. "Maybe you should have the rest of my champagne. Clearly, I had waaay too much."

A shadow fell on Jenny. "Ah, finally, girls, look..." She raised her head.

A redhead in a hooded green cloak stood over her. She smelled strongly of lavender and grass. Where had this woman come from on a deserted island? Hmm...strange.

"You smell nice," Jenny said. "Natural. I like it."

The woman beamed. "Oh, thank ye. No one has ever said that to me. How kind of ye."

"Do you see the glowing, or is it just me?" Jenny asked, pointing at the rock.

The woman giggled. "Oh, I see it, lass. 'Tis me who makes it glow."

Jenny swayed. "Really? How?"

"My name is Sìneag. I help people to go through the river of time and find the person they're destined for."

Jenny blinked. "Really? How?"

"Doesna matter how. What matters is why. There's a person for ye through that stone."

Jenny shook her head. She was *so* drunk. She put her glass down on the grass, and it fell and spilled its contents. "Um... At the expense of repeating myself...again... Really? And how?"

Sìneag bit her lip to stop a smile and sank to her knees next to Jenny. She was so pretty. A delicate, strawberry-shaped face, green eyes with long eyelashes, porcelain-white skin. And those cute freckles on her nose and cheeks. "You're beautiful," Jenny said. "Something about you is so...different. Are you from another time, too? Maybe you're a princess?"

Sìneag chuckled. "I'm nae a princess. I'm a faerie. And the man ye're destined for is the chief of clan MacDonald of Islay, Aulay. A true Highland laird with a big heart."

"And a big kilt…" Jenny giggled. "Sorry. Bad joke. So, he'd love me, you say? And yet, my husband said no man will love me until I stop being so selfish. And when he said selfish, he really meant independent. So, you're saying Aulay would love me even if I worked a lot and didn't give him babies?"

Sineag smiled, but her eyes were sad. "He'd love ye if ye were old and wrinkled and dinna have a hair on yer head, Jenny. A Highlander's love is forever. All ye need to do is place yer hand into the handprint."

Jenny raised her eyebrows and studied the handprint. How drunk was she that she was letting herself believe all this? "So, you're saying if I give a high five to this medieval hand, I'll time travel?"

Sineag nodded. "Aye."

"What about my girlfriends? Do they have a hot Highlander waiting for them? Well… two of them are taken, but Amanda…"

Sineag shrugged and said nothing. Jenny looked back over her shoulder. The three figures of her girlfriends were at the other edge of the island, a hundred or so feet away.

"Let's go time travel, girls!" Jenny cried.

When none of them reacted, she turned back to Sineag.

There was no one.

The seagull was still there, giving her an unblinking stink eye. Wind ruffled its feathers gently.

"Did you see where she went?" Jenny asked.

When the seagull didn't reply, she shrugged, looked at the glowing rock, and high-fived the hand.

Only, instead of solid, cold rock, her palm went through empty air and fell forward and down into darkness. She screamed and flapped her arms and legs, trying to hold on to something, but there was nothing but wet, cold, damp air. And then she sank into oblivion.

CHAPTER 2

Isle of Achleith, July 1313

Jenny woke up with a jerk. She was cold and her head hurt. The dry, pasty taste in her mouth told her she was dehydrated. Her head spun like the blades of a helicopter. She pushed herself up off the grass, and the wind threw her own hair into her face as she tried to untangle the long strands from her eyelashes.

"Oh gosh..." she murmured, holding on to her pounding head and looking around. "Where the hell am I?"

Next to her hand that pressed against the grass lay a coin covered in dirt. It was thick and the edge was uneven, not the perfect circle of modern coins. Her mind sluggish, she picked it up and looked at it, struggling to remember why she was here and what this coin had to do with it. She turned it around in her hand, thinking...

And then she remembered. Amanda and the girls... Champagne... Oh dear God, so much champagne... The boat broke down...

And then, a woman whose name she couldn't remember saying something about her true love being a Highlander who lived back in time, then high-fiving the stone, joking about traveling in time to meet her soul mate or whatever. There it was, the rock, a foot away from her.

Completely forgetting the coin in her hand, she put it into the pocket of her dress. She needed to find her friends. And the boat. Jenny groaned as she scrambled to her weak feet. There was nothing around her but a piece of mossy, grassy, and rocky land about a hundred feet wide and the sea—all around her as far as she could see.

Where was the boat? And the girls? "Amanda!" she called. "Natalie! Kyla!"

No one replied. They must be already on the boat. Why didn't they take her, especially if they saw she'd passed out? Seagulls squawked over her head, and she remembered something about a seagull sitting and watching her. As she walked to the edge of the cliff to see where the boat was, she realized something else was totally missing.

The surface of the island was completely empty. A cold droplet of sweat crawled down her spine.

"Where the hell is the lighthouse?" she cried, looking around.

But she wasn't completely alone. Some distance away, there was a ship. She narrowed her eyes, trying to make sure she was seeing what she was seeing... It had a sail. A single, square sail. Was that a sailboat? No, it looked like a Viking ship, not that she knew much about history... The sail looked yellowish, with some sort of a red symbol across it.

"What the hell?" she said to herself.

Her head pounded. Maybe she was still drunk, although what she felt was much more like a hangover. She looked down the cliff. The gravel beach lay at the base of the slope.

And there was no boat. No dinghy.

And not a single person in sight.

Panic paralyzed her.

Except for the seagulls that would feast on her dead body,

there was only one living thing in this vastness of sea and a tiny piece of barren land.

Whoever was on that damn Viking boat.

"Heeeeelp!"

AULAY BRACED HIS LEGS AGAINST THE MOVEMENT AS THE SHIP sank and rose on the waves. The sea was grayish blue around them, white-crested waves appearing here and there, like sheep in a field. The breeze blew into his face, tickling his beard and bringing the scent of the sea into his nostrils. The sail of his ship, *Tagradh*, which meant "claim," flapped above their heads. The men's eyes kept scanning the sea.

After days of searching, he was starting to worry they wouldn't find the wrecked English ship bearing a king's treasure of gold, armor, and weapons. But the Isle of Achleith had caught many a ship on its rocky shores. Mayhap his luck would finally change.

As his eyes focused on Achleith, he saw what appeared to be a single figure jumping and waving their hands.

"Do ye see that?" Aulay asked Colum. "Is that a person?"

Robert the Bruce's sources had reported that England had sent the treasure ship to Ireland, intending to start an invasion into the Western Highlands. But it had been caught in a storm that had thundered over the sea more than a sennight ago. The Bruce had asked Aulay and his men to find that ship and take its contents before the English recovered it.

An invasion from Ireland could mean that the English would start with Islay.

And he couldn't have that.

"Aye, I see that," said Colum. "Is that a woman?"

Aulay squinted his eyes. Something very green flapped around the person's figure. "Aye, she seems to wear a dress. She might be in distress since she's waving her arms and jumping up and down."

"Uncle, we must aid her."

"We dinna ken if she's alone. Or if she is in peril."

"We'll be careful."

Aulay ground his teeth. "Aye. Ye're right." He turned to his men and cried, "To the island!"

He squinted his eyes. "I see a beach there," he said to Colum. "We'll head there. The water is shallow enough for us to anchor nearby."

As the boat sailed towards the island, his eyes stayed on the figure. He could see now that she had long, red hair and a green dress so bright it seemed to radiate light. If she wanted attention, that color was successful.

The boat moved closer to the island and his mind drifted back into the past. Seven years since Leitis had died. Since that night that had wounded his soul and tortured his heart. He hadn't remarried or had any children. Having heirs had been his biggest wish. Someone to inherit the riches, the castles, the ships, and the secrets of a successful trading empire.

The closest heir he had was Colum.

"The ship may be somewhere around this island," said Colum as he raised his arm to the woman. They were so close now that she would be able to see that. "Mayhap the woman survived it."

"Aye," said Aulay as he watched her raise her own arm and then hurry down a steep path to the beach. Her dress came only to the middle of her calves, and her legs were so white they flashed like sun reflections against a mirror as she ran.

The shipwreck had been confirmed by Aulay's connections in Ireland, who claimed a part of the ship had washed ashore on one of the islands, though nothing more was found. Officially, Ireland was allied with England, but Aulay had Irish friends who traded with the MacDonalds despite the English embargo.

So, they knew the ship had crashed somewhere. They just had to find it.

If the English found it first, they could destroy all the progress Bruce had made.

Aulay watched the bottom of the sea to make sure they were deep enough to move away but shallow enough to be able to jump off the ship and move to the land.

Longships were part of the Viking heritage of his clan. Birlinns were designed after them and could be anchored in shallow water and even loaded and unloaded without the jetty if needed.

"Anchor!" he yelled when they reached the right depth.

The anchor—a wooden construction with a heavy rock in the middle—was dropped and the boat came to a stop.

Aulay barked the names of the men he wanted to take with him. They jumped off into the sea, chest-deep, and moved with their weapons unsheathed to the woman, who had come down to the beach. She froze and took a step back. An instinct in Aulay's stomach made him hurry towards her. The splashing of the water as the men ran through the surf was deafening. Ten steps away from her, Aulay saw her pretty, big eyes widen in her pale face. She took three more steps back, her hand jumping to her chest.

And Aulay knew something was not right.

She was dressed like...like...like no one he'd ever seen. The dress was too short, she had no undertunic on, no veil covering her hair. The fabric was so thin it floated on the air like a spider-web. And the color—now that he was close to her, it looked like real leaves and branches and flowers were placed right on the fabric of her dress. This was a masterwork, such as he'd never seen in his life. And he'd been trading with the Italians and French for decades. And her shoes... By God's feet, those shoes were three straps of leather attached to soles, shamelessly exposing her toes to the world.

She backed up the narrow path up the hill.

"My lady," said Aulay, walking quickly towards her.

She was ready to flee. He saw the panic in her eyes.

"Did ye cry for help?" he asked. "Is there anyone else here?"

As his men walked onto the beach behind him, her gaze fell on their swords and axes and shields, glistening with water and the dull light of the day.

She screamed, then turned and ran up the hill. But she didn't even make three steps before she slipped, her foot slid out of one of her shoes, and she fell on her stomach.

"She must be insane," said Colum, frowning and eyeing the woman. "But where the hell did she come from?"

As she scrambled to her feet, Aulay sighed. "There is something odd about her. And if there's something odd, she's nae one of us. And if she's nae one of us, she might be the enemy. Mayhap she's also looking for the treasure." He watched her round behind sway in the air as she tried to put on her odd shoes and keep running. But she kept losing her balance, and her shoe refused to slide back onto her foot. "Mayhap she's a spy. We must take her back to Islay and find out."

While they discussed her, she didn't get far. She kept running but slipping in her silly shoes.

He walked to her in ten long strides, his wet clothes stuck to his body and dripping. He sheathed his sword, bent down, picked her up, and flung her over his shoulder. She was small and nicely rounded. As he walked with her on his shoulder, his men turned and made their way to the ship.

Her weight was pleasant and soft on his body. But she kicked and screamed under his arm. "Let me go! Let me go!"

He needed to steady her, so he put his hand on her round arse as he walked through the water and jumped over the waves that crashed onto the beach.

And something within him squeezed at the thought that even if she wasn't an enemy, he was curious about her, and he liked the idea of her being in his castle on Islay.

CHAPTER 3

JENNY SCREAMED through the gag despite knowing all too well this was useless. She was sitting on the deck, her hands tied behind her back to the goddamn Viking ship mast, while the men around her handled the ship and talked about her.

Without any thought that she might hear…and not like it.

The gag tasted of dirt and salt, and she hoped it was sea salt and not the salt of some dude's old sweat. Her stomach flipped every time the ship sank and rose on the waves. The rope tying her wrists stung like it was made of nettles.

But none of that compared to the horror and the sheer animalistic urge to jump off this ship even if it would be into the depths of hell. She hadn't believed her eyes when the Viking ship had anchored and ten bearded dudes with muscles the sizes of islands, holding swords and axes, had jumped off it right into the sea and walked through the surf towards her as though they were strolling through some grass and undergrowth.

And then one of them—the biggest one—had walked to her like he was about to kill her with that sword, picked her up, flung her over his shoulder, and carried her as if she was a sack of potatoes.

And now, the men were looking at her like she was an odd creature in the zoo.

"'Tis odd woman's attire," said one of them. "So short and so...bright. How can a fabric be brighter than the real plants? Have ye ever seen anything like it, Seoras?"

She shifted on her ass. She wanted to cover herself, and was glad she had her green cardigan on, at least. She was definitely rethinking her choice of this dress now. It was very modest, sexually, but yes, quite colorful and bright. But it was in keeping with the theme of celebration that Amanda had wanted. Her flip-flops, though, were certainly the wrong choice.

"She must be Irish," said the man called Seoras, rubbing his bearded chin. He looked a little bit like the giant who had kidnapped her, though much younger. Same proud posture. Same sort of muscular body under the long, heavily quilted medieval coat. His dark beard was short, and his face was covered with smudges of dirt. "That red hair."

"It's the work of a great colorist in New York, you jackass!" she yelled through her gag.

Her naturally red hair started getting a few grays and she thought a brighter shade would be fun.

They frowned in confusion. They couldn't have understood anything unless they knew what "Mha mwha mahwa mahwa, mahrar!" meant.

That made her realize they weren't speaking English...

But neither was she—she yelled at them in Gaelic. How was it possible that she understood and spoke it? She'd heard the captain and the boatswain speak Gaelic with each other back in Scotland, and she'd understood nothing. How was it possible that she now knew what these men were saying?

"She might be English," said the third, younger man. "She may be looking for treasure, too."

The men were silent and stared at her, looking her up and down. Her dress covered her legs to the middle of her calves, and she became aware of her naked skin like never before.

"Stop staring, you idiots!" she yelled at them, and they frowned at her again.

"Is she a whore, do ye think?" asked the first man.

"She might be," said Seoras.

"I'm not!" she moaned. "And I'm going to kill you once your king of jackasses unties me!"

"But why would the laird take a whore back to Islay?"

"Mayhap he's finally ready to move on from Aunt Leitis."

The said laird of jackasses, unlike pretty much every man on this ship, was silent. He stood at the hull, and after he was done barking orders to take the ship away from the beach and they were in the open seas, he kept staring at her. Unlike his crew, he had no expression on his handsome face whatsoever.

Heat crawled into Jenny's cheeks as she remembered the way he'd lifted her up like she weighed nothing. The way his hard muscles had felt against her thighs when he'd held her in place. The way his manhandling palm on her ass had felt hot and heavy and big. And despite his incredible rudeness...part of her thawed and burned.

He was not just handsome, he was gorgeous—the way Zeus, the king of the gods of Mount Olympus, must be gorgeous. The way Sean Connery or George Clooney were even more handsome and sexy and pantie-melting the older they got. There was nothing old about that tall, muscular body with broad shoulders and narrow hips and the pure, palpable power that radiated from him. He must be in his late forties. Maybe early fifties. He had long, silvery hair tied back above his ears. His salt-and-pepper beard was short and groomed. He had high cheekbones and a straight nose with a little bump over the bridge. His eyebrows were dark and thick and hung in a strict, straight line. And those eyes...she was suddenly curious what color they were.

They stared at her. Assessing. Challenging.

Well, she couldn't budge. She couldn't speak, so she'd stare back. She'd show him she wasn't some bag of vegetables to manhandle and tie up and kidnap.

The staring contest kept going until they arrived at a big piece of land. Once they were approaching, he turned away from her and resumed barking orders to navigate the ship. This must be Islay. The landscape was still rough and rocky, with green and yellow moss and occasional trees and underbrush. They sailed into a harbor where more ships like this one were anchored, their sails down. The harbor was surrounded on two sides by rocks. On the right side, the rocks rose into a giant cliff with a castle on top of it. The massive stone walls surrounded a large, tall tower.

All the people on the wooden jetties had swords, pikes, and axes. All wore chain mail coifs and some sort of armor—either leather or heavily quilted fabric. A chill ran through her. She had never been on Islay, as they had hired the boat in Glasgow, but she was pretty sure there were no villages like this in the modern world.

The village on the shore was medieval. Scattered around the place were small houses made of rough stone, wattle and daub and wood, with thatched roofs. A single church tower was the tallest building in the village. Woodsmoke rose from every roof. A dog barked from somewhere. A few Highland cows with their broad horns and red fur ate peacefully in the cattle pens next to several houses. Triangular tepee-like shelters stood between the houses, containing large clay jars, pots, and wooden boxes, along with drying racks with fish and animal hides. Woodpiles lay under lean-tos. Horses tugged wooden carts full of hay, firewood, and stones. The air stank of animal manure, woodsmoke, and fish.

Where were the asphalt roads? Where were the electrical poles? As the men docked the ship and descended onto the jetty, the laird of jackasses came to her and untied her from the mast and undid her gag.

"Welcome to Islay, lass," he said.

His voice was soft, and soft currents of pleasure radiated through her skin where he'd touched her.

They were dark gray, his eyes. Like the sky before a storm.

"I have untied ye," he said, his eyes on her face, her neck, the modest cut of her dress on her chest. Her skin melted where he looked and she felt heat burning her skin. Goddamn, she was flushing. "I will bring ye to my castle and ye will tell me everything about who ye are."

"I'm not anyone…" she said. "Just—"

But before she could say anything, someone called after him and he took her by the elbow and led her out of the boat and onto the jetty. She tried to free her elbow, but it was like trying to pull herself from an iron vise. As she walked down the jetty, everyone stared at her. Men in long tunics—some to their ankles. Women in long tunics and dresses, wearing veils over their heads. Most of them wore cloaks. The clothes were simple, mostly in shades of dirty blue, red, and ochre. All their shoes had pointy toes.

Most of villagers stopped whatever they were doing—loading and unloading the ships, carrying sacks and heaps of wood, chopping and cleaning fish—to watch her pass. The sense that she was a zoo animal intensified, and she buttoned her cardigan over her chest with her free hand.

When she stepped onto the ground, her flip-flopped feet sank into the cold, wet mud mixed with stones, pebbles, and… she hoped not animal feces. She cried out, but the Viking king— well, this was Islay, so that made him a Highland laird—paid no attention to her, dragging her through the mud as if she were a wayward cow.

Something sharp pierced her toe, and she groaned and pulled the arm back that he had held.

With her effort, she managed to make him stop, and as he turned to her, cocking one eyebrow, she straightened her shoulders. "Am I allowed to talk now?" she demanded.

She was suddenly aware that more people had stopped what they were doing and gawked or gathered around them. She shivered, and not just from the chill that crept into her feet from the mud.

The giant Highlander crossed his muscular arms over his chest. Her heart skipped a beat despite her determination to ignore how handsome he was.

"Are ye allowed to talk?" he repeated. "Aye. If ye agree to speak calmly and nae to scream."

She tapped her index finger against her lower lip. "Hmm...let me think about that for a moment. A bunch of medieval dudes with swords gag me and tie me up like I'm a piece of property and then bring me to some place where it seems people ride horses, have no electricity, and look at me like they're ready to burn me at the stake... Oh...and...by the way, it seems I'm speaking a language I've never learned... Does it seem to you like I'm ready to talk? Do you know what I want to say?" She inhaled deeply and, pouring all her fear and her rage into it, screamed right into his face. "Let me go or I'll fucking call the cops!"

His face straightened. His eyes darkened, like a real storm gathered behind them. And his jaw muscles worked under his beard.

Bad idea, Jenny. That was such a bad idea.

"Madwoman," he mumbled as he leaned to her, picked her up, and flung her over his shoulder.

"Let me goooo!" she yelled as the mud and his feet flashed before her eyes. She hit his back and kicked her legs in the air, trying to free herself. "Let go, you barbarian!"

"Keep this up, lass, and ye might well find yerself burning at the stake."

He carried her through the village and then up the rocky hill. Several minutes later, when she had pretty much wasted all her energy trying to fight him, he put her back on the ground. She realized they were standing in front of a gate. They must be at a wall of the castle she'd seen from the ship. The goddamn giant hadn't even broken a sweat carrying her up the hill; he just glared at her with his dark, somber eyes.

"Ye can walk yerself here," he said, showing her through the giant gate.

She looked through it and saw that there were more thatched buildings and that big tower she'd seen from the ship. The two guards standing at the gate watched her, frowning.

She considered running back down the hill and looked at her feet. They were covered in mud and slippery against the rubber soles of her flip-flops. She was completely unsuited for this. Inside the bailey, she could see men with swords and spears, stone and timber houses with thatched roofs, as well as horses and chickens and geese. Her dress was thin and cold.

Something tugged at her dress from behind, and she looked back to see a goat chewing the fabric.

"Goddamn it!" she cried as she snatched her skirt away. "Never again a leaf pattern."

Her shoes were destroyed, her purse was back on the boat...back...wherever Amanda and her other friends were. The laird of jackasses shoved her gently forward, and she walked, her feet slipping and her ankles hurting as she tried to keep her balance.

As they passed through the gates, her captor was greeted by a gorgeous young woman in a long, beautiful medieval dress with a belt embroidered with gold and silver threads around her thin waist.

"Uncle Aulay, who is this?" the woman asked.

Aulay... That name rang a bell. Where had she heard it?

"Dinna concern yerself, Laoghaire."

"How canna I concern myself if our chief openly brings a whore to Dunyvaig? What will be of name MacDonald?"

Aulay MacDonald...

Through her still-cloudy mind, she remembered. That woman in the green dress. She had told Jenny she had a soul mate back in time... Aulay MacDonald, who'd love her even once she was wrinkled and old and...something.

Back in time?

Jenny was cold. As cold as if she had been turned into dry ice. Her feet hurt, her head hurt, her hands shook.

"You're Aulay MacDonald?" she asked.

He narrowed his eyes at her. "I am."

"Uncle, who is she?" insisted Laoghaire.

"We picked her up on Achleith," said a younger warrior, handsome and dark-haired. She remembered someone had addressed him as Colum.

"Achleith?" Laoghaire asked.

"'Tis where that rock is, the one that faeries visit," said another man, stopping by Laoghaire's side.

"Mayhap she was robbed," said an older woman with a kind face who had stopped her washing to watch them pass. "Who would wear this openly in their right mind?"

Laoghaire looked Jenny up and down with disgust. "Aye, her legs exposed like that...shameless."

Aulay took Jenny's elbow and gently pushed her to keep walking. "None of yer business, good people. Leave her alone."

"She may nae be human!" Jenny heard someone call out behind her back.

"Or mayhap she is witch," suggested a man, and when Jenny looked over her shoulder, she saw that it was one of Aulay's warriors from the ship.

When she looked up at Aulay to tell him she was human and she was not English and not a witch or a whore, there was a dark, thoughtful danger in his eyes.

She didn't like that look one bit.

"Ye must lock her up, Lord!" cried Laoghaire. "She is dangerous!"

"Aye, lock her up!" echoed a man's voice.

And then they all cried after them that she needed to be locked up and kept a prisoner.

And Aulay's fist around her elbow tightened.

CHAPTER 4

AULAY SAT in his great chair in the great hall of Dunyvaig Castle and stared at the most interesting woman he had ever seen in his life. The woman in the bright-green dress sat at one of the long tables that lined the huge hall and stared at the piece of boiled salmon on her trencher like she had no idea what to do with it. Thoughtfully, he rubbed his chin, watching the fires in the braziers play against her red hair.

A wee fox, wasn't she?

There were warriors drinking, talking, having a rest after the journey. As usual, Colum sat alone. Seoras sat with his heavily pregnant wife, Mhairi. Laoghaire sat next to her drinking wine, her back straight, throwing odd glances at the red-haired vixen.

Between the embroideries of the MacDonald crest, shields with MacDonald colors hung in neat rows. The shields were round with a single, square sail in the middle—once again, the Viking heritage his Nordic ancestors had left behind.

The great hall was full of quiet murmuring, warriors talking with one another and laughing as they ate.

Aulay noticed how they all looked at the strange woman. At the bare flesh exposed to the whole world. At her hair, long and bright and shining, a brilliant contrast against the unnatural green of her dress. Well, he supposed, it wasn't that unnatural. It was the color of the first newborn leaves in spring, when they are growing out of their tight buds and can't wait to feel the sun on their tender surfaces.

That, too, was how Aulay often felt. His soul was curled tight, hidden deep in the cold, waiting.

He took a long breath. He liked the smell that always seemed to live inside his great hall: woodsmoke from the braziers, stone, and leather. There were also rich embroideries he had acquired a dozen years ago in a monastery in the south of France, where he'd personally gone to trade. They depicted a large castle, bigger than Stirling, peasants working the fields under its massive walls, and a lady being courted by a knight. This embroidery had been his gift to Leitis, the symbol of his love, how he'd courted his wife. Even though their marriage had been arranged, he didn't touch her for months—not until he'd won her heart and she'd given herself to him willingly.

She had been the great love of his life. The woman he'd have happily died for.

He'd never even looked at any woman since Leitis.

Until this one.

And he didn't know her name or where she came from.

She picked up the carving knife and moved the salmon along the trencher, then leaned down and sniffed it. A wee fox indeed. Aulay hid a smile.

She was very pretty, with her small, straight stature, the curves under that thin, silky dress. What color were her eyes?

As though hearing his thoughts, she looked up at him. He couldn't see the color of her eyes from here, even though she glared straight at him.

Surprising himself, he stood and walked down the steps of the platform. He headed to her; the whole way, her glare was like a hail of nails showering over him.

When he stood one step away, he realized her eyes were brown and warm, almost yellow like the color of a late-summer honey. What would it be like if they didn't throw daggers but melted and looked at him with affection? As he walked around her, he craved to touch her again. He picked up a wavy piece of fabric right under her clavicle. It was warm from her body and felt like sheer silk, so soft and light, he thought it might be made of a faerie's wings.

"Why are ye dressed like this, lass?" he asked.

"Go to hell," she replied. "You realize how offensive you sound? Why wouldn't I be dressed like this?"

He chuckled and let go of the fabric. She smelled of something delicious and foreign, he noticed. Flowery and fresh. Like apples. And lemons, the fruit he'd once tried back in the kingdom of Galicia.

"For one," he said, "the goat thought yer dress was its meal."

She rolled her eyes. "Stupid goat."

"Nae fabric that I ken is so soft and light and so rich in color my eyes hurt."

"Oh yeah? Well, your clothes make me want to take them off and—"

Her whole face lit up in the color of flame. He stopped in front of her and couldn't stop an amused grin. "And what?"

"And burn them."

He cocked his head and looked at her feet. "I have never seen such ridiculous shoes. Three straps and a platform. Yer toes and feet are covered in mud and animal dung."

She swallowed and looked at her feet. "Can't argue there. I regret my choice of shoes more than you know."

He narrowed his eyes at her hair. There were two colors. One, this vibrant and rich fox red. The other, just a thin line at the roots, a paler, honey-red with a few silvery lines. How could one achieve such a vibrant color? He knew some women bleached their hair in the sun or with a mixture of wood ash and vinegar. Blondes were the standard of beauty and perfection. But he'd never heard of anyone trying to be red-haired.

There was a delicate bracelet on her wrist, a remarkable

craftsmanship of interwoven leaves. And she wore a thin ring on her right index finger.

He walked to stand by her side and crossed his arms over his chest. She was short and she was sitting, and he had an odd image of her kneeling before him, fisting his hard erection. God's blood, he hadn't had a lustful thought about a woman in seven years.

"Let's start with yer name," he said. "What do they call ye?"

"Right. *Now* you're asking my name. After you dragged me across the sea."

"Aye. *Now* I'm asking. What is yer name?"

She didn't answer at first, and he thought she wouldn't at all. Then she sighed, laid the cutting knife on the table, and said, "Dr. Jennifer Foster."

Jennifer... A beautiful name he'd never even heard in his life. It reminded him of the name Guinevere, the legendary King Arthur's wife. So, mayhap it was how they said it in England... But there was something else that surprised him even more about her answer.

He frowned. "Doctor? What does that mean?"

"You don't know what 'doctor' means?" She raised her eyebrows. "Really?"

"Really."

"Sure. And I thought I was supposed to be the one lying."

She was mocking him. He liked good banter with a female who knew her own mind, but he was starting to lose his patience.

He looked around. Warriors threw curious glances at them. The murmur in the great hall became quieter. Laoghaire stared at her with clear mistrust. This woman was bringing a lot of hubbub into the clan. He needed to be careful.

"Ye have two choices, lass," he said. "One, ye answer my questions truthfully. I will ken if ye lie to me. Then ye may eat with me. Two, ye keep on yer game of screaming, lying, and talking nonsense. In that case, ye go to the dungeon, and I lock ye up. Do ye understand?"

Oh, she hated him with her eyes then. The brown honey turned almost black. Slowly, she nodded.

"So, who are ye, Jennifer Foster, and what were ye doing on Achleith?"

"I got lost."

"Ye got lost. How do ye get lost on an island with nae other soul in sight?"

She looked at her feet and wrung her hands. He could see she was carefully choosing what to say.

"It's complicated."

"Where do ye come from? Ye speak Gaelic just fine, but I canna place yer accent."

"New York."

He leaned forward, attempting to catch her expression. "York? So ye admit ye're English?"

She frowned and shook her head. "I'm American, not English."

She was talking more nonsense. "What is American?"

"That is a good question! I've asked it myself my whole life. What does it mean to be an American? Well..." She put her hand in a fist and stuck out her index finger. "Freedom, for one. The right to have a voice, I guess, would be the second." She stuck out the next finger. "So, I guess you just really, um...restricted both things that mean that I'm American, which I really don't appreciate. People don't do that, you know. Normally, people use words, not force. Normal people. Well... Most people I know, that is. So... There are a lot of things that I wonder at this moment. Why did you need to tie me and gag me? What do you want with me? Where am I? And who actually are you? Et cetera."

Amused, he kept listening to her rambling, which brought an odd lightness to his chest. The sense of curiosity didn't die down. On the contrary, the more she talked, the more he longed to know.

She raised her eyebrows. "Please start answering."

When he kept silent, she cleared her throat. "An answer to aaany of my previous questions will do. I have many more. Just start."

The corners of his lips crawled up in a smile that he fought to suppress. In only a short time, she'd managed to make him smile twice. He didn't remember the last time he'd had a good laugh.

"As ye already guessed, I'm Aulay of Islay, chief of clan MacDonald. I tied and gagged ye because I didna ken if ye were a foe. If ye're English, ye ken why I was there and what I was searching for. If ye're nae English, then the reason shouldna matter to ye."

She made a satisfied facial expression with her mouth curved downward and her eyebrows raised. "Great start, Aulay. Now why are you keeping me here? Why don't you let me go?"

"Because ye may be a danger to my clan. And ye may ken something I need."

"Okay. That's easy. I don't want anything to do with your clan. Can I go now?"

"And how did ye get on the island?"

"On a boat, of course. My friends and I were on our way to Ireland, celebrating Amanda's divorce. Our boat broke down, and we had to make an emergency stop. Then a strange woman talked to me about...you. And the lighthouse disappeared."

"What woman?"

"I'm trying to remember her name... Gosh...what was it? I know she was Scottish, and she said... Um... No, I can't repeat that. She was joking. Anyway"—she snapped her fingers and pointed to the door—"if you could hook me up with a boat, that would be great!"

Ireland. A boat that had to be repaired. This couldn't be a coincidence. Somehow, she was connected to the shipwreck, and he had to find out how. Based on her appearance, she may be a whore brought on board the treasure ship to keep the men happy. Or she may have paid her passage that way.

"Nae yet. Ye must tell me about those friends and that boat that broke and why ye want to go to Ireland."

"No. I told you all I could. Please give me a phone. I'll call the police. I don't want to be here. I need to keep going. I have an important appointment in two weeks, and my friends are worried about me."

He looked back at the grand chair standing on the platform next to his. The grand chair that had been empty for the past seven years. Just like his, it was made of wood and had carvings of knots and crosses. It was the chair for his honorable guests. "Please, come with me and sit, lass, and tell me about those friends of yers and if they will be searching for ye here and why ye want to go to Ireland."

CHAPTER 5

THE PIECE of boiled salmon on the wooden trencher in front of Jenny was cold. The fish smelled fresh, but the scent turned her stomach. The great hall was filling with people, and servants brought trenchers of bread, cheese, and boiled meat and fish. Aulay chewed cheerfully sitting by her side, watching her with amusement.

"Is the fish nae to yer liking?" he asked.

"I usually like salmon," she said. "Somehow, I have no appetite."

"Oh?"

"Maybe it's all the squeezing my stomach got when a manhandling giant carried me over his shoulder. Twice!"

He chuckled and pushed a mug closer to her. "Mayhap some ale would soothe it."

She took the mug and sniffed. She wasn't hungover anymore, but the idea of alcohol wasn't particularly appealing. What if she started seeing glowing rocks and a woman who talked about time travel again? And even if she didn't, she had to stay on her toes. Her whole being was on edge, her nerves taut. She felt like a porcupine, bristled and ready to strike.

"I'll have some fish after all," she said, deciding she'd better bolster her strength for whatever was to come.

But there were no forks, only a knife. Everyone ate with their hands after cleaning them in a bowl of water. She copied a pregnant woman who sat at the other side of the great hall with the man called Seoras. She was dressed better than most women she'd seen in the village. The woman dipped her fingers into the water, then took the knife and cut a small piece of salmon.

Aulay followed her gaze and said, "'Tis Mhairi, the wife of my youngest nephew, Seoras."

"Oh," Jenny said. "Is she getting proper medical care? She'll soon give birth. She needs a good doctor. Or a midwife."

Mhairi used her fingers to put a piece salmon in her mouth. Jenny didn't want her fingers to smell like fish afterward, with no soap and no running water, so she stuck her knife into the salmon and was about to eat it from the tip of the knife when Aulay said, "I can see that whatever a 'doctor' means, it doesna mean 'lady.'"

Jenny put the fish down. "What did I do?"

"Ye speak like an educated woman, and yet ye are eating yer food from the knife?"

She sighed. Fingers it was. She picked up the piece of salmon and demonstratively put it in her mouth. As she chewed, his eyes dropped to her lips. Heat crept up her cheeks. She barely tasted the fish, which was seasoned only with herbs. Jenny missed salt and lemon and garlic.

Since the moment she'd opened her eyes on that island, everything had been off. Everything was strange and different. Everything confirmed the redheaded woman's claim about time travel. But how was it possible?

"It's healthier, anyway," she said with a forced smile.

"What?"

"No salt."

His dark eyes were attentive, watching her as though she was his sole focus. "Are ye missing salt? I can ask a servant to bring some for ye."

"Don't. I don't mind. I'm not really hungry, anyway."

Nervous jitters turned and twisted her stomach as questions spun inside her head. Had she really traveled in time? Was there some other reasonable explanation for all this? For meeting the man that woman had called the love of her life? For being dragged across the sea on an ancient ship, bound and gagged and pointed at? For being called a faerie and a whore because of the length of her dress?

No electricity. No cars. No running water. No technology of any kind.

And if this all was true—which she still couldn't believe—but if it was...

What about her appointment? Her last chance to have a baby?

She had to return to Achleith. If that rock had made her travel in time, it must work to send her forward once again. She felt her knees jiggle under the table, from nerves but also from the chill air. Despite it being summer and the fires in braziers all around, the great hall was cold.

"Who are those friends of yers?" Aulay asked, startling her.

What should she say? If she wanted to return to that island, she needed him to believe her. To relax around her and not think that she was some sort of a threat. His people had told him to lock her up in a dungeon—and if he did, any chance of escape would disappear. All those huge warriors would be very effective at keeping her in place. And she knew better than to provoke a band of armed men.

Which meant she probably shouldn't keep insisting she was American. And she definitely shouldn't say a word about time travel. She should tell him what he wanted to hear. Something believable and innocent.

Let him lower his guard. Then she'd run.

"They were women. Like I said, my friends and I were on our way to Ireland..."

"To celebrate something... Did ye say a divorce?"

"Yes. I did say a divorce. What I meant was that we were on a pilgrimage to Ireland to pray that the divorce doesn't happen for my friend."

"A pilgrimage?" He looked her all over, making her skin burn. "In this?"

She gave a long, heavy sigh. How many times can a person regret their choice of clothes?

"Yes," she said.

"All right." He eyed her carefully, his piercing gaze scanning her like an X-ray machine. "Where were ye headed for the pilgrimage?"

Well, shoot. She had no idea what pilgrimage sites there were in Ireland. She needed to do something with her hands to give herself time to think. She cut another piece of soft salmon and lifted it to her mouth with her fingers. She couldn't taste what she was chewing.

Ireland...

St. Patrick, of course!

"To the St. Patrick's site."

He leaned with his elbows over the table and pinned her with his gaze. Her feet grew cold. He was onto her. "And pray tell, where is that St. Patrick's site?"

Argh! With her hand shaking, she picked out a long fish bone between the flesh and laid it neatly on the trencher.

"On St. Patrick Mountain, of course," she said. "Have you not heard of it?"

"Nae."

She snatched the cup of ale and emptied it quickly. It tasted almost like root beer, not even that alcoholic. And surprisingly delicious. The beer made her head spin pleasantly. For better or for worse, she felt braver. "Well, who made you an expert on Ireland, anyway?"

He chuckled and took another sip. "Are ye always like this?"

"Like what?"

"Ye dinna let a man be right?"

Anger hit her in a scorching wave. That hit way too close home. Wasn't that exactly what Tom had told her over and over? He could never get a break with her. He could never feel relaxed with her. She always grilled him about things and never left him alone.

She should try to make Aulay like her. She should say things to placate him. Instead, she sputtered through her clenched teeth, "You have no idea what you're talking about."

Aulay's eyes darkened, and he leaned back in his chair, all humor gone. "All right. Let us assume there is a St. Patrick Mountain and it's a St. Patrick's pilgrimage site. What happened to yer boat?"

"It was wrecked, and we were stranded—"

Before she could finish, a swarm of loud, giggling kids ran into the great hall like a rainbow cloud and, with no regard to anyone else, hurried straight to Aulay. There must have been six or seven of them. As they jumped onto him, it was hard to say how many pairs of legs and arms stuck out of the wriggling heap. He laughed somewhere under them, and Jenny's heart melted like Nutella in the sun.

They wrestled and laughed and tickled. They yelled children's rhymes she didn't know, and Aulay's voice boomed from under them, happy and peaceful, like a dad with his big family. She must have spontaneously ovulated seeing this huge, powerful Highlander being soft like that...

And then all the goo and warmth within her washed away when her eyes fell on the open doors of the great hall. There were no guards there. Aulay was distracted by the kids. The warriors were busy eating.

This could be her only chance to escape. On weak legs, she stood up, expecting at any moment for him to notice her and grab her. As she walked down the stairs of his king-like platform, her mind raced. If he caught her, what explanation would she give him?

Bathroom. She needed a bathroom. A latrine... What was it called in the Middle Ages, anyway?

She might also say she needed to change her tampon. Men always faltered if there was any mention of a woman's period. And even medieval women must have some sort of menstrual hygiene practices.

As she walked down the aisle between the long tables, she wanted to run, but forced her legs to remain steady. The giggling and yelling kept going behind her, and none of the warriors she passed looked up from their meals.

Miraculously, she reached the doors to the great hall. As she entered the landing, she glanced back, but Aulay was still buried under the swarm of children. If her plan was successful, this would be the last time she'd see him.

She hurried down the stairs, one hand tracing the curved, rough stone wall for balance, her feet still dirty and slippery from the mud. Her footsteps against the stairs exploded in her ears as she ran. She was hyperaware of every sound coming from the great hall behind her.

As she opened the door of the tower and ran outside into the daylight, chickens and geese flew out from under her steps, squawking and hissing angrily. People watched her with frowns as she ran. Her lungs burned as she sped through the thatched-roof houses, heaps of firewood, shacks, carts, and warriors. She accelerated, despite the ache in her legs, despite slipping over and over again. She lost one flip-flop but kept going.

By the time she reached the outer gate of the castle, her rib cage hurt, feeling like it was too small for all the air she wanted to suck in. She ran down the rocky slope, zigzagging between the carts and the people who were on their way up carrying baskets of fish, ropes, bundles of sheep fleece...

When she reached the wooden jetty, her head was spinning and her throat hurt, and her lungs were about to burst. Just a little more. There was a man with a fishing boat who looked like he was about to depart.

She couldn't believe it. She'd made it this far. Just a bit farther.

But feet pounded behind her. With the last of her strength, she lengthened her short stride, lunging towards the fisherman.

She stopped abruptly before the man, gasping. His eyes rounded when he looked her over. Distantly, she remembered she had something like a coin...

"Please...take me...Achleith," she managed. "I have this—"

But before she could retrieve the coin, an iron fist clasped her arm then spun her around and pressed her against a chest as hard as stone.

"Where ye think ye're going, lass?" said Aulay.

His scent enveloped her. The sea, the whiff of metal and wood, and the subtle male musk of his warm skin. It made her knees weak. She kept gasping, unable to get enough air.

"I need to go back to Achleith!" she yelled into his face.

Big mistake. She should have said something about a bathroom or a tampon like she had planned...it might not have made sense, but it would have confused him and given her time to think.

She had just undone all the work of trying to get on his good side. Fury distorted his face like a storm and a chill ran through her body.

"And I need to be careful," he said as he clasped her elbow and dragged her back into the village. "I should have never believed ye. And they were right. Ye need to be locked up in the dungeon."

"Let me go, you jackass!" she yelled as the unstoppable force kept hauling her towards the castle. "You king of jackasses!"

"I dinna ken what that means!" he yelled back. "And I dinna want to ken."

She kept struggling to snatch her arm from his grip. She yelled at him to stop, but he ignored her. He dragged her through the mud, up the rocky slope, and through the inner bailey. In the tower, he took her down the stairs into a space illuminated by a brazier.

A dungeon.

He shoved her into a cell with metal bars and closed the door.

"Aulay, please!" she cried.

But without another look at her, he turned and left the dungeon. As the door closed behind him, so did her hope to return to her time and make it to her appointment.

Her only hope to have a baby.

CHAPTER 6

As Aulay descended from the main keep into the inner bailey of Dunyvaig Castle the next day, he kept thinking about the strange woman, Jennifer. He hadn't stopped thinking about her from the moment he'd seen her back on the Isle of Achleith.

As he walked to the sword-training site, feeling the morning sun on his skin, he wondered how she'd spent the night in the dungeon. It was warm here, but down there, it was freezing. He greeted his clansmen, every one of them nodding to him. The air in his castle always smelled of the sea mixed with the scent of horse dung and wet earth. The heavy, wooden door of the main keep was cold as he pushed it open.

Last night, he'd broken down and brought her a blanket. He'd found her shivering on the sleeping bench, and as he'd handed her the blanket through the gaps in the grating, she'd started all over again about letting her return to Achleith. He'd seen that she'd lost one of her ridiculous shoes, so he'd brought a pair of shoes for her that had belonged to his niece Anna when she was younger.

The woman had accepted both and stopped talking. In the light of the single brazier, their eyes locked; hers were like amber with light shining through them.

"Thank you," she whispered, as though stunned that an act of kindness like this could have come from him. He nodded and gave her a piece of bread and a horn flask of water. Then, before she could say anything else to break him down and let her out of the dungeon, he left and went upstairs to his bedchamber.

The training ground was already full of children who had just started learning sword fighting. Lads and lasses of ten to thirteen years of age. Some were from the orphanage Leitis had started, and the others were clan children whose parents did not have the time or skill to teach them at home. He admired women and knew that they could do so much more than cook and clean. Leitis and Anna had shown him that.

Mayhap it was the rebel in him that, at twenty-one years of age, had opposed his uncle and his despotic leadership, but he liked a person who stood up against norms. Against a bigger force.

That was why he supported the Bruce.

That was why he kept thinking about Jennifer. There was so much he didn't understand about her. Last night, he'd had a dream about her. He had been lusting for her, and it was the first time he'd had a dream like this since Leitis. Those legs of hers, flashing in the sun—her sculpted, seductive calves, the skin white and smooth. God's blood, he couldn't stop thinking about her legs.

He came to a stop before the children who were talking, playing, and running after one another.

"Well met!" he cried, and, as one, they stopped what they were doing and turned to him, grinning.

"Well met!" replied an uneven chorus of a dozen children's voices.

He grinned back. Something melted every time he saw them, the generation of MacDonalds that would remain long after his time had passed and make him proud.

"Stand in two rows facing each other," he called.

They did so. The shadow of the curtain wall fell on the

training grounds and shielded them from the summer sun. This was his favorite part of the day. To be with them, help them, train them, see them grow and improve.

They picked up their wooden training swords and held them vertically at their right shoulder. He cried, "Step forward and slash. Step forward and slash!"

As they kept going, a dull ache settled in his stomach with the wish that one of them was his own. A son or a daughter.

Colum came out of the main keep and waved at him, walking down the inner bailey and towards the gates.

If...most likely, *when* Aulay died childless, Colum would be an excellent laird. Aulay knew it, even though the clan still had their reservations about Colum's true loyalty. They had found him in English armor with an English sword back in Berwick when they'd stormed it to free him. He had sworn allegiance to Edward I.

But when they came for him, he had renounced the English king and left with them. Colum had confided in Aulay that he'd hated himself for doing it, and there was a reason for his actions he couldn't share. He'd never sworn that allegiance in his heart, and he'd done it to protect someone. But he still needed to prove he was loyal to his clan and to King Robert the Bruce before the clan would accept him as their laird.

As Aulay kept training the children, two young washer-women stopped with their baskets full of laundry and watched him with smiles, whispering. He knew those glances. Many unmarried young women of the clan were watching him like this. Ever since Leitis had died, some of them had hoped he'd take them to bed or marry them. He supposed it was nice to know he still had women's attention, even at fifty-one.

But he wasn't the sort of man who wanted to bed a lot of lasses. He was loyal to the bone.

He wanted one woman.

But the thought of loving again and risking losing that

person made his blood run cold. And he still missed Leitis. The thoughts about Jennifer Foster felt a wee bit like a betrayal.

Truth be told, he didn't like keeping anyone in that dungeon, so he wished he could free Jennifer. But he hoped a bit of time in the dungeon would convince her to stop lying. So, he would just let her sit.

~

AULAY WAS A DESPICABLE MAN. A MONSTER.

Jenny had spent what felt like a lifetime in this dungeon. There was no way to tell without windows. Had it been one day? Two? Three?

At some point, the fire in the brazier had gone out, and she'd been in complete darkness for a long, long time. Then someone had come and relit the brazier and brought her more stonelike bread and water. They hadn't replied to her questions about Aulay, her demands to be let go, to be seen by the laird.

Now, as she sat on the cold bench in the goddamn worst dress she could ever have chosen, wrapped in the blanket that Aulay had brought her and staring at the pointy medieval shoes —which, at least, were practical—she sighed.

She must have traveled in time. What other explanation to this insanity was there? Unless she had a brain tumor that gave her horrible hallucinations.

And if she had, indeed, traveled in time, what were her options? She needed to be back in New York on July 21, or she'd miss her appointment...and then she would need to wait for the clinic to have a cancelation. It could be months to get a new spot. And then her eggs might already be gone.

Tom and she had tried to get pregnant for a while when she was thirty-five, but nothing had worked because of her endometriosis.

Since IVF was not successful, her younger sister, Holly, had now agreed to become a surrogate and had an appointment to start taking hormones.

She imagined how it would be to have a baby and hold it. She'd always wanted to be a mother, to have a family.

She'd grown up in a happy family. Her mother and father loved each other and adored Jenny and her two sisters. Happy Christmases where no one felt forced to come out of obligation. Thanksgivings when Jenny felt truly thankful for her family. Her mom always said, "All we want is for you girls to be happy."

Even now, she talked to her mom and dad two to three times per week. She visited her nephews and nieces for their birthdays no matter what.

As she'd watched her sisters marrying men they loved, becoming mothers...

She'd wanted it, too.

She'd always thought she could have it all—a career and a family. And she loved her job treating sick children. She knew she was brought into this life to be a doctor, only she'd also always thought she was born to be a mother. She loved her nieces and nephews, and every time she saw her pregnant, glowing sisters, she had that ping in her stomach, that hope that one day it would be her. Ripe and pregnant and feeling life grow inside of her.

But maybe she'd never have that. She was thirty-nine and divorced...and locked in a medieval dungeon. Tears burned her eyes, and she rubbed them to stop herself from crying. What would the rest of her life be like if she could never be a mother?

Empty. Every child she'd ever treat in her clinic would be a small reminder of what she'd never have.

She really had to get out of here.

And for that, she needed Aulay's help. She'd failed yesterday, but she needed to convince him she was not a threat. She'd better start learning how not to die here...and perhaps find another way to get to Achleith. The clock was ticking, and if she didn't get back to her own time, it would be too late to have a baby.

In a few moments, the door to the dungeon creaked and someone came in. It was the same guard who had brought her food earlier. He handed her a bowl of porridge through the gaps in the grating, and she realized she was hungry. She curled her hands around the steaming bowl, absorbing the warmth, and ate hungrily.

She threw glances at the guard while he put more firewood into the brazier. He must be in his forties. He had a beard and wore that heavy armor that she'd seen on other warriors. He wasn't giving her evil smirks or anything.

"Do you have children...sir?" she asked.

Surprised, he looked up at her, a piece of firewood still in his hand. "Aye, I do."

"Oh. Nice. Are they great?"

"Nae all the time. But aye."

She slurped the porridge and nodded. "I don't have any. But I really want one."

The guard put the firewood into the brazier and straightened and turned to her. "Do ye have a husband?"

Way to destroy the mood, buddy. Her husband had betrayed her, cheated on her, and had a baby with another woman. And every time she thought of Tom, she still felt like a large stake was pierced right through the middle of her chest.

"No husband. I barely have my own sanity, friend. And I may soon lose the only thing that really matters to me. An opportunity to have my own child."

He was quiet for a while, studying her, then said, "Ye canna birth bairns, lass? Sometimes 'tis the family God lets ye find that matters the most."

She sighed. "Man, you're wise. It's true. My family is the best, and I love them. But I also have amazing friends that are like family. Still, they can't make up for having my own child that I can hold and love and take care of."

"I suppose ye may take it the way ye take it. But 'tis also possible to find nae just friends but children, too. There are many bairns with nae parents who need a family."

As the guard left the dungeon, she kept staring into empty space. If she didn't make it to her appointment and she had to accept the reality of never having her own children, she'd grieve her fertility like the loss of a limb. Did she want a baby so much that she'd try to adopt one?

She didn't want to think about that. She just wanted to hope for the best.

Was Tom right after all?

Perhaps she couldn't have it all.

CHAPTER 7

BRIGHT DAYLIGHT hurt Jenny's eyes as the same guard took her to Aulay on his summons. She'd spent two nights in the dungeon, as he'd explained to her, and so she had twelve days left till her appointment.

The day was grim, and the clouds were gray, and rain gathered somewhere on the farther side of the sky. After so many hours of smelling wet stone, damp wool, and her own sweat, she sucked in a lungful of fresh air. It was full of the scent of woodsmoke and horse dung and something baking in at least one of those thatched-roof houses scattered around the courtyard. Aulay stood with Colum and another man around a barrel studying something that looked like paper, vellum perhaps. Aulay leaned over it and drew something with a reed pen.

As she walked, part of their conversation reached her. "So, we looked at Achleith, and at the Isle of Fraoch, and here, at the Isle of Creag Uaine. Nae sign of the shipwreck."

"I think we should go to Clachgheur," said Colum. "'Tis notoriously difficult to dock there, and if the ship got wrecked and stuck, it could be on those cliffs."

"Aye," said Aulay as he wrote something. "'Tis a good suggestion. We must hurry. I expected to find the ship by now. With more time passing, the English might find it before us. The treasure and the weapons on that ship will give Scotland more power to use against the bastarts. Colum and Seoras, ye also need to double up training sessions for the warriors and prepare our defenses. Any repairs and maintenance to our ships must happen now."

"Aye, Uncle. And we will need to be at Bannockburn by June next year," said Colum. "'Tis when the English will come for Stirling. We need to be ready for an English attack here and keep our warriors strong to aid Bruce."

"If the English destroy us before the battle," said Seoras, "it will be a great blow to our king's forces."

Jenny's mind raced. That was why they were so afraid she was English and that she might know something they didn't. Was it about the ship they were searching for? Treasure and weapons, he'd said.

They were at war with England. She had heard about the Battle of Bannockburn, one of the most important victories in Scottish history. She didn't remember what year it had been exactly. But now she realized that it was even more important to make sure Aulay didn't think of her as an enemy. She needed him to let her go and help her get back to that island—and there was no way he'd do that if he thought she was in league with the English.

When she came near, Aulay's gaze felt heavy on her skin. He dismissed Colum and Seoras, who left and went to the castle gate. As he rolled up what she now saw was a large piece of vellum, which looked like a map, he turned to her.

Her guard raised his eyebrows at Aulay. "Do ye still need me to guard her, Laird?"

Aulay clasped his shoulder. There was a familiarity between the two, like between two old friends or brothers even. "Nae, Beathan. Go and start training the men. Thank ye for watching over her, I ken 'tis nae yer duty, but I appreciate it. Ye ken how much I trust ye, friend."

Beathan gave a crooked smile. "Aye, Laird. Go easy on her. I dinna think she's the enemy."

He winked at Jenny and walked away. Well, at least she had one person in this castle who didn't think she was the worst person in the world.

Then Jenny was left alone under the dark gaze that made her skin flush red hot.

"So, Jennifer Foster," he said. "After two days in the dungeon, are ye ready to tell the truth?"

"I was telling the truth this whole time," she said, crossing her arms over her chest. But she was ready to lie her ass off now to convince him she was no threat. "Is there a specific question?"

"Aye. I must ken more about that ship. Was there anything precious on it?"

She frowned. "Like what?"

"Armor. Swords. Shields. Gold."

She was thinking fast. Surely he wouldn't think a poor widow could be plotting with the English. "I don't know. I'm just a widow. If there was anything precious, I'd tell you."

"A widow?" Aulay asked as he clasped the sheath onto his belt. His movements made his tunic hug his chest and his broad shoulders and his flat stomach and his thin waist and hips... "Who was yer husband?"

Her mouth was dry. He looked insanely sexy in his medieval warrior outfit. She tried to get her horny brain to think of a reasonable explanation to go along with the widow story. "Um... he was a physician. So...I also learned about medicine, and how to run his business."

"A woman running a physician's business? I thought we agreed ye wilna lie."

Nerves trembled within her like a feather on the wind. In cases like this, she always fell back to her defense mechanism —bubbliness.

"You know what, at my work, I see twenty to thirty children every day. I spent years studying medicine and surgery and years building my practice...my husband's practice, I mean. And get this. While I was working hard, my dear husband cheated on me!"

Aulay's face darkened. "Ye worked in his business while he was bedding other lasses?"

But she didn't get to reply. A woman passed by her, coughing violently. She held a baby in her arms. The baby was probably about six months old. It was crying and had a dry, chesty cough that made her desperately wish for her stethoscope. She needed to listen to its chest because it might have a chest infection.

Following, despite Aulay's protests, Jenny saw the woman sit with the baby in her lap on a heap of firewood by one of the houses in the inner bailey. The small homes were hidden behind the kitchen building with a small garden, chicken coop, and a cow barn, as well the stables and barrack buildings where the warriors slept.

Jenny knelt on the dirt-packed ground before the mother and the baby, the earth cold against her knees.

The baby was swaddled in a woolen blanket, but it cried so hard its chin trembled. Its cheeks were red, and its eyes were feverish, but no tears came.

"I'm a physician," she said to the woman. "I want to help you."

The woman didn't look well. She was tall and red-haired, her eyelashes and eyebrows were light and almost golden. Her pale green eyes were red, and her gaze was milky, like the woman didn't understand completely what was going on around her. She must be exhausted.

"There's nae need," said the woman. "I already have a physician."

"What's your name?" Jenny asked.

"Ailis," said the mother. "And this is Una."

"Jennifer, please let Ailis alone," boomed Aulay's voice behind Jenny. She turned over her shoulder to find him glaring at her with his trademark stare of death. "She's Beathan's wife."

Jenny looked up at Aulay, who towered over her, almost as tall as the thatched-roof stone house.

"I'm sure Beathan wants the best care for his wife and daughter. Besides," Jenny said, "based on how bad their coughs are, her physician isn't much help."

"Are ye sure ye are a physician?" asked Ailis, and Jenny turned back around.

Jenny sat down next to her on the pile of firewood. Splinters pricked her skin through the thin fabric of her green dress, which now bore a few dirty smudges. She guessed it was good. She was blending into the surroundings where everything was dirt and stone and wood. The pointy shoes Aulay had given her kept her feet warmer than her flip-flops, small mercy at least.

"What do you mean?" she said. "Of course I'm sure I'm a physician."

"'Tis just ye look more like an expensive whore than a physician."

Jenny sighed. Right. No time to reflect on something she could do nothing about. She needed to be a doctor for this baby and this woman. She straightened her back and looked at the baby again. She needed to listen to its chest even without the stethoscope, measure its pulse, and so on.

"Ailis, may I touch Una?" she asked.

"Jennifer..." Aulay said in a warning. Jenny threw a glare at him.

Ailis's eyes widened. "Bhatair never asks this."

"Is Bhatair your physician?" Jenny asked.

"Aye."

"I will check her fever and her vital signs, look into her throat and so on. Is that all right with you?"

Ailis looked at Una and her eyes filled with worry. "She isna getting well. I suppose this wilna harm. Aye, ye may."

People were gathering around in a wall and watching her with somber faces. They stared at her like she was a threat. She was a stranger who looked like nothing they'd ever seen. And now she wanted to try to heal one of their own...

Behind them, the actual walls of the castle shot into the sky like a granite prison. Guards and warriors patrolled on the gallery over the walls. Down the slope, hidden behind the barracks, stables, and other buildings were the gatehouse and the gate.

Unreachable.

Was it just her or did the walls seem to shrink and narrow around her? The main keep was rectangular and six floors high, with tiny slit windows cutting the surface like eyes.

Unease washed over her. She was on a very thin ice. They thought she was a whore, a faerie, an English enemy. What did she really know about the medieval world? And even if she could diagnose Una without a thermometer, a stethoscope, and an otoscope, she had no access to modern medicine. There were no antibiotics, no syringes, no acetaminophen. So she wouldn't be able to treat her in the way she knew would work.

And yet, she'd sworn the Hippocratic oath, and she couldn't stand by and do nothing when she saw a sick baby. Even if she was putting herself in danger, she had to try.

"I'm going to touch her now," she said to Ailis, and a murmur went over the gathered crowd.

She laid the back of her hand on the baby's forehead. Scalding. Through the coarse, linen folds of the swaddling blanket, she found the baby's little hand. It was small, soft, and burning. She needed to measure the pulse on her wrist, but the girl kept shuffling her hands and feet as she cried.

One good thing about the crying was that Jenny could easily see the throat. "Does Una nurse?" she asked as she looked deep into the baby's mouth. The tonsils were red and inflamed. Una had a fever, a dry cough, and was fussy. Her upper lip was wet with mucus.

"Oh, nae," Ailis said weakly. "Poor wee thing hasna the strength."

Una must have a sore throat. Most babies ate and drank less if they had a cold, ear infection, or flu.

Una needed some way to stay hydrated. Jenny would normally prescribe an oral rehydration therapy drink from a drugstore. There was also a homemade version with a bit of refined sugar and salt mixed in water. But refined sugar wasn't available in the Middle Ages. She could ask Aulay for salt; he had offered her some when they ate in the great hall.

"We need to keep her hydrated and find a way to lower her fever," said Jenny. "How long has she been like this?"

"A sennight. What is hydra...?" asked Ailis.

"Keep her drinking liquids, it's very important for her to get better."

She needed her otoscope to properly check for an ear infection, but she looked into the child's ears, anyway. There was no fluid oozing out, thankfully.

"How long has her nose been congested?" she asked.

A strong, dry cough exploded from Ailis's chest. Just like Una's. "Oh, a few days," Ailis said once her coughing fit stopped. "The healer thinks 'tis too much phlegm, ye ken. 'Tis why she needs to be outside."

This could be the flu, too. The influenza virus was much deadlier without modern medical care.

"Nonsense," Jenny said. "Cold wind will make her lungs worse. What she needs is a warm and humid space to ease the dry cough, something to help with the fever, and plenty of fluids."

Ailis shook her head. "Nae."

Being aware of Aulay's heavy stare, Jenny licked her lips nervously. She didn't remember the last time she'd had to work so hard to convince a patient to take the treatment. "Please, Ailis. At least let me help you get her to take some milk...or even water."

"Nae. I thought mayhap ye kent something Bhatair didna.

But what ye're suggesting is what he said to nae do. And he said she'd get worse first. 'Tis the sweating sickness."

"I did say she has an excess of sanguine humor," said a man as he made his way through the crowd.

She turned her head. Coming to stand next to Aulay, the man was dark blond and of average height, which, next to Aulay, made him look short. He wore a long, brown tunic that fell to the edges of his pointy shoes. A wide leather belt wrapped around his waist. He didn't have a cross on his chest, but there was something monk-like about him. He had a basket in his hands and watched Jenny with a frown in his intelligent, piercing blue eyes.

Ah. This must be Bhatair, the physician. Jenny stood up. He eyed her up and down, puzzled.

"And to balance the sanguine humor, Una needs to go outside into the cold, dry environment. So 'tis working."

Humors...what were the humors again? She did remember something about that from the history of medicine classes.

"Laird," Bhatair demanded, "why is a whore looking at my patients and talking nonsense?"

Jenny opened her mouth to say something, as did Aulay, but Ailis interrupted, "She said she is a physician, and she touched Una. Then she said Una needs some hydra..."

"Liquids," said Jenny firmly. "Una needs her mother's milk or water. She also needs to have her fever reduced, and she needs to have some sort of a steam—"

Bhatair raised his hand. "Silence."

Jenny gasped. "How dare you silence me? This baby needs help, and all you've been doing is making her worse. She may have the flu. And if she has an ear infection, being outside in the cold is dangerous."

Bhatair shook his head. "Ear infection," he scoffed. "There's nae such thing as an ear infection. Ye say ye're a physician. But if ye kent anything about medicine like an educated physician, ye'd ken the baby and the mother have the sweating sickness, and need to be outside to cool down the hot humor of sanguine. Ye should keep out of my way and do yer womanly duties... Which"—he swept his disgusted gaze over her clothes—"ye are clearly interpreting as whoredom." He turned to Aulay. "She needs to be punished like any whore should."

Jenny took a shaky breath. She'd never been so insulted in her life. Her hands shook as he approached Ailis and Una, pushed Jenny to the side, and sank to his knees in front of them. Tears burned Jenny's eyes as helplessness swept over her. She should say something. She should keep fighting. But the strength was sucked out of her with every breath she took. The medieval world was cruel and unfair and so misogynistic.

They thought she was a whore. They thought she should be punished, kept in a prison...perhaps even killed. What could she do to make them change their minds when it would take centuries for humanity to evolve?

Something felt warm on her skin, and she realized Aulay was staring at her with a mixture of confusion and empathy. A big jump from his usual "one wrong word and I'll kill you" glare.

Bhatair took a clay cup with a closed lid out of the basket and handed it to Ailis. "'Tis for the pain. Mead mixed with willow bark and some uisge."

Jenny opened her mouth in shock. As she was thinking about how to stop this, he took out an empty animal horn with some sort of a nipple attached to its pointy end...made of leather, she thought. Ailis inserted the nipple into the baby's mouth, and Bhatair poured the liquid from the cup.

The baby became quiet and sucked. It was like watching a car accident. She knew it was a disaster but couldn't look away.

Once Una drank the liquid, she only fussed for a bit, and in a matter of minutes dozed off.

"I have the same for ye," said Bhatair and gave Ailis another cup.

While Ailis drank, Jenny couldn't stand back anymore. "How

could you give a six-month-old baby alcohol and honey? You must want to kill her."

Bhatair sighed and stood up, his fists on his waist. "And why are they bad for a bairn, pray tell?"

"The bacteria in honey can lead to infant botulism, which can be deadly. Willow bark has acetylsalicylic acid and can cause Reye's syndrome. And mead and uisge are both alcohol! Alcohol is toxic. You're damaging the baby's brain."

Silence fell over the crowd, and in a moment, Bhatair as well as the people gathered around them burst out laughing. Humiliation washed over Jenny like heavy rain.

It seemed like his treatment had helped. The baby was knocked out from the alcohol. And, of course, she knew chances were slim that the bacteria was in this honey and for acetylsalicylic acid, otherwise known as aspirin, to cause real harm. And she supposed in medieval conditions, this was probably one of the best available treatments...

So maybe they were right to laugh, and she should let the healer who knew this time do his job.

"Now, Ailis, let us go inside, and I'll let yer blood," Bhatair said.

CHAPTER 8

AULAY WATCHED Jennifer with a sort of regret and anger that he didn't understand himself. He saw the hurt and humiliation in her big amber eyes as everyone laughed at her. He didn't. He supposed he'd always been soft-hearted to the rejected and the misunderstood. And her humiliation, her anger had been sincere.

He could see she wasn't used to being treated this way, and he remembered that she'd run her husband's practice for years. He couldn't help but respect a strong woman who managed her husband's affairs. As a loyal man himself, he felt sorry for her and angry with her husband who'd been a whoremonger while she worked for him.

If Aulay was honest, he'd always thought Bhatair was a wee bit of a fool about himself. He was a Highlander who had gone to Paris to study modern medicine, and when Aulay had hired him to stay in Islay and work for the MacDonald clan, he'd asked an immoderate amount of money. Which Aulay was happy to pay to keep his people healthy. But the man could be harsh and arrogant.

Aulay realized, against his better judgment, he'd been cheering for the feisty wee fox.

Until her advice had made no sense, and Bhatair had actually helped the baby like he was supposed to.

Aulay had wanted her to be right and to be able to heal the baby with her strange notions.

But after she'd said some words that made no sense at all, he'd realized she was just lying. Inventing things. Trying to fool everyone.

And he'd had enough. What was that word, "bacteria"? What did that even mean?

No, she must have lied all along about being a healer. She was trying to charm them, like some charlatans did, selling miraculous remedies that never worked. And if she had lied about that, she may be lying about what ship she was on when she was crossing the sea to Ireland.

He couldn't stand charlatans. Seven years ago, about three weeks after he'd returned to Dunyvaig with Robert the Bruce, one such "healer" had come to Islay. He'd had a cart full of potions and exotic roots. Dried bat wings. Amulets. Potions that smelled like heaven and hell mixed together.

Leitis had been in pain for months by then. She was weak. And she desperately wanted that child because she knew how much Aulay wanted an heir.

Aulay had seen how every time the tiny body of one of their dead babies had been buried, the light in her eyes grew dimmer. She'd taken it as a sign from God that this man had come to Islay, and she'd bought a potion from him for a healthy labor and delivery.

Both Bhatair and Aulay had told her not to. Bhatair had never heard of the potion and didn't want to put her in danger. Aulay just didn't trust the man. And she'd told them she wouldn't take it. But the potion had disappeared. And then she got worse. And then the babe didn't even make it out during the labor. And Aulay had almost hunted down and killed the charlatan.

Bhatair told him that had she not taken that potion, maybe she and the baby could have been saved.

So, if Jenny was one of those charlatans who got rich on empty promises and lies—

The feel of his wife's dead body, still warm, on his lap... The belly that was round but as still as she. The babe that didn't move inside her anymore... She'd been buried still pregnant, his dead lad or lass still inside of her.

Fury slapped him in an icy-cold shock.

God forgive him, he'd rather die than let another charlatan harm any of his people. While Bhatair led Ailis and Una away for the bloodletting, Aulay grabbed Jennifer by her elbow and dragged her out of the crowd. He saw red, darkness mixed with fury, that made the world around him sharp and bright.

"What are you doing!" she yelled, trying to free herself. "Let me go!"

He turned the corner of the stables, away from the gazes of the crowd, and cornered her. She was pressed against the wall, he a step away.

"Tell me once and for all, lass, do ye take me for a fool?"

"What?"

"Ye are nae a physician. Just confess."

"I am a physician!"

He shook his head. "Ye are nae. All that nonsense ye told. I ken yer sort. Empty words. Empty promises. What is it to ye if one more fool dies, deceived by yer lies?"

A tremor went through her like wind over still water. "I am a doctor! I took an oath to do no harm. How dare you? I have helped thousands of children in my lifetime."

God, the way her eyes shone as she said that...like a knight on a horse, waving the banner, calling for the troops to charge. His blood answered the call, heat washing through him like an army. "Aye, ye 'helped,' did ye? And did ye defy yer husband like this, too?"

"Defied? Of course I defied him. Who was he to tell me what to do, and who are you?"

He took a moment to look her over. Her dress was torn at

the edges and dirty in places, but still the bright-green color shone like sunlight through the first spring leaves. Her breasts rose and fell quickly, luscious and heaving. Her cheeks were flushed, eyes bright and glistening with her own fury and fire. Her lips... Good God, her lips were like cherries he'd once tried in the south...

"Do ye ken," he said slowly, "what is done to women who keep behaving like ye do?"

"I didn't do anything wrong, you giant oaf."

One step closer, and he was pinning her to the wall, his chest to hers, her cherry lips just an inch away. Her sweet breath reached him, and he craved to kiss her. "Women are their husbands' property," he said slowly, marveling at how smooth her skin was. "To discipline and to put in their place."

She raised her chin high. "I'm not anyone's property. You think you can intimidate me? Well, you can't. All you are is an arrogant, self-righteous man who thinks he can do anything just because he was born male." The feel of her soft breasts moving as she breathed against his rib cage was like warm uisge, making him dizzy, weak, and hot from desire. "Who gave you the right to manhandle me and kidnap me? If it weren't for you, I'd be back in my time now."

Mesmerized by the movement of her lips, he didn't understand what "back in my time" meant, didn't even think it mattered. Just more of her odd words and notions.

"Who gave me the right to touch ye?" he growled. "Nae one, lass. The laird doesna need permission to do as he likes. If I want to, ye'll be mine by right."

God's bones, he'd never met anyone so strange and defiant and so beautiful. And suddenly the thought of her being his felt like the only right thing there was.

And so, it seemed, did it for her. Because there was that glint in her eyes.

And they came together, her cherry lips finally on him.

CHAPTER 9

HIS LIPS DEMANDED. Claimed. Ravished. The glide of his mouth against hers was a revelation.

It was the heat of the sun and the downpour of rain. His tongue possessed her. Devoured her.

His scent was like a drug. She was helpless. Shameless.

Her back ground against the hard rock wall of the stables, and she didn't care. Let it. All she wanted was him—closer, closer...so close there wouldn't be any distinction between where he ended and she began.

Then his hands massaged her ass, and her leg was hooked around his hip, and her hands were in his hair. They were one aching, needing ball of tangled limbs, unable to let go.

Never had she feel anything like this. Not with Tom. Not with the couple of boyfriends she'd gone out with before Tom.

She throbbed, aching and wet, and she felt him, long and hard, as she melted against him. He growled like a bear, and when he began thrusting, pleasure spilled through her from the sweet friction. She wanted him inside her, here and now. Against the wall. Part of her thought distantly that this was what Amanda must have been talking about when she'd recommended sex with a Highlander...

"Lass, I want ye..." he growled. "Tell me ye want to be mine."

Yes, her body wanted to say. It was the only thing it could say.

But someone cleared their throat loudly, and they both froze and slowly looked in the direction of the cough. It was that tall, handsome man. Colum. With his arms crossed over his chest and a puzzled frown on his face.

Several things became clear to Jenny at once. One, her dress was pretty much up to her waist, so Colum was staring at her bare leg hooked around his uncle's hip. Two, Aulay's hips were firmly pressed against her very aroused sex. Both Aulay and she were panting. And she was high above the ground, pinned to the wall by Aulay. Three, even though they were both clothed, it must have looked to Colum as though he'd interrupted them while they were having sex.

Four, behind Colum, several of the locals peered around the corner, faces astonished and disapproving.

Oh, God, no. Now they would all be sure she was a whore, wouldn't they?

Slowly, Aulay set her on the ground and, thankfully, her dress slid down. She straightened her clothes, still hot and aroused, still unable to shake the incredible high of being in this man's arms.

"What is the matter?" said Aulay. "What couldna wait?"

"The bairn... Una..." said one of the women behind Colum. "She got worse."

"What?" Jenny stepped forward. "But he just gave her the potion."

Another woman pinned her angry eyes on Jenny. "Aye, he did. But ye touched Una before, didna ye?"

Silence fell as Jenny realized they were all staring at her accusatorily.

"I just examined her," said Jenny, feeling their aggression and fear pulsating like an engorged vein.

"But Ailis," said a man, "said she got worse because ye're a witch. And ye did something to hurt Una when ye touched her."

Jenny gasped. Helplessness and anger churned within her like a sickening mixture. "What? That's ridiculous... Let me see..."

Without giving anyone another glance, she marched from behind the stables towards where Bhatair had just led Ailis and Una. With much hubbub, the crowd followed her.

"Jennifer!" cried Aulay as he drew level with her. "Dinna ye think ye've done enough?"

"Apparently not. If the baby got worse, it wasn't because of my touch. It was because she wasn't treated properly!"

Or because it may be too late for her to recover...

The door of a house opened and Bhatair stepped out. His face was somber, but when he saw her, his nostrils flared.

"Ye," he growled.

"What is going on with Una?" she asked. "Let me pass."

He stood in front of the door, and when she stepped forward to enter, he blocked her way. "Ye did this. Ye are a witch and a charlatan. Ye made Una worse when ye examined her with yer strange ways and strange speeches. Mayhap ye called upon the faeries or cursed the bairn. Who kens what ye're capable of when ye're dressed like that and speak lies about being a physician?"

"And she's seducing the laird!" called one of the women behind them.

"Aye!" cried another. "She poisoned his mind! He doesna see her clearly for what she is. A curse to all of us."

Jenny looked over her shoulder. The gathering consisted of about twenty people, and all of them were in an uproar. Shaking their fists in the air. Faces furious and mean under their coifs and veils.

"Whip her, Lord!"

"Whip her for whoredom!"

"Kill her!"

"Get her off of the island!"

The cries made Jenny dizzy. All that hatred, all that rejection. She'd never felt anything like this in her life—not this humiliation, not this judgment. And so unfairly. She was just trying to help. Part of her wanted to give up, do anything to get away from here.

She was in hell.

She turned to Bhatair, who eyed her with furious contempt. "Is she running a fever again?" Jenny asked. "Just let me look at her. I promise you, I know what I'm doing. If she develops pneumonia, she'll need antibiotics..."

Bhatair's nostrils flared. "Ye've done enough, whore. Laird, do something. Listen to yer people. Ye canna let her go around lying and promising people empty cures when she canna truly do anything."

Jenny glanced at Aulay. She should have gotten on his good side by now. She should have made him like her...believe her... help her. Aulay's dark eyes were on her. There was a glimmer in that darkness that she didn't understand. His jaw muscles worked, but he didn't say anything. Then when the uproar reached the next level, he turned to his people and raised his hands to the sides.

He opened his mouth to say something, but a horn sounded from the wall.

"Attack!" cried a voice that brought a chill to Jenny's bones.

CHAPTER 10

"To the walls!" Aulay yelled as he ran down towards the gates. "Close the gates!"

Who was attacking? What was happening? His blood was still pumping hard from the maddening kiss that Jennifer and he had shared, then by the danger she seemed to be putting herself into.

And now this.

Following his men, he climbed the stone stairs leading to the wall gallery. They should have trained harder. They should have made the repairs to the birlinns that still needed them.

It was too late.

The English? The Irish that had found the English treasure ship before them? Another Lowland clan siding with the enemy?

Who was it?

When he stood on top of the curtain wall, his heart dropped.

The sea was calm and empty, no one headed down to the secluded Lagavulin Bay. The ships floated peacefully. But in the village below, people ran towards their houses.

And then he saw it.

From the woods behind the village, a band of men charged

towards them. Swords and axes were drawn, shields at the ready. And they were well armored: chain mail coifs, helmets, breastplates, and boiled leather. Not léintean-cròich—thick, quilted coats—like most of Highlanders had. The English. The unmistakable yellow surcoat with three red lions flashed between the gray rock of the houses.

Must be about five dozen of them. He muttered an oath and looked around. Colum and Seoras were there, so was Beathan.

"Archers, ready!" he commanded, and twenty archers pulled the strings of their bows. They had time to shoot at the enemy while they were still running towards the village through the open field. "Shoot!"

A swarm of arrows flew into the air with a swoosh. Some of the enemy fell, but most kept running. "Ready! Shoot!" he roared.

They repeated the shooting until the enemy was too close to the village.

"Swordsmen!" He turned around and unsheathed his claymore and stabbed the air with it. "Down to the village!"

The men down below in the bailey waited. Every MacDonald warrior knew when that horn sounded, they had to be ready to fight. As Aulay hurried down the stone stairs, he scanned the inner bailey. Jennifer stood a wee bit away, her face worried. He felt his expression harden. She could try to get away in the chaos and get herself in danger.

"Beathan," he said over his shoulder, "go and lock her in my bedchamber, then return to the battle, aye?"

He didn't need to say to his friend who "her" was.

"Aye, Lord," Beathan said and sprinted towards Jennifer. Aulay turned to his men. "Let us go and protect our people and our land! Protect yer families, yer wives, and yer home! Clann Domnhnaill! Clann Domnhnaill!"

"Clann Domnhnaill! Clann Domnhnaill!" echoed his men, pumping their fists, holding their claymores high up in the air.

Then they were off, sprinting like wolves down the inner

bailey and through the gatehouse and down the road to the village. Aulay could already see the first enemy warriors clashing with the villagers. Every MacDonald—farmer, shepherd, or blacksmith—had a sword and knew at least the basics of how to wield it. He had made sure of it.

But most people who lived in the village were not true warriors. Their daily business wasn't to train on the sword or the bow. It was work that sustained the everyday life of the clan.

But in cases like this, they could protect themselves at least for a short time.

Aulay and his men hurtled through the village.

Goddamn it to hell, how had the English arrived here? Did they land on the other side of the island and come here on foot?

A dozen villagers fought and were losing against two dozen enemy warriors. One villager held his sword at the level of his head while the Englishman forced his sword down on him. Another, backed against a wall, had a bad gash on his right shoulder and slashed with his sword poorly at the enemy.

Aulay roared, "Clann Domnhnaill! Clann Domnhnaill!"

The villagers heard him. "Clann Domnhnaill!" they echoed.

"Clann Domnhnaill!" Aulay's warriors shouted.

They ran at the enemy with full force and clashed. Aulay pushed one Englishman off Conn, the tanner, and swung his sword at the man's head. The man deflected it and slashed with his own blade. It was Aulay's turn to deflect, and he knocked the sword back with no difficulty. The warrior was young and strong but inexperienced. Aulay could see right away with pups like him where his weakness was.

Aulay made a small lunge to his right, but instead, went left and thrust his sword into the bearded face. The Englishman fell and didn't stand up again.

Aulay clapped Conn's shoulder. "Thanks, Lord," the tanner said.

Around him, his men hurled spears, wielded their axes and swords, sliced at limbs and heads. Warriors circled each other, came together, and clashed swords. Steel glistened, and as flesh tore and blood spilled, men cried in pain.

There were more of the English than Aulay had thought. It must have been a ship or two full of warriors. He knew he had seven dozen warriors by his side. Their numbers were fairly evenly matched, but the English were far better armed. Still, they were Highlanders and they were fighting for their home and their honor. It would take more than several dozen Englishmen to bring them to their knees.

The iron tang of blood was so thick around him, he could taste it on his tongue. The earth of Islay was being generously fed with gore today. Then all was a blur of gore and the rage of a battle that took him over like a full goblet of fiery uisge. He jabbed and cut and ripped his blade into the chain mail. He twirled and ducked and avoided bad blows.

Until he didn't. He had just clashed swords with another Englishman when his back prickled with an acute sense of danger. But he couldn't turn, or he would be killed.

Then there was something like a soft push. He took a step to his side and thrust his sword belly-deep into the Englishman right through his boiled armor.

Then he looked.

Nae!

It was Beathan.

He lay on the ground with a spear thrust through his chest. His eyes were unmoving, and blood bloomed through his léine-chròich, around the wooden sheath.

He had taken the death meant for Aulay. Disregarding the chaos of the battle around him, Aulay dropped to his knees in front of his loyal friend. He lowered his head and pressed it against Beathan's chest. Pain tore at his gut.

"Nae ye, Beathan. Nae ye!"

Countless times Aulay had saved Beathan's life. Countless times Beathan had saved his. Beathan was ten years younger than Aulay, and he had been one Aulay's first students to train in sword fighting. He had been late to take a wife, but Ailis was the love of his life, and Una was the very center of his happiness.

What would he tell Ailis? How could he go and tell her that her husband and the father of her bairn would not return to her?

He straightened his back, closed Beathan's unseeing eyes, and laid his friend's sword on his stomach, pressing his still-warm fists around the handle.

"Rest in peace, my friend," he said. "Ye are with God now."

$\sim$

AULAY'S ARMS ACHED AS HE HELD THE ROUGH WOODEN handles of the stretcher. His whole body was aching and sweaty under his tunic. The sky grayed, and rain had started drizzling, as though God was mourning Beathan, too. The way up the hill towards Dunyvaig Castle had become slick and muddy. The castle loomed over him, silent and solemn.

Like his own heart.

The English had lost and retreated. Before he had killed one of them, Aulay had learned the attackers were sent to discover if Aulay had found the shipwreck, and to retrieve the treasure if possible.

That meant the English hadn't found it. The treasure was still out there.

It meant he needed to have a serious conversation with the sole survivor of the shipwreck...Jennifer Foster.

They needed that treasure, or this attack would be only a small taste of what the English and their Irish allies would do to Islay and the Highlands.

He looked up at the gatehouse as they came through. The rough stone glistened with rain. Colum held the back handles of Beathan's stretcher. The other Highlanders walked up with nine more stretchers with three wounded and six dead. Seven warriors he'd lost today. All of them were his pride and his friends.

But Beathan was someone he'd fought with for the past twenty years.

They passed through the gate and kept walking up the slope of the inner bailey, the scent of rain replaced the iron tang of blood, and Aulay raised his face to the sky, letting rain fall onto his face and become the tears he didn't let himself shed.

They stopped in front of Beathan's house, and Aulay and Colum put the stretcher on the ground to inform a sick woman with a six-moon-old bairn that she had just become a widow.

CHAPTER 11

IT WAS ALREADY LATE when Aulay shut the door of his bedchamber, confining himself with the copper-haired woman.

Exhaustion weighed on his body—from the battle, from holding himself steady while he talked to Ailis. Grief and anger fought within him, and he didn't think he'd have it in him to talk to Jennifer like he should.

But the moment he saw her, something lightened in his chest. With her dress so bright it seemed to glow, she looked foreign against rough stone walls, the muted red of the canopy curtains over his bed, and the fire reflecting from the swords and shields on the wall.

Seeing her bonnie face, he remembered how warm and delicious her body had felt in his arms earlier today. How her curves fit right into his hands as though made for him. How the need for her had consumed him, as though nothing else existed. He hadn't felt that since he was with Leitis... No, he couldn't remember a time even with her that he'd been so overtaken by desire. The mad, all-powerful drive to claim her for his own. Like a lad before he had his first woman.

"What happened?" she asked. "Who attacked? Are you all

right?" Her eyes scanned him as if looking for injuries. He was covered in blood, but it was all the blood of the enemy.

"English, looking for the shipwreck," he said, advancing on her. "The shipwreck ye refuse to talk about. They killed Beathan and six other men. Ye've been here for three days, and until ye tell me everything ye ken, it doesna look like ye're leaving anytime soon."

She opened her mouth, no doubt to protest, but he raised his hand to silence her and walked to the last in the row of chests standing in the corner. The one he hadn't touched for seven years. The wooden surface, the carved ornamentation of a romantic scene with a lady and a knight in a garden, was regularly cleaned by the servants so it didn't look like it had been untouched. He had bought this chest in the Kingdom of Galicia, a present for his beloved wife, and he remembered the bright smile on her face as he gave it to her. He'd sworn then to keep showering her with gifts as long as they would keep making her smile like that.

The slit window above the chest cast silvery moonlight, the shadows on the carvings dark.

"What are you doing?" Jennifer asked, her voice pulling him out of his thoughts.

He unlocked the chest, asking internally if what he was about to do was right. He was sure Leitis wouldn't want a woman to be cowed and to freeze in her completely unsuitable clothes when there was a whole chest of perfectly good clothing that no one used.

And no one would use. He wasn't going to marry. He wasn't going to lose anyone again.

"I'm giving ye some attire that is more suited," he said and lifted the lid.

It didn't smell like Leitis anymore. His servants put in lavender to keep moths away. He picked up a green dress that Leitis had worn during pregnancy and that had more room, since Jennifer had a more ample bosom and arse, he thought with his mouth going dry. He picked up an undertunic as well, a girdle, and another pair of shoes.

He stood and handed them to her. Jennifer took them with a frown. "Whose are they?"

"They belonged to my late wife, Leitis," he said. "She was taller and thinner, but they lie unused, and this way ye have something warmer. And people wilna be bothered by ye as much."

Jennifer looked at the garments like they were a dangerous animal. "Are you sure about this?"

Truth be told, he wasn't sure. It hurt to see another woman with Leitis's clothes. But it was for the peace of the village and to help this woman fit in. "Aye. 'Tis what she would have done in the first place had she been alive. I should have offered sooner."

"Look, I appreciate it, but are there any other clothes I could wear? I'm really not sure you're good with this—"

Something snapped within him. She was right, he was not entirely comfortable, but he was holding to his decision, because this was the right thing. If she kept insisting, she was increasing the heaviness and guilt in his chest.

"Just wear them!" he barked.

He didn't want to snap at her. He had a glass bottle of uisge on the table against the opposite wall, and he walked there briskly and poured a goblet for himself and for her, then handed it to her. She sniffed it while he downed his drink. She tasted it and grimaced and gave the goblet back to him.

"There's no need to spit fire, Aulay," she said. "I just mean, I understand it can't be easy for you to let another woman wear your wife's clothes."

He studied her, the creamy white of her skin, the lush breasts, the beautiful curve of her waist going into her round hips. "Mayhap ye understand," he said. "But I canna trust anything ye say until I am sure ye're telling the truth."

He would get the truth out of her about the shipwreck, whatever it required.

Seeing her in his bedchamber was intoxicating—he couldn't stop envisioning himself throwing her onto the bed and covering her with his body. If he tore that ridiculous dress to pieces, would her skin underneath it be just as soft as the skin on her face when he cupped it? He could fish the truth out of her that way...

Her chest rose and fell quickly, her gaze falling onto his bed and returning to him, dark and glossy.

She wanted him, too.

Slowly, he put the goblet back on the table and walked around her. She was standing with the clothes clutched to her stomach, breathing heavily.

"Stop pacing around me like a lion," she said. "You won't scare me."

"Ye should be scared. I'm this close to doing something I very much want to but shouldn't. Why did ye come up with all those strange lies? Do ye think I'm stupid? I didna build the richest clan of Scotland from nothing because I lack wits."

Aye, his goblets were made of gold, his bed had a rich drapery and nice blankets, furs. A Persian rug lay on the floor. The chairs, the table, and the bed were made by master carpenters, with beautiful carvings on the handles and backs. An intricately carved ivory box that came all the way from the Orient stood on the table. The cross over the door was silver with golden decorations and rubies, emeralds, and diamonds. The swords and shields that hung on the walls dated back to Somerled himself, the great Norse-Gaelic warlord who, two hundred years ago, through his conquests, created the Kingdom of Argyll and the Isles. Somerled's sons had started the MacDonald, Ruaidhrí, and MacDougall clans. These weapons were Aulay's pride and glory. He'd hoped to give them to his son—a futile hope, it seemed.

She raised her chin and then did something that completely threw him off guard. She reached out to him with her hand and touched his lips with her fingertips. The touch was like a kiss, the brush delicate and sending a jolt of desire straight into his groin. Her eyes glistened with the heat he remembered from their kiss.

"I don't care about your wealth," she said. "Just let me leave this island."

Let her go? He'd show her to tease him like that.

He took her by the hand, threw her onto his bed, and covered her with his body. She gasped and wriggled, trying to get out. So bonnie, with her cheeks flushed and her mouth red, her eyes glistening under her long lashes. Her body was soft and warm under him, all curves. He could feel her lush thighs that he'd like to spread with his knees and pleasure her, and watch her cheeks gain more color as she screamed his name in ecstasy.

"I have this wealth on this island ye want to leave so badly because I'm a trader. Because I have the fastest and best ships."

With his arm supporting him and his hips holding her firmly in place, he painted a map on her chest. "We sell fleece to Bruges and Dordrecht in the Low Countries." He made a long route down to her left breast. "We trade with Norway and France and Galicia. Other Mediterranean countries." He gently brought his finger down between her breasts and then went back up again and circled her nipple, and she inhaled sharply. "We go as far as Iceland and Hamburg." His finger went back up to her neck, and he gently traced it up to her chin.

Her chest rose and fell quickly, her skin flushed. He felt heat rush to his cock. God's bones she was bonnie. "Great," she said, her voice low and breathy. "What does this have to do with me?"

"Behind England's back"—he brought his fingers higher and cupped her face—"I trade with the Irish. Edward II has been hunting MacDonald ships in the Irish Sea, but we ken how to evade them and how to fight."

He pressed his thumb against her lush lower lip. It reddened and became fuller. Oh, she wanted him like he wanted her. He craved to bite that lip gently and suck on it.

She wriggled under him, breathing heavily. "So? What are you trying to say?"

She felt so good under him. Christ, if he kissed her now, they wouldn't be able to stop. He shouldn't take advantage of her being his prisoner. He shouldn't abuse that power, even though he really wanted to. He still didn't trust her, but taking her would be about pleasure, not trust.

"I'm trying to say there's nae people more skilled at sea than clan MacDonald. And yet, with all my ships and all my men, I canna find the English shipwreck. The shipwreck that ye survived. How?"

"I..." There was doubt in her eyes. A question. And fear. "I don't know how to explain it."

"What are ye hiding, lass?"

She was silent for a while, seemingly having lost her breath. She pushed against him, and he let her go right away.

She stood up and paced the room, putting some distance between them. He sat up and leaned over his knees, watching her every move.

"You want to intimidate the shit out of me," she said. "But it won't work. You think I'm lying. But I want to tell you the truth, actually. Only, this truth will make you think I'm crazy."

For the first time, he believed her. Whatever she was about to say would be true. He folded his arms and nodded. "Aye. I am listening."

She blew a long breath out through her lush, O-shaped mouth that made him think of her lips curving around something else... "I came from the future," she said, and all pleasant images evaporated from his head.

"What?" he asked.

"I traveled through time. From the year 2022. I was traveling with my friends, just a vacation, and we got stranded on that damned island. There was a lighthouse...and yes, I was a little drunk...and then there was this woman who came and told me about you. And when I touched that rock with a hand carved into it, I fell through time. And when I opened my eyes, there was no lighthouse on the island. My friends and the boat that brought us there were gone. There was just your ship out in the distance, and I was terrified and called to you."

When she grew silent, there was so much hope in her eyes, his heart ached. But he had never heard a more ridiculous story in his life. It wasn't even well thought out. He laughed. "Time travel? Dear woman, 'tis a jest, surely. I could have believed ye about the shipwreck—there was a big storm ten days ago. But ye canna expect me to believe ye come from another time."

The hope in her eyes died. "Yes, I was in a shipwreck," she said. "On my way to Ireland to see my family."

"The English treasure ship?"

"No. It was a regular ship. I don't know anything about the treasure."

"Are ye sure? What was its name?"

"*Victoria*," she said.

Victoria? Strange name.

"What happened exactly?"

She cleared her throat and looked down at her feet. "There was a storm. We got turned over. I woke up on the shore of that island."

He studied her for a while. She kept looking at him silently, withdrawn, and quiet. So unlike her. He didn't like that the fire in her was extinguished. But something felt wrong about this Ireland story just like the previous one. Could he really believe her that she wasn't on the English treasure ship? He wasn't willing to torture her to get that information. Maybe he had to win her trust instead.

"I will help ye navigate here until I ken what to do with ye. Are ye really a healer? Did you tell me the truth about that?"

"I am."

"All right, lass." He went to his table and poured more uisge into his goblet. "I will tell ye how to behave and ye must listen carefully and dinna interrupt or question this. Clearly ye canna be doing what ye're doing on purpose."

"I appreciate the tips, but I can't promise not to interrupt or question."

He drank the uisge and shook his head, chuckling. "Of course ye canna. Look, lass, ye canna be insulting people and talking back to men. Ye assume ye're right in everything. Ye saw what yer behavior can lead to. I may be forced to punish ye. Ye must learn to be humble. I enjoy the fire in ye, but if ye want to fit in, 'tis what ye have to do."

She shook her head in exasperation and blew a long breath out. "I know you're right...it's just..."

"Aye."

He liked that she could be flexible and wouldn't just defy him. He could claim her as his mistress. If she only gave herself to him, how sweet her body would feel... She was no virgin; she'd had a husband. They were both experienced. This could be a very pleasant arrangement.

But no. He couldn't do it. Knowing himself, he'd get attached far too quickly. He was not interested in female conquests. And what would that lead to, anyway? He didn't trust this woman completely. She was a stranger and wanted to leave. If he fell in love with her and she left one day...he'd be devastated. And he didn't think he would be able to sustain a broken heart again.

"Join me tomorrow to break the fast. I will find ye a place to stay, a bedchamber."

CHAPTER 12

THE NEXT MORNING, Jenny went down to the great hall, but the servants told her Aulay was in the courtyard. As she descended the stairs, the linen undertunic scratched her body. The dress he had given her was too long for her, but she had asked a kitchen maid to help her shorten it. The woman may have been too nice to refuse to help or maybe she didn't know who Jenny was. Before hemming the dress, she shortened it with the rough, medieval scissors that looked like they belonged in a torture chamber.

The dress was pretty, and now that it was the right length, it fit her well, even though it was a little tight in the bust. But it did the job of helping her blend in, unlike her own dress, which screamed to everyone she was an outsider.

But the best part was the shoes. Unlike the shoes Aulay had brought her in the dungeon, these were made of soft leather and felt like nothing on her feet. They also protected her feet from dirt and mud. She marveled at how a simple change of dress altered the way she felt. She could imagine she was a medieval lady. Only that prospect wasn't very bright. In fact, all she'd known of this time until now was danger.

The courtyard of the castle was gray under the dark, grim

clouds. The chaos of activity greeted her—bleating sheep, clucking chickens, honking geese. Servants carried firewood, pushed carts with hay and branches. Warriors sparred on swords and spears and shot arrows into targets.

The air was humid and cold, lush with the scent of the sea and wet mud, manure, and woodsmoke. Rhythmic sounds of metal banging against metal as the men sparred and the ring of a distant hammer hitting an anvil filled the air. Men cried out as they trained.

And then she saw Aulay. He stood in front of a group of children with a sword and demonstrated a movement. The boys and girls, standing in two rows, repeated his movement. There were about twenty of them, between the ages of ten and twelve.

With her heart melting, she slowly walked towards the group. The pregnant woman she'd seen with Seoras sat nearby and weaved a basket, throwing smiling glances at the children from time to time.

"...and then Somerled came down from his ship," proclaimed Aulay, "and he and his brave band of warriors stormed the castle of Glasgow..."

The children giggled and roared. Their faces were full of fierce joy, and Jenny's heart lit up like a bulb. Aulay took a step forward, and simultaneously brought his sword down diagonally with an exaggerated grunt. Echoing him, the children all took a step forward and swung their swords with a grunt.

Jenny must have spontaneously ovulated another one of her last eggs. It was too bad she couldn't get pregnant from regular sex, or maybe she'd let the Scottish giant have his way with her. He was older than her, but clearly still in his prime. The way his muscles played under his tunic as he slashed the sword, the way his thighs bulged, tightening the fabric of the breeches, the way the wind threw strands of long hair into his handsome, fierce face made her breathless. But with every minute and every hour, the appointment at the clinic was approaching. And her chances of having a baby were decreasing.

Aulay locked eyes with her, and the ground shifted under her. He told the kids to keep training and walked to Jenny.

"Lady Jennifer," he said as he stood by her side.

Just his presence next to her made her skin buzz. "Laird Aulay. Please, call me Jenny."

He smiled a crooked grin. "Aye. Jenny."

He said her name slowly, and it rolled off his tongue like candy.

Jenny bit her lip to stop herself from smiling. "Who are the children?" she asked.

"Children of the clan including those who have nae parents nae more. I only teach them what their own fathers would have if they were still alive."

Oh, wow. Did he care about children like she did?

His face darkened, and he added, "What I will one day teach Una, too."

Jenny's heart sank. When he'd told her Beathan had died protecting him, her heart bled for Ailis and for Una. She gave him a reassuring smile. She saw how hard he took Beathan's death.

"Is it common that you're teaching girls to fight on swords, too?"

He sighed and chuckled, almost shaking off the sadness. "Girls' main priority is to learn household chores, but MacDonald women should always be able to defend themselves. It's in our blood. Viking roots. Celts and Picts. Pictish kings were chosen from the woman's bloodline. Viking women often knew how to use a short sword and a bow. The women who my clan came from were fierce, and I want that to be part of the legacy I leave for future generations."

This was kind of forward thinking for the Middle Ages, wasn't it? Empowering girls and treating them equally... Clearly not in all regards, based on how he had treated her. But, it seemed, he respected their right to fight and defend themselves. How could he be so arrogant and bossy and bark commands at her but, at the same time, have this softer side that she could admire and respect?

"And there's Mhairi." He nodded to the pregnant woman who was weaving the basket. "She watches over the children."

Roaring, one of the younger boys ran to Aulay with his wooden sword, but before he could ram into the laird, Aulay picked him up and swung him around. The boy burst out in delighted giggles that only children could. Jenny saw sad children who didn't feel well every day of her life—she didn't get to see much of this side of their lives, and this moment was like the sun rising after a long night. That was what she lived for, to have her own child and give them moments like these...a million moments like these. She melted, watching this big, brawny High-lander lose all his fierceness and be raw and happy.

Mhairi left her basket and hurried to them. "Artur," she cried. "Get off the laird this minute!"

"'Tis all right!" Aulay put Artur down, and they both giggled. It was impossible to say who had a bigger grin, Artur or Aulay.

Jenny's own lips spread in a giant smile but then fell. A yellow crust formed around the child's lips and under his nose. Impetigo. It was a mild bacterial infection that sometimes occurred in children. She could easily treat it with an antibiotic cream.

"Wait..." She sank to a crouch in front of Artur. "Artur, how long have you had this around your lips?"

The boy stopped smiling and looked suspiciously at her. "I dinna ken...three...four sennights."

That was textbook impetigo. "Do you have sores on your skin anywhere else?"

Artur looked at Aulay, who gave him a short nod. "'Tis all right, lad. Ye may tell her." After a long pause, he added, "She may be able to help."

Something warmed in Jenny's chest. Was he finally trusting her, believing in her abilities?

Artur nodded and rolled up the sleeve of his tunic. There

were more small sores, and dark-red and yellowish crusts formed over most of them. Normally, children between the ages of two and five got it, but Artur was probably ten. She thought it must be because of the lack of hygiene. If they all lived in an orphanage, more children were probably infected. Impetigo spread in day cares and preschools every year, in summers and winters.

"Are there more of your friends with this?" she asked.

"Aye," said Artur.

She nodded. What could she use instead of antibiotic cream? She wished she knew more about herbal medicine. Something about garlic and onion came to mind.

"Did you notice these sores, Mhairi?" Jenny asked.

"Aye. God is putting them through a test. 'Tis a miasma they're carrying."

"Miasma?" Jenny asked. "Like, a smell?"

"Aye. It comes from the orphanage."

"Can you please show me?"

"Aye." Mhairi exchanged a glance with Aulay. "I suppose I can."

"Come," Aulay said. "I'll show ye myself."

They walked behind the keep and towards a timber building with a thatched roof. As Mhairi opened the door and stepped in, Jenny could smell a combination of dust and rotting food and vegetation. There were ten big beds and chests lining the walls. The windows were without glass, and daylight shone through them. There was a long hearth in the middle, a hole in the roof above it. The floor was covered in reeds. The sheets on the beds and the blankets could use a good wash—they looked gray brown with yellowish stains.

"Nae matter how much lavender I throw on the floor reeds, nothing helps," said Mhairi.

No doubt bacteria gathered here; it must be in the floor reeds. Who knew how many years they had been here and what was underneath.

"What do you use against infection on wounds?" Jenny asked.

"Infection?" Mhairi pronounced the word awkwardly.

"Umm...rot?" Jenny guessed.

"Ah, rot-wound. Wild garlic and honey."

"Oh, this is perfect! Honey will work great and will probably soften the sting of the garlic. The children have impetigo. It's a disease..." She thought about how to put it in terms they'd understand. "That's the miasma that they all have. We should try garlic mixed with honey."

"I only have wild garlic."

"That will work. I can help you."

"Aye. Thank ye, my lady. I have those things in my medicinal basket." She showed them to the opposite end of the room and approached a table with a basket on top of it. Aulay came in, too. The woman retrieved a glass bottle with a green liquid in it. Pieces of a green plant swam in the liquid. "'Tis the wild garlic tincture that Bhatair made. Jenny, would ye pour some into the bowl and some honey and mix the two together?"

While Mhairi rummaged in the chest with jars and pouches standing by the table, Jenny did as asked. "The floor needs to be cleaned of those reeds," Jenny said. "There's where the miasma comes from. The sheets will need to be washed well. The mattresses beaten out. All that holds the sickness that afflicted them."

Aulay looked around the floor. "Mhairi alone canna do all that."

"I'll help," Jenny said as she stirred the honey and the wild garlic tincture. "I'm happy to. And if you can, it would really help it if you could make wooden floors for the children. They will keep warm better, will be easier to clean, too, and will keep miasma away. Is it possible, do you think?"

Aulay nodded and pushed the reeds with his foot. "If 'tis better for the children, everything is possible. Timber is always an expensive resource, but we have the woods on Islay. Most of the timber goes into shipbuilding, but I can spare men to take some timber they already have and build the wooden floors. I promise ye."

Jenny studied him. He was so handsome with his strong jaw and chiseled cheekbones, plus all those bulging muscles, threatening to tear the seams of his tunic.

"Let me get the rake and start on cleaning this," he said and walked out. When he came back, he worked the rake, clearing the reeds out of the building.

Jenny started clearing them out as well. Under the reeds, on the packed-dirt floor, there were little corpses of mice along with dry and rotting pieces of food. Children came into the house and watched them work.

"What are ye doing, Lady?" asked Artur.

"Cleaning your home," said Jenny as she stopped and turned to the boy.

"Oh. I thought floor reeds were supposed to do that."

"The salve is ready, Jenny," said Mhairi. "I added bear fat, too, to protect the children's skin. Pure wild garlic can be harsh on the skin. If ye want to start treating the children, I'll get the beds cleaned."

"Would you call your friends, Artur?" Jenny asked as she took the bowl from Mhairi's hands. It smelled like honey and sharply of something between garlic and onion.

"Aye," said Artur and ran out.

Jenny went outside, into the daylight. The children quickly gathered around her and stood watching her carefully. Aulay was still clearing the reeds out of the building.

"Who wants to go first?" asked Jenny, and when no one volunteered, she said, "Who's the bravest of you all? The bravest son or daughter of Somerled?"

Everyone raised their hands. "I!" cried every child in the group, and Jenny smiled.

"Artur," she said. "You have the name of a legendary king. Why don't you go first?"

Artur nodded and stepped forward. "Aye."

Sticking his chest out, he stood calmly as Jenny dipped her finger into the salve and applied the mixture around the boy's mouth and onto his sores on his hands. "Do not lick it," she warned. "Well done, you."

The next child came, and she applied more of the salve. "What's your name?" she asked.

"Ceana," said the girl.

"Beautiful name, sweetheart. How old are you?"

"Ten winters."

"Oh, and already learning sword fighting." She finished the girl's mouth and looked at her hands. There were sores on the backs of her palms, and Jenny spread the salve over the yellow crusts. "How do you like living here?"

"I like it fine. 'Tis my home."

"And what do you do for fun here?"

The girl shrugged. "We run. We play tag. We go to the woods and pick berries, go fishing and swimming in the sea. Play with dolls."

Jenny beamed. "Sounds delightful. You're good to go. We'll fix your home, and you won't be sick as much."

Jenny was delighted she was finally doing something right. And Aulay was finally backing her up. She felt useful. She felt like she was in her right place. She could help the children in Middle Ages also.

As she treated the rest of the children, the stack of reeds rose next to the orphanage. She was so impressed that Aulay cared for these children. Was it his way to fill the void that was left in him because he was childless just like her? She recognized a similar void in her own heart. That was one reason why being a pediatrician was so fulfilling.

As he went in and out of the orphanage, their eyes met from time to time, and she found it hard to look away.

CHAPTER 13

"PLEASE, listen to me. She has a chance to get better, I promise," the sound of Jenny's strange accent rolled to Aulay's ears from the corner of the building in the courtyard. Her voice did something to him. It sent a tremor of joy through his veins, and there was that pull that tugged him to her.

It was the day after he and Jenny had worked all day on the orphanage. Yesterday, she and Mhairi had personally stripped the dirty bed linens and washed them in the stream under the guard of one of his men-at-arms. The orphan girls went with them to help. The linens had dried before the sunset, and the children had slept in clean beds. Aulay had ordered one of his carpenters to work on a wooden floor for the orphanage, and he said he'd do it in two sennights.

As Aulay stepped from behind the building, he saw Jenny crouching before Ailis, who held Una in her hands. The bairn was wailing. Ailis sat on the same pile of firewood in front of her home, which was one of the first in a group of similar houses. Behind Jenny, following the main path in the bailey from the gatehouse to the main keep, a chicken strutted past them and leaned down to peck at the ground. Workers and servants walked up and down the path with sacks, baskets of produce, and carts with firewood.

A gust of strong wind blew a cloud away and a ray of sunshine fell on Jenny, setting her red hair ablaze.

"Step away from me, witch," said Ailis angrily. Her voice was raw, and she coughed out every word. "Bhatair told ye"—*cough*—"nae to"—*cough*—"interfe—" *Cough, cough, cough.*

Poor Una's crying also rasped as she wailed.

"Please, I'm just trying to help," said Jennifer. "You've just lost your husband, and you're grieving. Maybe that's why you're getting worse. You're burning up. Both you and Una need medical help urgently."

"She told ye nae to interfere," said Laoghaire, who was passing by with her maid and a bunch of flowers in her hands. "And how dare ye wear my aunt's dress?"

Jenny faltered, opening and closing her mouth. Leitis's dress was clearly not made for her figure, but the color was beautiful against her hair. Seeing her in his wife's dress was even more difficult than having to give the clothes to her, but it was all worth it since the antagonism of the people had dissolved—well, most of them. Many of them didn't pay attention to her or didn't recognize her. He was glad that peace had returned to Dunyvaig. If only his niece would go on her way.

"I gave it to her," he said loudly as he made his way towards Jenny and Laoghaire. "The lady didn't have anything to wear. We all should have more compassion for her instead of judging her."

"Why are ye protecting this woman, laird?" asked Bhatair, who walked from his little surgery briskly towards them, his medicinal basket in his hands. "She speaks nonsense and must have bewitched ye because ye would have never believed a charlatan. Ye ken they can bring death."

Bhatair stared at Aulay, his eyes bulging. The word "charlatan" hung between them, heavy and dark. They both shared the guilt of Leitis's death.

Only, there was a difference between that charlatan and

Jenny. "There's no proof she's a charlatan," Aulay said in a low voice. "MacDonald is a strong clan, and a strong clan has a big heart and doesna need to treat every newcomer with hostility."

"Laird, she clearly impaired yer judgment—"

"Did ye see the orphans today?" Aulay asked. "I saw Artur and his yellow crusts got better after Jenny's treatment. The sores on the other children's faces and hands diminished. She made the miasma leave the orphanage."

Jenny slowly rose from the ground. Her face lit up as he said that, and something in his chest ached. He liked the brightness in her eyes, the confidence in her straight back.

Bhatair glared at her. "The children have a yellow crust disease. 'Tis nae dangerous."

Jenny crossed her arms over her chest. "True. But it doesn't mean children should suffer if there's help available."

Ailis looked up at Aulay with a glimmer of hope. "Artur got bett"—*cough*—"er?"

"Aye. Give Jenny the benefit of the doubt, people."

To his disappointment, no one agreed or nodded, but at least there were no loud protests thrown around. He wasn't sure why he was defending her so fiercely. She had told him the most outrageous story about time travel two days ago, but yesterday, after her salve worked and her simple logic about cleaning made the children feel better, he'd wondered for a moment if she was telling the truth. After all, she'd also told him two different stories of why she was going to Ireland. Was it pilgrimage or was it to see her family? Were either of those true or anything else she'd said? And why would she come up with an unbelievable tale about time travel?

But then he dismissed his doubt again. He had decided to trust her. She was a healer, as he had witnessed himself when she'd treated the orphans.

Jenny took a step closer to him. "Thank you," she said quietly, her voice gentle and pleasant. Then she walked away. He liked not arguing with her, and her appreciation felt like a precious gift.

She went to a large cauldron that steamed over the fire and stirred it with a long stick. There were rags and cloth lying in a basket on the ground. Aulay watched Bhatair follow her.

"What are ye doing, woman?" he demanded.

"I'm cleaning miasma from linen cloths," she said calmly and without looking at Bhatair. "To bandage wounds and such."

Bhatair was a highly respected member of the clan, and his words carried a lot of weight, but he could be arrogant and rash. Aulay watched them, wanting to see if Jenny would follow his advice and know her place as a woman and as an outsider.

Bhatair scoffed. "This wouldna stop the miasma."

"It would, actually," she said softly. "Boiling water kills it. It's good for your surgical instruments, too."

"My surgical instruments do nae have miasma on them!" cried Bhatair in outrage.

Alarmed by Bhatair's yelling, people stopped and looked at them. Aulay needed to intervene. He strode towards them. "Bhatair—" he said.

But Bhatair kept going, "I'd never agree to give anything medical into yer hands. I didn't learn in the most advanced medical school in the world for nothing. I am a highly qualified physician, and I would never believe a strange woman saying such outrageous things!"

His voice got louder and louder. Jenny's face got paler and paler, but she kept her mouth shut and listened to him with a straight back.

"Bhatair—" Aulay said.

"I will prove to everyone ye're wrong and ye're a liar. Because ye are hiding something!" With that, Bhatair finally took his leave, his long tunic flapping violently around his legs as he marched towards Ailis.

He met Jenny's eyes. She said nothing, only scoffed. Then she returned to her task of stirring the cloth in the cauldron. The fire was seething in her eyes, he could see it. He wished he hadn't told her to keep her mouth shut; he wished she was in a position to defend herself against Bhatair. But it wouldn't do her any good since more people would be on Bhatair's side.

"Do ye have children?" he asked. "Ye seem to have a good way with them. Ye ken the diseases..."

"No," she said. "Not right now, anyway... I want them, though. More than anything. At least one."

The words were like an arrow shot straight through his heart. "Oh." He felt like he'd swallowed a handful of gravel, and he cleared his throat. "So do I."

She stopped stirring and met his gaze. Time stopped around them. He forgot he was in the middle of the inner bailey with dozens of people walking, training, talking, working around them. He knew that need. More than anything he wanted a child of his own to care for, to love and protect and spoil.

"I've always wanted one," she said.

"Why didna ye have one?"

"Well... While I was working on building the clinic...the practice...I had no time. And then my husband was gone, and there was no one left to have them with. What about you?"

"Um... My wife...Leitis...she got pregnant seven times. But none of the children survived. And the seventh pregnancy killed her."

She stopped stirring and laid her hand on his forearm. He stared at her hand, the warmth of her seeping through his veins. "I'm so sorry, Aulay. I'm so terribly sorry." Her eyes glistened with tears. "I admire your strength. Something like that can destroy a person forever. But you're still strong."

He nodded curtly. Nothing would return his seven dead babies or Leitis, but her compassion was palpable, and it soothed the ache in his chest.

"Listen," she said as she returned to stirring. "I know you didn't believe me when I said I was from another time. But you also asked me to tell you the truth. And the truth is"—she picked up another long stick and put it into the water, then with two sticks lifted the steaming, almost boiling pieces of linen and carefully laid them in a large, empty basket—"that I did."

He watched as she returned the sticks the water to get more of the steaming cloth and put it into the basket. Was she lying again? Or was she really insane to keep insisting on this?

"I'm nae so sure 'tis a lie anymore."

"I became a pediatrician...a children's doctor...because I love children and always knew I wanted them. But I worked hard, first studying to be a doctor, going through my residency, then building my clinic. When my husband cheated on me, I asked for a divorce. I'm sorry I lied about him being dead."

He listened, not really believing his ears. It all sounded so incredibly outrageous. She was lying, his reason cried. Women didn't study to be physicians. Women didn't build their own practice. And women certainly didn't divorce.

"It's very difficult for me to have my own baby," she said as she now put dry linen cloths into the boiling water. "Because of my age... And my body just decided it was done, I guess. I still have a chance to have a baby with the help of other physicians. But I need to return to my time for that. I only have ten days left to return home."

Aulay's mind reeled. "How does that work?" he asked through a dry throat.

"Um..." She put more dry linen into the cauldron. "They will extract my eggs. Then fertilize them with a sperm in a glass plate and then put the embryos back inside."

"Yer...eggs?"

Her face was blank for a moment as she looked at him, then her cheeks flushed. "Gosh, that must sound odd to you." She shifted uncomfortably, and her hand shot to her throat. "Yeah. Eggs. Well, they're not like...chicken eggs...or goose eggs... You can't see them, let alone make an omelet with them. They're—"

Rage boiled inside him. He was a fool to even try to believe her. "Women have invisible eggs? What are ye talking about?"

Her face blushed even more. "Um...it's science. My body will never be able to bear a child without modern medical help, so they will implant the embryo into my sister, and she will carry it for me."

He couldn't believe what he was hearing. That wasn't possible. "'Tis witchcraft! How dare ye!"

She gaped at him. "Aulay!"

"I've been protecting ye, asking for the benefit of the doubt from my people. I've given ye my wife's clothes. But even I have my limits."

She put the sticks aside. There was a hurt in her eyes. "Aulay—"

"Such outrageous lies wilna get me to let ye go. Ye have eggs that need to be taken out and then put into yer sister? And ye'll make a child out of that? Ye must be mad if ye think I believe it. Nae a word of this. Another laird would be already trying ye for witchcraft. If ye tell me one more word of this, I will put ye back into the dungeon."

CHAPTER 14

As Jenny walked out of the main keep the next day, she saw Aulay, Colum, and a band of twenty or so men walk down towards the gate of the castle. They were all armored from head to toe, wearing leather and iron plates and chain mail coifs, and carrying spears and swords. The fierce, unyielding faces were hard as they walked past a group of about fifty men and some women from the village who trained with wooden swords.

Her heart beating faster, she followed about ten steps behind them thinking maybe she could sneak out and go with them. But as she approached the gates, the guards stopped her. "Dinna take me for a fool," said one of them, blocking her way with a spear. "The laird warned every warrior about ye."

With a heaviness growing in her chest, she watched the warriors leave down the slope. Aulay looked at her over his shoulder. Their gazes met and something tore and exploded in her chest. She'd hoped he'd forget their stupid conversation about eggs and how disgusted and disappointed with her he'd been. But on the other hand, she didn't regret speaking the truth. She'd had enough of Tom telling her their whole marriage that she should change and be more submissive and let him provide for her. The Bhatairs, Aulays, and Toms of the world wouldn't have power over her. Even if she sometimes needed to pretend that they did.

She'd never let another man make her feel bad about herself, her passion, and what she thought was the right thing.

Aulay reminded her of Zeus again, all powerful and all knowing, with his shoulders as broad as a boat and his chest as thick as a tree trunk...and yet there was a helpless sadness in his eyes as he held her gaze for a moment.

And then he turned back and disappeared behind the curve of the slope leading down to the village and to the port.

Well, it was what it was. She couldn't leave yet. Nine days till her appointment. Nine days...

She walked up the slope towards the main keep. She was tired. She'd barely slept last night after... Good God, Amanda was right—those Highlanders knew their way with women, at least in her dream one of them had.

She'd dreamed of Aulay last night.

She'd been deep in the woods; it was warm and dark. She stood in a meadow full of night flowers, grass tickling her bare feet. Large, moss-covered trees surrounded the meadow, and Aulay had appeared from the woods, bare-chested and in only a kilt. He strode to her, his face dangerous, like a wolf spotting his prey. The powerful muscles of his thighs rolled, showing through the gap in the kilt as he marched to her.

There was no hesitation. She knew he would come to her because he wanted to claim her as his own, and that was right and good. When he kissed her and wrapped his arms around her, it was like coming home. Her dress slid off her like water, and she was naked against him, skin to skin. She was hot, her sex wet and burning and achy for him.

He picked her up and lowered her onto the soft carpet of moss. His body, large and hard, covered hers.

"I ken what ye need, lass," he growled. "I'll give ye what ye need."

Then he slid deep inside of her, and he was right. That was

exactly what she needed. He stretched her to the very edge, and pleasure shot through her. Then he angled himself and slid in and out of her, speeding up. Then he was fucking her like a wild animal. She came, screaming his name...and the moment he did, she knew she was pregnant.

Remembering the dream, Jenny felt her cheeks heat as she walked, and she looked around. Had anyone seen her blush brighter than the sun? God, that feeling she'd had in her dream, of being pregnant...the fullness, the tightness deep within her, the endless love that came from knowing she was growing a life...

When she'd woken up, the devastation of knowing she was empty. That this feeling would never come in her real life. That she'd never grow a child inside her and then hold it and love it and kiss it and see it grow into an amazing, beautiful human being, giving it all of her, every last drop of her soul so that it would be happy and healthy and live a wonderful life...

Her life may always remain incomplete, and even if she could have a baby, she wouldn't be able to carry it within her own body. Her eyes burned with tears, and she wiped one away with the back of her hand.

If she wanted to have a child, she needed to get out of here and go back to her own time. So, come on, Jenny, fight. Kiss damned Bhatair's feet if you have to. Sleep with Aulay if that brings you any closer to returning. Anything to make them believe you're safe and trustworthy. Anything to fit in.

Because a human life may be at stake—the life of the child she'd always wanted. Her last chance.

Jenny really liked Aulay. In her restless night, she'd wondered if he had been from her time, who would he be? A businessman, probably. If he hadn't kept her captive, if he hadn't been bossy and stubborn and such an alpha, she could fall for him. It was easy to see that he had a heart. And a smoking body.

She should have been more careful yesterday. She could tell the truth without spooking him by talking about eggs and undoing all the progress she'd made. At least on the surface, she needed to work with him to navigate this strange medieval world. If anyone would give her a boat and help her get back on Achleith, it would be him.

But while he was away, she assumed to go and look for the treasure ship again, she needed to check up on her patients. The orphans needed fresh salve, and Una and Ailis hadn't left her thoughts, though Bhatair wouldn't let her get near them. So, she needed to get on his good side, even if meeting him wasn't on her list of favorite activities.

She sighed and promised herself to try to not make it worse. She needed to fit in to get out of here, and if she could convince Bhatair she belonged, the rest would follow. She went to the stone house two buildings away and opened the door. Inside, three windows barely illuminated a small space with a single bed and a large table covered with boxes, bottles, cups, and bowls. Shelves hung on the wall above the table with similar stuff filling them. Bunches of herbs hung from the ceiling on the other side of the house. A fireplace held a lit fire with a cauldron steaming over it. The room smelled pungent, like herbs and dust and something earthy.

The good doctor himself stood at the table and poured dried chamomile flowers into a jar with what looked like oil. He looked at her over his shoulder, and his gaze darkened. He turned back to his task and poured another handful into the jar.

"What do ye want?" he said.

"May I come in?" Jenny asked.

"Only if ye promise to nae anger me with yer silly notions."

Jenny's teeth clenched. Silly notions... "We got off on the wrong foot, Bhatair. I was wondering if I could be helpful to you."

He scoffed. "Help from ye? Never."

She entered the room. There was another large table in the middle of the room that looked like it had bloodstains on it. Was that where he did surgeries? A shiver ran through her. This was as unsterile as it could be. And what about light? Only a little light came from the windows. She'd have hated being a surgeon who needed to perform in such conditions.

"Come on. I know you don't like me. But you're clearly busy. And I have a pair of freely available hands. I will only do what you tell me."

Bhatair snorted as he stirred the jar that was now full of chamomile flowers and oil.

"I can clean for you, if you like. I couldn't help but notice your instruments might need some scrubbing." In a wooden box on the table lay huge iron knives, scissors, tongs, drills. They were made of iron and had rust stains...or blood on them. They looked like torture tools.

"I suppose there's nae harm in that," he said. "Water is in the corner."

She nodded, picked up the box of instruments, and walked towards the bucket of water. "Do you have soap?" she asked.

"Nae, dinna be silly."

"Right. What about alcohol...uisge?" she asked.

"Cleaning instruments with uisge?" He frowned at her and shook his head.

"How do you usually clean them?" she asked.

"Fire." He shrugged.

She raised her eyebrows. She shouldn't be surprised. Fire was everything in the Middle Ages. It meant food. It meant heat. It meant protection. The gruel or oatmeal she got every morning for breakfast, the coarse bread was baked using fire. Even in her tiny bedroom, where she had the luxury of being alone, there was a small brazier that kept the chill of Scottish nights away.

"You're right. That will work, too."

He gave a victorious "hmm," plugged the jar with a large cork, and started working on the next jar.

"You know," she said as she picked up a large bowl and dipped it into the bucket. "I'm really not a charlatan. I did learn medicine."

"All right. I will listen. Where and how?"

How could she put it into terms he would understand and that wouldn't get her into trouble? "Books," she said. That was true and safe enough. "Observing other doct—healers. Listening to them."

"Ye can read?" He threw a curious glance at her.

She put the bowl of water on the reed-covered floor before her, wondering how many dead mice lay underneath. "Yes, I can read."

"'Tis unusual for a woman..." he said. "Did ye also learn astrology?"

Jenny picked up a clean cloth from the chest near her and ducked her head as she tried to force down laughter. "Astrology?"

"Aye, of course, 'tis how you determine how to heal the patient."

Jenny dipped the cloth into the water and carefully rubbed the sides of a knife blade. The water turned dark brown. Who had Bhatair used it on last? It wasn't even that sharp. "I admit," she said, "I didn't learn astrology to cure patients."

"Aye, of course ye didna. What did I expect from a woman?"

Anger shot through her, but before she could say anything, the door opened, and Mhairi came in.

"Ah, Jennifer...Bhatair...are ye busy?"

He wiped his hands on his apron and turned to her. "Nae. What is it?"

Boiling the instruments would have been more effective, but Jenny didn't want to argue with him. Baby steps. As she held the knife she'd just cleaned in the open fire of the fireplace, Mhairi came closer to him. "'Tis my legs again, Bhatair. They swell so much. Last time, yer wee leeches helped greatly."

"Aye," he said and gestured at a chair. "Sit. Let me take a look."

Mhairi slowly lowered her heavily pregnant body into the chair, and Bhatair rolled the skirt of her dress higher, exposing her legs. They were swollen, and varicose veins bulged from her calves. Even a young woman like Mhairi could get varicose veins during pregnancy, depending on a variety of factors, and medieval conditions weren't helping anyone.

"Aye," Bhatair said with a concerned nod. "Leeches."

Jennifer didn't deal with varicose veins in her practice, but she sometimes had heard new mothers complain of them. She'd also heard that leeches had recently made a comeback in modern medicine. Plastic surgery as well as cardiology used them more and more. New research suggested that there was something in the saliva of the little beasts that helped with healing and preventing clots.

While the knife was in the fire, she watched Bhatair find a dark clay jar, open the lid, and use a large pair of tweezers to pick up a small, wriggling dark leech and place it on the raised vein. Jennifer shuddered but forced herself to watch. One by one, he used about a dozen of them.

"Do they really get better, Mhairi?" she asked. "Your veins?"

"Oh, aye," Mhairi said. "Wee disgusting buggers, but they are a miracle. The swelling gets better. Nae more pain."

Well, who knew? Maybe the leeches could be a useful tool in reducing inflammation. "How are the children?" she asked.

"Well. Yer salve is a miracle. Their yellow crusts are getting smaller."

"What salve?" Bhatair asked.

"Well, just honey, garlic, and bear fat," Jenny said. "And it wasn't mine. It was Mhairi's. I just suggested to use something that helped to keep infection...um, rot-wound away."

"Hmm," Bhatair said, looking doubtful.

He didn't say it was a good idea, but he also didn't chastise her and try to humiliate her.

As she removed the knife from the fire and put into a clean basket on a clean cloth, she struggled to remember what little knowledge she had about other herbal antibiotics. She didn't know much about herbal medicine, but she had an expert here that did.

"What else do you use against rot, Bhatair?" she asked. "What is available on Islay?"

"What ye mentioned," he said. "'Tis what's available."

"Right. What about the chamomile oil that you're making now? What do you use it for?"

Bhatair shrugged. "Joint pain. Red skin. Painful gas. Indigestion."

She cleaned another knife in water and put it into the fire.

"What about cough? What helps with dry cough?"

"Licorice root. Garlic. Honey."

She was almost shaking when she was brave enough to ask the questions she'd been dying to ask. "May I take those things and go with you to check on Una and Ailis? Please? I am worried about them."

Bhatair held her in his gaze for a long time. "Nae. Ye may help with cleaning, but dinna go near my patients."

CHAPTER 15

JENNY STARED at the heavy wooden door of Ailis's house, which was down the bailey and closer to the curtain wall.

Bhatair had just told her not to go near his patents. But Jenny was a doctor, and if someone needed her, she'd be there for them. Even if Bhatair would spit fire at her later.

She pulled open the door and entered. Inside, a dying fire played in the hearth. There was a large bed in the other corner of the room. A single small window cast light on a kitchen that consisted of one table, a sack of what looked like flour, and a basket of vegetables. A cauldron stood on the table. Jenny wondered if the poor woman had any strength to cook at all. And yet, the cauldron steamed with something appetizing. Maybe a neighbor or family member helped her.

Ailis sat on the bed, Una in her arms.

"May I come in?" Jenny asked.

Ailis gave her a long, empty look. "Ye... I had hoped ye might come. Nothing Bhatair did helped."

Concern mixed with hope twinged in Jenny's chest. "Is it all right if I look at Una?" Jenny asked.

"Aye," Ailis said.

Jenny took the baby in her arms and her stomach churned.

She was a very pretty little girl, but she was not all right. She was sleeping now. Her skin looked ashen, her lips were chapped, and she had dark circles under her eyes. Long red eyelashes cast shadows on her red cheeks.

"She looks dehydrated again," said Jenny. "Has she been nursing?"

"Nae, she refuses to take the breast, poor"—*cough*—"wee thing. I've been throwing my milk. Have been so full, I couldna take it nae more."

"Right. Maybe she has no strength to nurse. And plus, she has no appetite because of her fever and her illness. She must have terrible throat pain, and it probably hurts to swallow. I see it often with babies. First thing we need to do is to rehydrate her urgently." Jenny went to the kitchen area and saw a clean, clay bowl. Still holding Una, she carefully picked up the bowl and brought it to Ailis. "Can you express your milk in here? But we won't throw it away. We need to spoon-feed it to Una."

"Aye."

Ailis turned away and started working on squeezing her mother's milk out. While she was doing that, Jenny pressed her ear to Una's rib cage. The baby's breathing was shallow and there was a clear peeping sound coming from her little lungs. Not good.

Jenny laid the baby into the wooden crib, which looked more like a box for vegetables. With her hands free, she picked up firewood and threw the pieces into the dying fire. Ailis kept up her terrible, dry cough, which reached the point of almost retching. Una, too, coughed in her sleep, a dry cough that sounded almost like barking. Jenny took a clean cauldron and poured water from a bucket that stood by the fire, then set it onto a hook over the flames.

"Did Bhatair give you anything for the cough?"

"Aye. Honey and garlic. There's still some coltsfoot root and foxglove leaves in the pouch there." She pointed at the kitchen table. Jenny found the pouches, and once Ailis confirmed that they were right, she poured the leaves into the cauldron. For dry cough, she wanted to make sure both Ailis and Una could breathe over the steam with the leaves. Any warm vapors would help.

While the cauldron was heating up, Ailis finished expressing her milk and handed Jenny the bowl. Jenny gave a cup of water to Ailis, and she drank it thirstily, then she huddled up in the blankets on the bed and lay there shivering, no doubt from fever. She kept coughing and moaning a little.

Jenny gently woke Una up. She was whimpering and shivering and then started crying, her voice raspy. The poor baby didn't even have enough moisture for tears.

Softly shushing, Jenny sat at the table. Using a small spoon, she fed Una the milk. Her mouth was wide open from crying, so it worked well. The tiny thing had to stop her wailing to swallow, and Jenny hated doing it, but this would keep her hydrated and allow for a chance to save her life.

By the time all the milk was fed to Una, she was a little calmer, and her eyes seemed a little brighter. She clung to Jenny and whimpered a little and kept coughing. Mother's milk would give Una Ailis's antibodies, which would help the little girl fight off this flu. Jenny sat with Una and rocked her gently, feeling the pleasant little weight of her body, inhaling the scent of a baby.

Finally, when the water boiled, Jenny put Una in her crib and went to take the cauldron off the fire. She put it on the ground, took a free blanket from the bed, then picked up Una once again. Holding the baby in one arm, she sat on the floor in front of the cauldron and covered them both with the blanket, making a sort of steam room.

It was dark under the blanket, and the vapors from the water brought the scents of herbs and flowers. "Don't touch the cauldron," Jenny said to Una. "It's hot. Ouch..."

To her amazement, Una smiled, then coughed. As they sat together, steaming, sweating, breathing in the hot steam, and the little girl's body shook and strained in her arms as she coughed,

Jenny wondered if this was how it would feel with her own baby. Holding it like this, protecting it, fighting against the world for it if needed. To love this little being with its pouty mouth and snot and coughing little body.

She kissed the little head. Una's soft curls that protruded from under the baby's coif dampened from the steam.

Nine days... Nine days until her last chance to have it all...

And all that stood between her and that life was Aulay. Aulay, with his storm-cloud eyes and his high cheekbones and his lips, so full within his beard. He had such long, curling eyelashes. A brush of softness below his thick, straight brows.

When she thought about ten minutes had passed, she came out from under the blanket with Una.

"Ailis, there's still enough steam. You should go and breathe it, too," she said as she sat on the edge of the bed.

Ailis nodded weakly. "I dinna think I can, mistress."

Una coughed, and it sounded a bit wetter, like she was almost coughing out some phlegm, which was a good sign. "Okay, but you should do it later. You both should breathe steam about two to three times per day. Look, Una is already feeling better."

"Aye." Ailis smiled weakly. "Thank ye. I'm glad ye came. I think they're all wrong about ye. Bhatair especially. I am sorry I accused ye of witchcraft. But ye should stay away from the laird, mistress. Everyone notices how he looks at ye, but we all ken nae one would be good enough for our laird."

The warning squeezed her stomach painfully. "Believe me, you're very wrong, Ailis. He has no interest in me."

"My deceased husband, Beathan, was one of Aulay's closest friends and warriors. Aulay saved his life several times. He treated him like a brother and gave him this house for his service."

The baby in Jenny's arms was very sweet and held Jenny's finger, and her heart melted. She was used to seeing many children in her practice, but there was something special about this girl.

"I'm sorry, Ailis," Jenny said. "I'm so sorry about Beathan. He was kind to me."

"Aye... He's with God now."

"You're tired. Go to sleep. I'll watch Una, don't you worry."

Ailis nodded and closed her eyes. The poor woman looked worse. In a few moments, she dozed off.

As Jenny kept playing with Una and rocking her, her mind drifted back to Aulay. He was clearly a great leader and a kind man, and she realized she'd never been so attracted to a man in her life, not even her ex-husband.

CHAPTER 16

"SAIL!" came a loud call from Colum.

Though the sun shone overhead, the sea spread around them like a vast, gray blanket. Wind filled *Tagradh*'s sail and roared in his ears. Waves crashed hard against the hull. The horizon was clear, the dark gray blue of the sea a sharp line against the cerulean of the sky. In the midst of this vastness was a single piece of land. From a distance, it looked like a giant stone head popping out of the sea. This was where he'd found Jennifer.

Coming from behind the green hills and barren rocks of the Isle of Achleith, about one mile away, was a big ship, a cog. It bore a single mast with a square sail. A merchant?

Watching the Isle of Achleith had been heart-wrenching because every curve and every crease reminded him of the beautiful spoils he'd found on the island and had left back in the castle. Even now in the sea, with danger facing him, he couldn't stop thinking about Jennifer. Beautiful Jennifer saying preposterous things and making him feel things he didn't want to feel. Bringing urges to the surface he didn't want to follow.

Urges for her body, the need to be in her company and touch her, have her nearby.

In the very early morn, before the Matins, they'd buried

Beathan and the other fallen warriors. Their absence on the ship, but especially that of Beathan, was an aching void, a dark hole in Aulay's heart. All he could do now was to honor their memory by protecting their families in Islay.

Especially by protecting Ailis and Una. Beathan would have wanted that.

After the burial, they'd gone to sea. *Tagradh* had already been repaired and reinforced, and his shipbuilders now worked on the rest of the birlinns. Back in Dunyvaig, the farmers and tradesmen from the village, as well as the young warriors, kept training on swords, bows, and Lochaber axes.

They'd sailed *Tagradh* around Clachgheur—a good place for a shipwreck, as Colum had suggested—but they'd seen nothing on either side. They'd been in the open seas since early morning. They have passed by Rathlin Island and Portrush, seeing Ireland from afar, but staying far enough away not to attract any unnecessary attention.

After that unsuccessful search, they came back to the Isle of Achleith because they had never searched its other side. Aulay wanted to circle around it to see if there was any sign of the shipwreck on the southern coast.

But that was where the ship had come from. As their birlinn drew closer to the cog, Aulay saw a crow's nest on top of the mast with the draping of a flag: a red square with three golden lions.

Not a merchant. An English warship.

"God's arse," Aulay muttered. Colum was already on his way to him. There were thirty men on *Tagradh*. They were all in full armor and ten of those warriors were bowmen.

"English," Colum said as he stood next to Aulay.

The ship dipped with a strong wave, and Aulay gripped the gunwale. "Aye."

"That ship is big," Colum said.

"Aye. 'Tis a cog. A merchant vessel originally, nae doubt."

"Which means 'tis much slower and less maneuverable than

Tagradh."

"True. If there are a hundred warriors in there, I wouldna be surprised. 'Tis three men for one of ours."

"God's arse," Colum echoed. "They didna find the treasure ship, surely?"

The other ship was drawing closer and closer. Aulay strained his eyes to see who was on the vessel and what their intentions were.

"Only one way to find out," Aulay said. "Politely ask them."

He squeezed the handle of his claymore. He was not one to run from a fight, even outnumbered, especially if it meant taking that treasure away from the enemy. Something flew into the air and landed in the water about three hundred yards away from the English ship.

"A longbow," said Colum through gritted teeth. "Only a longbow arrow can fly three hundred yards."

"Aye. A warning shot. They're ready to attack."

"What do we do?" Colum asked. "We're still too distant for them to reach us. Those English longbows can destroy us. I've seen the arrows pierce a man through armor and exit out the other side."

Aulay's teeth clenched. "Aye. But we're the lords of the seas. We will win in close combat, and we're swift enough to run from them if needed. I say we greet them."

Colum nodded, his eyes darkening, his face gaining that haunted, resolved expression that he wore every time there was mention of the English.

"Get ready for battle!" Aulay yelled to his men. "Prepare to take cover from the arrows. Archers, at positions!"

The men roared and thumped their swords against their shields and *Tagradh* filled with MacDonald war cries. "Clann Domnhnaill! Clann Domnhnaill!" The waves roared around them, crashing against the ship.

They must have been about four hundred yards away when Aulay could distinguish the row of the longbowmen along the port side of the ship, as it slowly started turning. Their arrows flew like a dark rain cloud, but none of them reached *Tagradh*. Closer and closer the two ships approached, the sea driving them towards an inevitable clash. The longbow arrows started hitting the ship around them. Aulay and the men crouched and raised shields over their heads. The arrows hit the shields with loud thonks, splinters flying.

"Archers!" roared Aulay when the attack stopped for a few moments as the enemy nocked their arrows.

Scottish arrows flew through the air and hit the English ship, but a new rush of the arrows was already coming for them. This time, one of Aulay's archers didn't manage to hide in time. There was a sound of cloth and flesh ripping and a pained groan and a splash of water... Damnation.

"Shoot!" yelled Aulay the moment there was a break in the assault of arrows.

Kneeling under the shields, with the deck rising and sinking, they approached their enemy. The scent of death was here—in their pungent sweat and the angry thumps of their hearts—but they refused to succumb to fear.

And too soon...or not soon enough...they came alongside the cog. Aulay could hear the roar of the enemy warriors and knights, see the deadly edges of their swords glinting as they shook them in the air, hear the flapping of their sail.

"Chains!" cried Aulay. His warriors threw chains with hooks and pulled the ships tight together. They were so close, they could look their enemy in the eyes, count the links of their chain mail.

"Ye pigs came for what's ours!" yelled Aulay, and his men roared behind him. "Ye will learn a lesson to never do that again!"

"I will laugh at your grave, you dirty barbarian!" cried a man who must have been the captain. He wore a red surcoat bearing three golden lions.

"Ramparts!" roared Aulay.

His men threw wooden ramparts that hooked on to the other ship and then ran across them. "Clann Domnhnaill! Clann Domnhnaill!" they roared.

Their archers kept shooting at the enemy to cover the first Highlanders boarding the cog. Aulay rushed across with his men, and as soon as his feet touched the enemy deck, he plunged into battle. Swords flashed, strikes came one after another. His men with Lochaber axes were deadly beasts. With powerful strikes, MacDonald axes cut through chain mail.

Metal rang against metal. Wounded men grunted and groaned. Water splashed as they were thrown overboard.

And then the English captain stepped in front of him. He raised his sword and slashed at Aulay, who deflected the thrust and attacked. Steel sang with each hit as they sparred.

The English captain was younger, but Aulay was stronger and had years of battle behind him. He knew the man was trained in the typical English way. Hit after hit, Aulay let him believe he was winning by stepping back, and then when the bastard got cocky, Aulay stepped away from his opponent's sword and sent a thrust into his shoulder that crushed the chain mail and pierced the flesh, albeit not as much as Aulay needed.

But it gave him an opening to press the moaning Englishman against the gunwale. "Did ye find it?" Aulay demanded through gritted teeth.

"Ah...found...what?" The Englishman was hurt but perhaps not in quite enough pain.

"The goddamn treasure ship."

The captain's upper lip curled up in contempt. "Go to hell, you wild animal."

Aulay grinned and chuckled. "Wild animal? I'll show ye a wild animal." He pressed the edge of his sword underneath the man's chin. "Did ye find the lost treasure?"

The man's eyes darted quickly behind Aulay, which told him there was someone there. "No." Then his gaze grew from fearful to triumphant. "And neither will you."

Aulay grabbed the man by the hauberk and pivoted so that his enemy became his shield.

It worked, but the move came too late to fully protect him, only knocking aside the man's sword—making it a wounding blow rather than a killing one. White-hot pain flared through his left shoulder, and something wet flowed down his arm.

The captain fell on the deck, and Colum thrust his sword right into the man's face. Colum looked up at Aulay's shoulder and his face went blank with fear.

"'Tis nothing," Aulay said. "I'm fine."

But it wasn't nothing. He knew it. He had been in enough battles to know a serious wound. And despite killing the captain, the battle was not in the MacDonalds' favor. There were simply too many English warriors.

More than a hundred, he estimated.

"Retreat!" yelled Aulay. "Retreat!"

Colum and the others picked up their wounded clansmen and helped whoever could walk. While the English were trying to see if their captain could be saved, Aulay and his best warriors fought, enabling the rest to take the wounded back to their ship.

As soon as the last of the MacDonalds were on *Tagradh*'s deck, Aulay yelled, "Throw the bridges!"

Even though the English followed them, the MacDonalds lifted the wooden platforms that connected the two ships. English warriors fell into the sea with loud splashes.

"Cut the ropes!" cried Aulay as he hastily made his way to the rudder.

Using their axes, the men cut the ropes with the hooks. "To the oars!" Aulay roared.

And as thirty men sat at the oars and arrows began hitting their ship again, Aulay put all the power that he had into a single command.

"Row!"

CHAPTER 17

HOT WATER BURNED Aulay's wound as he lowered himself into the bath, and he let out a sharp hiss. The tub was large and looked like an oversize wine barrel with three steps to climb inside. He had refused Bhatair treating him. Six of his warriors were wounded very badly and needed the physician more than he did. Out of thirty, five hadn't come back home today. Five of his great men who wouldn't hug and kiss their wives and mothers. Two more children would be fatherless.

Aulay leaned against the wall of the tub and closed his eyes, letting the guilt and the sadness take him. He didn't think he would ever come to terms with the deaths of the men he led into battle. Aye, death was always the risk of a soldier's life. But that didn't make it any easier. He'd been desperate to know if the English had found the treasure ship, at the cost of being outnumbered three to one.

Blood oozed into the water from his shoulder wound. He'd get it treated once he was sure the men had been taken care of. He'd noticed Jennifer bringing Bhatair clean linens and water. And he'd seen genuine concern in her eyes. An enemy wouldn't look worried for his men. Seeing her focused, efficient, and so caring made him feel better, breathe easier. Aulay regretted that he had spoken so harshly to her yesterday.

He didn't believe the nonsense about time travel, but it was possible she was convinced she was telling the truth. Maybe in reality, she was a wee different...or had too wild an imagination...

Or what if she was right?

No. Mayhap it was his desire for her that clouded his mind. Even as they'd sailed, he'd kept thinking about her. He'd never wanted anyone like he wanted her. With Leitis, it had been an arranged marriage, and they had come to love each other deeply. It was never this burning, unyielding need to have her. It was almost like a sickness.

There was a knock at the door.

"Aye," he said as he picked up a washcloth, wincing when a sharp pain pierced his shoulder.

He heard the door open and light steps came inside. "I just wanted to check on you..."

It was her voice, her sweet, melodic accent, and he turned his head to her. Her red hair stuck out of a wee headscarf with blood smudges on it. There were also bloodstains on Leitis's dress, but her hands were clean.

Her gaze felt like the bubbles of a hot spring on his skin. Surprising himself, he felt nervous, something he hadn't felt since he was an adolescent lad having his first encounter with a woman. He was naked in front a woman he desired.

And he felt another desire that was new and strange... He wanted her to like him.

"I heard you were wounded," she said. "Did Bhatair treat you?"

"Dinna ye fash about me. If ye want to help, go and help my men instead."

"They're all patched up and are resting. May I see?"

He chuckled. "Lass, ye're seeing everything already. I have nothing to hide."

To his satisfaction, her face lit up red as a torch. "Show me your wound, I mean," she said.

He nodded and leaned forward. She approached the tub. When she touched him around the wound, it felt like knives piercing him. "It's not deep, but it needs cleaning and stitches and a dressing. Main thing is that it doesn't get infected. Is it all right if I stitch it?"

"Can ye?"

"Yes of course, I'm a doctor...um...a healer." She chuckled. "I borrowed some thread and a needle from Bhatair. I thought you might need them."

He shook his head. "Lass, ye dinna give up, do ye?"

"No. I told you. I took an oath."

As she worked on his shoulder, he clenched his teeth to stop from groaning and screaming. To distract himself from the pain, which felt like small teeth tearing his muscles apart, he rubbed the clean cloth over his body. Warm water helped to dull the pain. When she was finally finished, he sighed with relief.

"You should get out of the tub," she said. "And I'll dress the wound. You should keep the wound out of water for a few days after."

He met her sparkling eyes, and without looking away from her, he stood up. All his previous hesitation melted away when her eyes slowly went down his body. They widened in surprise, and she bit her lip. When they dropped to his crotch, her mouth fell open.

Her chest rose and fell quicker, her eyes darkened, her lips were lush and red.

She liked what she saw. She wanted him.

And he sure as hell wanted her.

"Would ye like to join me, Jenny?"

She took a barely audible sharp inhale and met his eyes. Hers were wide, her cheeks red.

"No." She tore her eyes away from his body, breathing fast. "I mean..."

He stretched out his arm. "Towel."

She threw a blazing gaze at him, with no sign of being intimidated. "Excuse me?"

"Give me the towel." He pointed at the cloth his servants had left him, which hung over the back of the chair.

She folded her arms over her ample bosom. "You're like a three-year-old. What about a please and a thank-you?"

He exhaled and chuckled. He loved it when she had this fire in her. "Please. And thank ye."

She reached out and gave it to him. As he began rubbing water off himself, she stared at the water with longing. "I haven't had a shower for five days."

He frowned. "A shower? Ye werena in the rain for five days?"

"I mean, a bath."

He stepped out of the water and onto the floor. He wrapped the towel around his waist. Only two steps away from her, he could just close the distance between them and kiss her.

"Ye're welcome to take a bath, Jenny," he said.

She bit her bottom lip, looking at his bath the way he wanted her to look at him.

"Really?" she asked. "Are you sure?"

"Aye, lass."

She eyed him for a few moments. "Right. Then turn around and don't get any ideas. Got it?"

He chuckled softly but didn't move. He was going to enjoy this. Turning around? That was the last thing he wanted.

"Turn around," she said, lifting her chin.

He cocked his head. "Are ye certain ye want me to?"

Her chin rose higher. "Yes of course I want you to."

He nodded and walked past her and towards an iron cauldron with hot water his servants had brought earlier. He wanted to watch her strip her dress off. Hell, he wanted to help her, unlace the dress and see her milky, silken skin emerge and kiss every inch.

Ignoring the pain in his wound, he filled a bucket with hot

water and heard the soft rustle of skin against linen. Red-hot images burned his mind...her generous breasts springing out the dress...her narrow waist and full hips with her gorgeous arse he could tease and bite and...

A splash told him she was in the water. He turned around and the water was up to her chin, her knees pulled in to her chest.

He approached the tub. "Hot water is coming in. Careful."

He poured the water into the corner, and he thought he heard a satisfied moan from her as the fresh water reached her body.

"Another?" he asked.

"Oh, God, yes, please!" she said, her voice throaty. "This is heaven."

Heaven, he thought as he got another bucket. He'd show her heaven. He'd make her forget anything else if only she agreed to come into his arms.

When the last drop was inside the bath, he watched her glistening back. His fingers itched to touch her, to feel her skin. And then his hands moved before he could stop himself. He brushed his arms against her back, on both sides of her spine, up and down. He'd expected her to say stop and he was ready to do so the moment she did.

But no word came from her.

He ran his hands up her smooth skin. A wave of wee lightning strikes stormed under his fingers. He curved his hands around her shoulders and massaged her tight flesh. Her head fell back as he did. He watched her eyes close and her lips part.

She felt it, too. No matter how much she would say no to his words with her own, her body enjoyed his touch. He knew it from their kiss, and he saw it now. Just like his own body loved touching hers. A moan escaped her lips as he kept kneading her tight muscles. They softened and warmed. Oh aye, she enjoyed this all right. He kept working her tired muscles in the back, and as she began to relax, he moved lower and lower. He couldn't see her lower back deep in the tub in the dim light of the fires in his bedchamber.

But as he went lower, he could feel the dimples just above her pelvis, and when he reached the top of her buttocks, and knew he was touching her ample arse, he started hardening. She didn't stop him—on the contrary, he could see her breathing slower, her arms going limper around her knees. And when he went lower and brushed against the crack of her gorgeous arse, she moaned again.

He was burning for her, ready to go back into the water with her and give her a massage in all the right places that would make her squirm and beg for more.

"Lass..." he rasped. "Stay with me tonight."

"Um..."

"Stay. Be mine. I want ye like I never wanted anyone in my life. I wilna do anything ye wouldna want me to."

She turned her head to him, and her eyes were dark, glinting with meaning. "Okay."

He frowned. "Okay?"

"I will stay, Aulay."

He kissed her then, abandoned her back and claimed her mouth like he was a goddamn barbarian starving for food and spoils.

A loud knock sounded at the door. He ignored it, coming back for her mouth again and again, drinking her taste. He cupped her delicious breast and fire seethed through his groin.

Another knock, louder, more insistent this time.

"Laird!" He heard Colum's voice. "We need ye!"

He withdrew from her for a moment, cursing. She was so delicious with her mouth swollen from the kiss, her cheeks flushed, her breasts beautiful and luscious under the water. "What?" he barked at the door.

"'Tis the English. The sentinels thought they saw the ship."

He let out a long growl, his blood chilling. The ship they'd left behind had never reached them, but that didn't mean it wouldn't have followed them.

"Coming," he replied as he unwrapped the towel around his hips and pulled on his braies. "Wait for me, lass..."

She nodded. "I will."

When he was dressed, he left her in his bedchamber and went out. The coldness never left his chest. In the dying light of the day, he watched the English ship sailing about three miles away. Before the sun set, it turned and disappeared behind the horizon. It seemed it only scouted.

But the coldness in his chest was replaced with worry. With the previous attack on the village, and the encounter at sea earlier today, was there a larger force behind it? They needed to be careful.

When he returned to his bedchamber, the beautiful vixen was asleep in his bed, her red hair spilled on his pillow like liquid honey.

CHAPTER 18

SOMETHING heavy and hot was wrapped around her. She had the odd sensation of being snuggled by a bear. Her eyes flew open.

Not a bear. Whew.

Aulay.

His scent was in her nostrils. His huge arm wrapped tightly around her, his heavy leg over her hips. She didn't move for a moment, inhaling his manly musk and marveling at his handsome, peaceful face. His long eyelashes cast shadows from the pink-golden light that came from the slit window. He had a pale bruise on his cheekbone, and she longed to press her lips there, to soothe any hurt.

This was nice. Jenny sighed deeply, melting into his heat. Had she really agreed to sleep with him last night? Was she crazy?

She must have fallen asleep when he'd gone, and he hadn't woken her up when he'd returned.

This was a mistake. Yes, the man looked like Scottish Zeus—or whatever the equivalent of Zeus would be in Scotland. MacZeus? So of course, it was hard for a mortal woman to resist him.

But she had to. She needed to pretend like that conversation had never happened. Like his hands massaging her in the hot bath hadn't almost made her come. Like she didn't want those hands to massage her...everywhere.

Her lady parts started simmering again, especially given that her behind was comfortably tucked right into his crotch, and she could feel something big and hot pressing against her butt cheeks...

Enough. She needed to leave before he woke up. Slowly, she crawled out from under his arms and stood up next to the bed. He sighed a long, deep breath out and went back to sleep. She was cold without his embrace...and sort of lonely. But thankfully, she was still in her undertunic or whatever it was called. As quietly as she could, she put on her dress, her stockings and her shoes and left the room.

When she walked out of the main keep, the first rays of sun shone behind the curtain walls. She breathed in the fresh air that smelled like wet earth and morning dew. Coffee and a croissant... what wouldn't she give for a cappuccino right now.

She missed her warm, soft bed. She missed wearing underwear. She missed shoes without pointy toes. She missed brushing her teeth with a good toothbrush, and she even missed the taste of a toothpaste. She hadn't shaved the hair on her legs and under her armpits since she'd left her hotel in Glasgow. Soon, her graying roots would need a touch-up at her favorite hair salon. She missed modern toilets. The tiny closet in the castle with a chair and a hole that led all the way down into the sea wasn't the most hygienic or convenient. And, oh dear God, she didn't even want to think about when her period would come. How did women manage without tampons? And the pain...good grief. She might need to beg Bhatair for some herbal pain relief. All she wanted on those days was to lie in her bed curled into a ball and binge-watch soap operas.

And she missed her clinic. The kids...the morning ritual she and Amanda had of drinking a coffee together and chatting about complicated cases they wanted each other's opinion on.

Medieval life was hard. Everything needed to be done by hand: grinding flour, baking bread, cleaning fish and poultry, cutting firewood. It seemed people in the village provided the castle and the village with produce, wood, and any work that was necessary. The church bell tolled every three hours, starting from Matins—which was, Jenny thought, around 6 a.m. —and finishing with Compline, which was after sunset, probably around 9 p.m.

But most importantly... Eight days until her appointment. She needed at least one day to get to Edinburgh and get on a flight and fly back.

Unconcerned about her struggles, birds chirped cheerfully from behind the walls. Seagulls squawked above. The sea behind the castle murmured. And then it was all drowned out by children's joyful cries. The little crowd of them spilled out of the orphanage and ran around, swinging their wooden swords. Artur waved to her, and Jenny's chest lightened. She hurried to the children.

"How is everyone?" she asked as they gathered in a circle around her.

"Good!" came a distorted chorus of voices.

She beamed. "Great! Let me see how your skin is."

She examined them one by one. The sores were better. Not completely gone, but they looked drier, smaller, and the redness reduced. Of course, a modern-day antibiotic would be stronger, but the garlic was working.

"We'll do another round," she said. "Come on, everyone, let's go and get your sores treated."

As they went into the orphanage, she noticed the scent was earthy and clean. The kids slept two or three in one bed, so it was especially important to maintain good hygiene.

"Ah, Jenny," said Mhairi as she lifted a blanket to make a bed. "The children look better, aye?"

Jenny picked up the rest of the antibiotic salve. "Yes, definitely on the right track."

Mhairi frowned. "Forgive me? Track?"

"Um..." Jenny laughed uncomfortably as she sank to her knees and spread the salve over Artur's sores with a spoon. "I mean, on the mend."

She worked the salve into the children's sores one by one, talking cheerfully to them and to Mhairi.

When she finished, Mhairi said, "I was going to take the children to gather raspberries. Would ye come with us, Jenny?"

Jenny nodded. The thought of scurvy in Dunyvaig village and the castle worried her, though she hadn't seen any signs yet. She wondered if it was because people had a supply of fresh fruit and veggies in the summer. "Raspberries would be very good for them. I'd love to come, but the laird commanded the guards not to let me out."

"Ah, 'tis all right. I'll tell them ye're with me. What nonsense, to keep ye within the walls."

Hope bloomed in Jenny's chest. If she could just leave these walls, she might be able to go to another part of the island, and maybe find a boat to take her to Achleith. Of course, if she escaped on Mhairi's watch, the woman might get in trouble with Aulay. But she knew he would not be harsh with Seoras's pregnant wife.

As they walked down the slope towards the gate, she looked over her shoulder at the keep. The tower was a dark, rectangular mass of rocks, as menacing against the blue sky as its commander. She may never see him again if she got away today. A sense of loss and sadness weighed heavily in her chest instead of relief. For a moment, she wished she could stay.

To her surprise, the guard let her pass. Maybe they feared Mhairi as much as Aulay. Or maybe the guards didn't think that Jenny would dare to escape under Mhairi's watch. But a moment later, she was walking down the steep road leading to the village of Dunyvaig.

There was a brook coming out of a collection of rocks. It pooled first in an oval and then kept flowing down the slope and into the sea. The oval pool was next to what looked like a waste pit with carcasses of rats and bones floating in the dirty brown water.

"Is that a waste pit?" she asked Mhairi.

"Aye, 'tis. Chamber pots from the village need to be emptied somewhere."

"Do people take water from that brook?"

"Aye, sometimes. If 'tis nae possible to take it from the village and the castle wells."

That was a recipe for all kinds of nasty diseases. Something had to be done about it.

As the children skipped and chattered happily in front of them, Jenny looked at Mhairi, who had placed her hand on her watermelon belly. So pregnant, so happy. So round and full of life, with her cheeks plush and rosy. She wobbled slowly as she walked, pretty much like a penguin, the head of her baby no doubt deep in her pelvis now, getting ready to be born. If there was a perfect image of a woman full of life and fertility, it was Mhairi.

Mhairi had no idea what Jenny would have given to be like that. She'd take the varicose veins; she'd take pelvic pain and back pain and achy boobs. She'd take it all for a chance to hold her own baby in her arms.

She shouldn't be jealous. She should be a doctor and watch this pregnant woman in case of any complications. "Are you sure you're fine walking that far?" Jenny asked as they walked slowly side by side.

"Aye," said Mhairi, smiling. "My bones ache, but my ankles and veins are better after the leeches. And Bhatair said 'tis good to walk to get the bairn to be born."

Jenny chuckled. Some truths were universal through time and generations. Walking was still advised in the twenty-first century to get the baby to drop and start labor.

"Are you very uncomfortable?" Jenny asked.

"A wee bit. I have been having the tightening in my womb for three days now," said Mhairi, making the face of someone who was trying to appear stronger than they were.

"You've been having contractions?" Jenny looked her over. "Should you be going to the woods?"

Mhairi chuckled. Her rosy cheeks dimpled, but the smile didn't reach her gray eyes. "The bairn isna in the right position still. So, walking might help."

That worried Jenny. The baby may still turn, but chances of it turning head down were smaller and smaller the closer to due date they were. They passed by the house of a tanner, which was one of the last houses in the village. The sweet and disgusting odor of old urine assaulted her nostrils.

As they entered the fields, Mhairi stopped and closed her eyes and put her hand on her lower back, breathing deeply.

Jenny stopped and waited with her. When Mhairi opened her eyes and smiled, Jenny said, "Sweetheart, you might be in labor already. How close together are your contractions...your tightenings?"

They resumed walking. "Nae very close. Let us keep going, I want the bairn to turn. My ma had the same problem. And I told Seoras before he marrit me. Nae matter how much I love him, I may never be a good wife. I may die giving birth." She chuckled nervously.

Jenny glanced at her sharply. Breech babies were not caused by genetics. "Don't say that."

The grass of the field tickled her ankles as they walked. The children yelled and screamed as they ran through the oat field towards the dark gathering of trees up at the edge.

"'Tis out of our hands, ye're right," said Mhairi. "'Tis God's will what happens to us."

Jenny knew now was not the best time to educate anyone about medicine. She needed to think about herself and her own baby...who may not ever be conceived, especially if she stayed here too long. And yet, she couldn't just leave a woman who may be in mortal danger.

She picked a stalk of oats. "How did you meet Seoras?"

Mhairi threw her an odd look and picked an oat stalk of her own. "We didna meet before we stood in front of a priest."

Jenny raised her brows. Arranged marriage. A chill went through her. What would it be like to stand in front of a man she'd never met and have to commit to him for the rest of her life?

She couldn't imagine that. She had thought Tom was the love of her life. She had thought her marriage would last forever. And yet, here she was, divorced and betrayed and left because of something she never could have given Tom. She wondered if it would have been the same had she married Aulay.

Jenny said, "And how was that for you? Did you like him right away when you saw him?"

Mhairi chuckled. "Nae. Ours was a marriage of alliance. I'm of clan Ruaidhrí, of the Isle of Skye. I was bound to marry a MacDonald to strengthen the ties of Somerled, our great Norse ancestor, between us. Colum is the eldest, but my ma and da were advised against him... He betrayed the clan, I was told. So, I marrit Seoras, his younger brother. And to answer yer question..." Mhairi ran the oats through her fingers thoughtfully. "I didna think much of him at first. I said aye when the priest asked if I took him for a husband, but 'twas mayhap two sennights after the wedding that I kent I loved him."

Two weeks after marrying someone to fall in love with them... And what if Mhairi had never fallen in love? What if her husband had been unkind or abusive? This was such a different reality to what Jenny knew—the world of dating where a swipe left or right only meant a potential meeting, and everyone was free to date anyone they wanted.

"And are you happy?" Jenny asked.

"Aye." Mhairi beamed as they kept trudging through the field of oats. "I didna think I'd fall in love with my husband. Ye ken. Ye've been marrit. Love is never the purpose. 'Tis never the reason, either. 'Tis something that hopefully happens. Marriage is for strengthening the clans, the ties between families. But we fell in love. And now we're about to have a bairn..."

Jenny looked at her. "How's your life, then?" she asked. "You're a pregnant woman, married to the man you love, living in a castle... Do you like it?"

Mhairi chuckled and looked away, at the kids running towards the woods. "Aye, Jenny." She rubbed her bump and smiled cheerfully. "Seoras makes me so happy. We're blessed that we found each other, and I like my life on Islay." She brushed her hand along her belly. "I canna wait for my bairn to arrive and to hold it in my arms." She sighed. "Also, because my body hurts."

Jenny gave her an empathetic smile. "I don't know how you do it. You're on your feet all day and with such a huge belly. Is your pregnancy going well?"

"Aye. I canna complain."

As they walked, Jenny asked her more questions about her pregnancy and the baby and heard nothing alarming aside from the child being in the breech position. Still, she wanted to keep an eye on Mhairi, especially closer to the birth. They kept chatting, and Jenny found herself liking Mhairi more and more. She reminded her of her girlfriends back in New York. They stopped several times when Mhairi had contractions. Every instinct told Jenny to make sure Mhairi made it back home. She was in early labor for sure.

And so, she didn't run off, and she didn't ask Mhairi for help getting away. Part of her didn't want to leave. The thought of abandoning Aulay and the kids and Ailis and little Una made her stomach hurt. She felt needed here. She had started liking it here.

She still had time to get back. She didn't need to leave today.

In the woods, it was quiet and dark after the blinding sun. Moss was everywhere—on tree trunks, on stones, on the ground. Jenny inhaled the rich scent of greenery and earth. The kids ran in different directions. Several of them gathered around raspberry bushes and quieted for the first time as they picked the berries and shoved them into their mouths. Most of the berries didn't make it into their baskets, but Jenny gathered all the berries she could for Una and Ailis. Vitamin C would be very good for their immune systems to fight this flu off.

On their way back to the castle, she saw kids as young as seven years old working the fields of oats with their parents. Some of them gathered fallen branches for firewood and put them into a basket on their backs. Small crofts stood at the edges of the fields. Behind them, sheep grazed on the slopes of hills.

By the time they were passing the village, Mhairi was having to stop more often and for longer. She held on to Jenny's arms as she breathed through the contractions.

"You're definitely in labor, Mhairi," Jenny said when the next one passed. "We must return to your home immediately. If you let me, I'll stay with you."

Mhairi shook her head. "Nae, thank ye. Bhatair will be with me."

Jenny sent Artur to find Bhatair as soon as possible. As they passed the church, people exited from Mass. Many of them were coughing, and Jenny saw blood on the handkerchief of one of them.

"Tuberculosis?" she murmured.

The BCG vaccine had been invented only at the beginning of the twentieth century. Tuberculosis bacteria were spread through air and may have accumulated in the church for years. While tuberculosis was no longer very common in the States, she knew it was still a big concern in other parts of the world. It was deadly without a long and complex treatment. She needed to talk to the priest and suggest a good cleaning like she had done in the orphanage.

There was so much she could do here to help.

Jenny needed to talk to Aulay about that. She helped Mhairi to the main keep, where Bhatair was already waiting for her. He scowled at Jenny and took Mhairi by the elbow, helping her inside.

"Can I help?" asked Jenny.

"Nae. Ye wilna go near my patient." With that, he closed the door.

Jenny was worried. If the baby didn't turn, it meant all kinds of complications that without modern medicine might mean death for the baby and the mother.

She couldn't do much to help now, but what she could do was speak with Aulay. She looked for him everywhere, but she was told he was down in the village. While she waited for him to return, she went to the orphanage to make more of the impetigo salve and to tidy up. The children chatted and played around her as she worked.

When she left the orphanage, it must have been hours later. There was still light in the sky, but it was clearly evening, and the inner bailey was full of the scents of cooking meals. She would take some raspberries to Ailis and Una, then look for Aulay again.

But she didn't need to search. MacZeus stood a hundred feet away, barking orders at the warriors who were standing in a row with their swords. He looked angry.

Her stomach fluttered as she approached him.

She picked several raspberries from her basket. "Raspberry?" she asked.

He turned to her, his steely eyes blazing.

CHAPTER 19

AULAY'S FISTS clenched and unclenched. He'd almost died when he'd woken up to an empty bed. Then he'd almost died again when after searching every corner of the castle, he had finally been told by the guard that Jennifer, Mhairi, and the orphans had gone to gather raspberries. He had never been so close to whipping the arse of one of his men. The English had attacked from that forest.

"I said to nae let her leave the castle," he'd growled into the face of the paling man.

Then he'd sent another man on horseback to find her and bring her back because as much as he would have rather ridden out himself, he was needed for sword training. The attack from the forest had showed that even the workers who lived in the village needed to be better trained.

He still needed to go down to the port and supervise the repair and reinforcement of other birlinns to prepare them for the battles to come. Some of the people who lived on the other side of the island had reported an English ship not far off their shore.

But before the man he'd sent had returned to the castle,

Jenny, Mhairi, and the children came back. Shortly after Jenny took Mhairi to the physician, she'd disappeared again.

He put his sword back into the sheath. He was so goddamn furious with her. After last night... He'd thought they shared something. For seven years he hadn't allowed a woman to come close to him. He'd been terrified of falling in love and losing another woman like he'd lost Leitis.

But with Jennifer, he couldn't resist. She pulled him to her, made him feel things he'd thought he'd never feel again.

He'd thought with Leitis, the great love of his life was dead. That he was destined to be alone for the rest of his life.

So, he wasn't furious with Jenny because she had left the castle against his word.

He'd been terrified harm would come to her. What if the English decided to land on Islay again? Or outlaws arrived without him knowing?

What if they hurt her? Something broke in him at the thought. Whether he liked or not, he felt so much more for Jenny than he wanted to admit.

He looked at the raspberries in the open palm of her hand, threw a cautious glance around him. Several curious gazes rested on them. The wound in his left shoulder pained him sharply as he grabbed her by the upper arm, more roughly than he'd intended, and dragged her away behind the stables, far from prying eyes.

"What's wrong with you?" Jenny exclaimed, snatching her arm away. The berries scattered on the ground, and she leaned down and picked them up one by one. "Ruining perfectly good raspberries. They're delicious, by the way."

"I couldna give two horse shites about the raspberries. Ye left."

She glared at him. The strands of her hair were framing her face. Her warm brown eyes were dark and glistening. "And you are behaving like a caveman."

"I woke up this morn and ye were gone," he grated out through clenched teeth.

Her cheeks blazed. "Deal with it. I do not belong to you."

She did not belong to him... But how he wished that she did.

He took a step closer to her. She was small and now in direct proximity to his body. He could smell the scent of sun and flowers from her head, and her own womanly smell he wanted to inhale and make part of his body and his soul.

"Maybe ye should," he said. "I made my intentions clear last night. And I didna make them lightly."

Her eyelashes fluttered. She opened her mouth and closed it. Then she stepped away from him and waved her hand towards the village. "How can you keep chasing me when you have so many issues in your little kingdom that need immediate attention?"

He frowned. "Issues?"

"The orphanage was a disaster. A breeding ground for bacteria...miasma, I mean."

"I already have a man that's dealing with that."

"Yes, but what about the church? The sewage pit?"

He blinked. "What is wrong with the church?"

"It needs to be cleaned and aired out. Many of the people coming out of there have tuberculosis."

He blinked. "Tubercu— What?"

"Um. Consumption, I guess that's what it used to called."

"Aye. There's consumption in the village."

"The drinking water is right next to the sewage pit. It means disease. People are basically drinking their own excrement."

His face paled. "'Tis far enough."

"No. It's not. Not anymore."

He nodded. "I will take a look. And what about scurvy?"

"People need to eat raw fruit and vegetables. Even if they just chew on raw leaves that are edible, like cabbage...right, it's not in season...but even dandelion leaves. I can show your cook a wonderful salad..."

She was bossy. He liked it. "Ye tell me I behave like a caveman. Ye behave like a mistress of the house."

Their gazes locked. The idea of the little fox being the bossy wee wife of his house was strangely sweet and beautiful.

With a long breath out, he took her palm in his, marveling at the rush of tingles that ran through his body at the touch of her skin against his. He gently opened her palm and brought it to his lips, then opened his mouth and took the raspberries into it. He watched her eyes widen and her pupils dilate as he licked her palm in the process and kissed her skin. The sweet taste of raspberries exploded in his mouth, but it was nothing compared to the feel of her skin against his.

When he let go of her hand, she looked disappointed. He was, too.

"How did ye travel in time, lass?" he asked.

"What? You believe me now suddenly?"

He crossed his arms over his chest. "I dinna ken. But if ye did travel in time, that would explain yer outrageous ideas. Nothing else can."

"I told you, I was by that rock, with the handprint and some strange symbols carved into it. Then a woman came, Sìneag, who told me she was a faerie. She told me about traveling in time. And about you being the man destined for me. And then I put my hand into the handprint...and poof. I was gone. Fell through the rock like it was air."

This all sounded like nonsense. Like a child's wild imagination. And yet, she seemed so convinced, so sure. And he supposed he knew exactly which rock she spoke of. There was a rock just like that over on the hill near Dunyvaig at the old Pictish fort. People avoided it like it was possessed. They said faeries live there, and if they didn't like a human, they took the person into their faerie kingdom to keep as a slave.

Should he tell her about that rock? God almighty, what if her way back home was right there, and she didn't know it? Then she would leave right away. And he was a selfish, sinful man, but he couldn't part with her yet.

God's bones, not yet.

"Do ye love yer husband?" he asked. His voice was like gravel.

"*Ex*-husband," she said. "He's not my husband anymore. And no, I don't."

"Are ye sure 'tis nae why ye want to return?" he asked.

"I used to love him, but he broke my heart. Over and over again, he chose other women over me."

Aulay's heart beat faster. If she only wanted to go back to have a bairn, he could get her pregnant... He could give her that. He didn't know anything about female eggs and such, but he knew the traditional way of making babies worked just fine. Would that be enough for her to stay?

"Only an idiot would do that. I havna met anyone like ye in all my life. I loved my wife. I was happy with her. I've achieved much, seen the world through my trade and through war. And yet, never in all my years have I met someone as precious and beautiful as ye. If I had ye, Jenny, I'd never let ye go."

She didn't say anything, just stared at him, her eyes glistening.

"Mayhap that faerie was right, Jenny, and ye and I are meant to be together. Mayhap she was right to send ye here through time. Mayhap ye dinna need to return to yer time. I can get ye pregnant. Let me give ye a child. I want one, too."

"Aulay, that's not how—" she said finally.

But he didn't let her finish that rejection.

He backed her against the wall of the stables, planted his hands at either side of her face, and sealed his mouth with hers. She tasted and smelled like raspberries, and he wanted to inhale her whole. Her mouth was so tender, it was like falling into a cloud. She was all silky and smooth and warm and soft. He loved her curves, the feminine flesh he ached to kiss and bite and grab and hold. His blood boiled as the need to claim her, to own her, made his heart thump and desire pulsate in his groin.

"Mistress..." came a shy voice from behind him.

Aulay groaned against her mouth. Maybe behind the stables wasn't such a good place to kiss a woman. Unwillingly, he lifted his lips from hers and looked over his shoulder.

It was Artur. He did look much better—his sores were smaller, and he was clearly on the mend. His mouth was stained with raspberry juice.

"'Tis Mhairi. 'Tisna good! Bhatair wilna want ye there, but ye helped us so much. Mayhap ye can help her. Please come."

CHAPTER 20

SEORAS PACED the windowless landing before the bedchamber he and Mhairi shared in the main keep. Torchlight jumped off the rough stone walls, barely illuminating the stairs that led both up and down. Aulay's chest tightened as he remembered himself doing the same during each of Leitis's labors.

Just like the last time, a woman's pained screams and moans sounded from behind the door. Seoras looked older. Not a lad of eight and twenty. As Jenny hurried inside the bedchamber, Aulay squeezed his nephew's shoulder and said the words he didn't necessarily believe, but the words Seoras needed. "Have faith, lad," he said.

"Uncle— But what if—"

What if she was like Leitis, unable to give birth to a live and healthy child. What if she died tonight, just like Leitis. What if Seoras would be like Aulay.

A widower after this day. A man with his heart forever broken.

"I ken," Aulay said. "But have faith."

Seoras nodded. Aulay opened his mouth to say he'd stay with him and keep him company, but Bhatair's angry yells came from behind the door.

"...leave! Dinna ye dare come to me with yer outlandish—"

"She'll die if we don't act!" came Jenny's angry voice.

Aulay didn't want to do this. He didn't want to leave Seoras alone to deal with his anxiety, and he didn't want to be another pair of eyes witnessing Mhairi's labor struggles and make her even more uncomfortable than she might be.

But Bhatair and Jenny needed someone to intervene.

He opened the door. "What is going on?" he barked.

Bhatair knelt next to the bed where Mhairi was kneeling on all fours and moaning in pain. Jenny was next to the bed, and Bhatair was blocking her way with his arm. His face was a pure outrage, his eyebrows drawn together, his mouth a disgusted chasm.

"Aulay, he won't let me examine her," Jenny said.

"She is a charlatan!" Bhatair roared. "I told her to stay away. Nae patient of mine will—"

"Bhatair, you must let Jenny help. She's capable, I assure ye."

"I will be the judge of that."

"Ahhhh..." came a pained moan from the woman. "With all respect, Bhatair, 'tis me who should be the judge of that. I've been pushing for hours. Nothing is happening. Mayhap the female healer will ken better... I trust Jenny."

"But Mhairi—" Bhatair contradicted.

"Ye couldna help," insisted Mhairi. "I should have asked her to stay with me in the first place."

Jenny exchanged a thankful glance with Aulay and sat on the bed. Bhatair didn't block her way anymore, only stood and helplessly opened and closed his mouth. A grimace of worry crossed his face.

Seoras came in, and Aulay moved inside the room and closed the door behind him. Seoras was pale, and it seemed he couldn't breathe. Both men stood by the door with their arms crossed. Aulay didn't want to be here, but he needed to intervene if Bhatair and Jenny had struggles again, which, by the looks of Bhatair, might happen at any moment.

Jenny asked Mhairi to lie on her back and examined her.

"She's fully dilated," she said. "But the baby is still breech."

"Aye, I already ken that," said Bhatair. "Mhairi, the only way ye can give birth is to push."

"I canna," Mhairi said weakly.

Seoras turned to Aulay and asked, "Uncle. Tell me how did you keep living?"

How, indeed? Aulay was at a loss. Normally he always knew what to do and what to say. This was his Achilles' heel. "Ye keep existing, lad. Living has ended with her."

And it may have started again with Jenny.

Mhairi, usually sweet and kind and talkative, was pale and weak. There were blood smears on the bed around her. Her blond hair was pasted against her face like wet seaweed. Seoras and she had been married for a year, and this bairn would be the first child of the next generation. And if it was a lad, it could be one of the next lairds of clan MacDonald.

Seoras was Aulay's nephew, but without children of his own, this was as close as Aulay would get to having grandchildren.

"Sweetheart, are you sure you can't push?" Jenny asked.

"Ahhhhh!" a terrible cry came from Mhairi. "Aaaaah!"

Bhatair marched to Aulay and stood by him, shaking his head. He whispered, "She wilna make it, laird. The bairn may already be dead. Prepare yer nephew."

Jenny stood up and walked to Bhatair. She lowered her voice as she spoke to him. She had that look he knew, when she was all focused and efficient and helping people. "Okay," she said. "I have an idea. It's risky. But I think I can help. I can do a C-section. It's extremely dangerous, and I've only done it twice, but I observed it many times done by gynecologists. It's her and the baby's only chance."

"A C-section?" asked Bhatair.

"Cesarean section. Have you heard of it?"

His eyes widened. "I have heard it done when the bairn must live but the mother wilna. This will kill her."

Shock washed through Aulay like cold poison straight into his blood. "Jenny, ye canna be serious..."

"I may be able to save her...I hope so!" Jenny said. "But, Bhatair, you must do everything I say. We need everything clean. Sterile. Lots of light, alcohol, and all instruments must be treated with alcohol beforehand. And quickly. I can't promise you she'll survive this. It will be extremely painful for her without anesthetic. But it's her only chance. Can you help me? Can you follow my every instruction? For her and the baby's sake?"

Bhatair shook his head. "'Tis madness."

"Is that a no?" she asked. "Tell me now. We don't have time."

"Aye. I will help. But only if she and Seoras ken what it means."

"Great. I will talk to them. Please bring all the uisge you can find and your surgical instruments. Aulay, clean the table and put it next to the window, and wipe it with uisge. Do you have any on you?"

Aulay nodded, struck dumb. Was she really about to cut into the woman to get the bairn and then expect Mhairi to live? Was he going to trust her enough to let her do that?

As Jenny walked to Seoras and Mhairi and started talking to them softly, Aulay moved to the table. He didn't realize what he was doing, still shocked he would allow Jenny, whom he had suspected to be a charlatan only a few days ago, to do this.

He cleaned the table of things. His shoulder ached sharply as he pushed the table closer to the window where, thankfully, sunlight was still coming through. He then took his horn flask of uisge and a clean cloth that lay in Bhatair's basket and generously poured uisge over the table, then wiped it with the cloth till it was dry. The room filled with the sharp scent of alcohol. Why he needed to do that, he didn't know.

"I dinna give ye permission to kill my wife!" Seoras exclaimed.

"I'm just saying it's a risk," Jenny said. "But that's why we're doing it. If we don't do anything, she'll likely die, and so will your child. If you allow me to do the surgery, it'll give her and the baby a chance to live."

"I give ye my permission," Mhairi said. "Do anything to save my bairn. Even if I have to die, do it."

"No!" Seoras cried.

It was all like knives slashing against Aulay's very soul. This conversation had never even been an option for Aulay.

"Aye," said Mhairi as she squeezed Jenny's hand. "Do it."

Bhatair barged into the room with another basket.

Jenny nodded to him. "Please wipe all the instruments quickly with uisge and lay them here." She pointed at another small table. "Aulay, please move this small table here." She pointed next to the big table.

While he did as she asked, Jenny found a clean bed linen and put it on the large, clean table.

"And now, Seoras, please pick up Mhairi and lay her here." While Seoras brought Mhairi onto the table, Jenny looked at Bhatair, who was wiping the knives with a cloth. "Bhatair, do you have opium, by any chance?"

"Never heard of it," Bhatair said.

"That's too bad," Jenny mumbled as she scratched her head. "It's the only anesthetic I can think of that wouldn't harm the baby."

"Anesthetic?" asked Bhatair.

"To knock her unconscious. For the pain. She'll be in so much pain."

Bhatair nodded at the cask he'd brought. "Uisge."

"Yes, that might be our only option. Alcohol should be avoided, of course, I don't want the baby to be born drunk, but it shouldn't affect its development too much. And I suppose herbs might have side effects on the baby."

She nodded. "Okay. I suppose that's our only option. Mhairi, sweetheart, you'll need to drink a lot of uisge."

As Seoras gave the exhausted Mhairi the cask, and she diligently drank the amount that two grown men could sustain, Jenny poured more uisge right onto the woman's round belly. Then she poured it all over her own hands and Bhatair's. He mumbled something angrily but allowed her to do it.

"Scalpel, Bhatair," she said as she stretched out her hand.

"What?"

"That knife, please. The sharpest one you have."

He handed it to her.

"Now please prepare the needle and the thread in the same way. Lots of uisge. Soak them in it if you have to."

He nodded and began cleaning the hooked needles and the threads, then inserted the thread in one of the needles. As he did, Mhairi's cries became weaker and weaker, and she finally dozed off.

Jenny breathed out and looked at everyone in the room. "Be prepared, everyone," she said. "She will probably wake up from pain, so Aulay and Seoras, you both must be strong and hold her in place. Her life will depend on you holding her in place. If you don't, I might accidentally cut the baby... Are you ready?"

"Aye," said Seoras.

Aulay nodded.

"Making the incision." She nodded and brought the knife to the belly and cut it. Aulay couldn't watch. It was butchery, and there was so much blood he only had seen the like on battlefields. Mhairi opened her eyes and gave such an agonized cry, Aulay's heart wrenched. He and Seoras held her down on the table. They'd both seen men scream like that on the battlefield and after as their wounds were cauterized, limbs amputated, and arrows pulled from their bodies.

But it was different when a woman cried like that, the one you loved.

He held her tightly for her own life.

Then there was another cry.

A newborn's.

Aulay and Seoras lifted their heads. Jenny was giving Bhatair a baby. He was bloody and wriggling and crying his wee arse off.

Bhatair took the bairn and looked at Seoras. "Ye must take yer son, I need to tend to yer wife."

As Seoras left her and took the baby into a clean swaddling cloth, Aulay's eyes watered. "Hold on, lass," he whispered to Mhairi, who looked more and more ashen but had stopped screaming, and was watching her son with tears. "Just hold on a wee bit longer."

The bairn was still attached to the mother through the cord. Bhatair tied the cord in two places with strings, and Jenny cut it with scissors. Then they kept working and using linen, and other things—it was all a blur to Aulay. He kept holding Mhairi down and saying calming things. She kept whimpering and moaning, but she sounded weaker and weaker.

After a while, the afterbirth was delivered and Jenny and Bhatair became agitated.

"Hemorrhage!" Jenny muttered. "Bhatair! Clamp!"

Mhairi resumed whimpering and screaming.

Jenny kept throwing out commands like a wee general.

"More linen. We must control the bleeding. Okay, this is good. This should hold. Feel her pulse."

"Her what?" asked Bhatair.

"The beating of her pulse on her wrist."

"Why is that even—"

"Just do it."

While he did it, Jenny worked with the needle over the bloody gap in the woman's body. Aulay kept muttering to Mhairi that she was going to be all right and holding her shoulders down. While the wee bairn screamed and his father wept happy tears over him, Aulay watched Jenny's precise, quick movements with fascination.

Soon, the gap was closed, and she dressed the wound. "Sweetheart, you can't move..." But Mhairi was asleep again.

She wiped her forehead with her hand and looked at Bhatair,

who studied the dressed wound and the patient with fascination. He listened to her heart and nodded, bewildered. "She's still alive."

Jenny asked him to pour water over her hands, and while Bhatair did that, she asked Aulay to put a clean sheet over Mhairi's bed and carry her back to bed. While Aulay did that, she cleaned her hands with uisge once again and went to Seoras.

"May I see the baby?" she asked. "I'd like to make sure he's okay."

Seoras nodded, his eyes teary. Aulay put Mhairi into her bed and covered her with a clean blanket. He came close to Jenny. As she took the newborn, who was now quiet and watched her with interested dark-blue eyes, Aulay's heart lurched. She cooed and talked to the bairn as she carefully looked him over and counted the fingers and toes.

She looked at them with shining eyes. "He's perfect. Congratulations, Seoras, you have a beautiful, healthy son. And your wife lives."

Seoras nodded as he accepted the baby from her arms, tears in his eyes. "Is Mhairi going to be all right?"

She exchanged a glance with Bhatair, who still eyed Mhairi like she was the next Ascension of Christ. "We will see. It's important to keep an eye on her wound. She had a major surgery. If you have a wet nurse lined up, it's best if she feeds the baby. I'll check on Mhairi regularly."

Aulay's heart kept doing something strange...like soaring, warm and light, as he watched this wondrous woman. But it was painful, like a needle kept poking his heart and digging deeper and deeper.

"May I have a word, Jenny?" Aulay asked as he took her hand in his.

Jenny smiled at him and nodded. "Only for a moment. I still need to clean and make sure Mhairi is all right."

He led her out of the room and onto the landing, then closed the door. In the dim light, she was like a mysterious creature from another world.

"I...I just wanted to say thank ye." He felt tears prickle the backs of his eyes. "I am in agony...and ye... Seven years ago, had ye been here, ye could have saved my wife and my own bairn."

Her eyes filled with tears, and she squeezed his hand. "I'm so sorry, Aulay. I'm sorry I couldn't have saved Leitis and your baby."

He nodded and pulled her into his arms. Godly benediction flowed through his veins. Only why God would have sent her to him so late, he didn't know.

CHAPTER 21

AULAY OPENED the door to his bedchamber before Jenny and let her in. The scents of roses and meadowsweet filled her nostrils. A bath stood in the middle of his room, reflected flames of the surrounding tallow candles dancing off the water. Steam rose from it, and Jenny's tired muscles ached to get in there.

"A bath..." Jenny murmured dreamily and turned to him. Her lips spread in a huge smile, and he returned it, wrinkles forming around his eyes.

"For ye, lass," he said.

She gasped and, despite her exhausted muscles, went to the large barrel and climbed the stairs and dipped her hand into the water. The scent of flowers and herbs came from there. The hot liquid burned her fingers pleasantly.

"Oh, it's like you read my mind, Aulay..."

Something lightened and bubbled in her chest. He was a kind man. Bossy, yes, but she now understood why his whole clan worshipped him. He went above and beyond for them...and for her.

"I thought ye might want one, after a day like today," he said as he came closer. "Ye must be exhausted after the birth and cleaning everything."

"That's so thoughtful of you. I am grimy, and I'm sure my hands need another good scrub to fully remove the blood. But main thing is, Mhairi and the baby are all right."

Mhairi had woken up with a huge hangover. But now that she wasn't pregnant, she could take some willow bark tincture, which dulled her pain somewhat. Of course, she was still in a lot of pain and in shock after enduring a major surgery, but Aulay had asked one of the women from the village to step in as a nurse and helper for her, and, with time, the poor woman would heal.

"I'm still in shock myself that we pulled it off," Jenny said.

She didn't want to say it out loud, but she was not a surgeon. And even though her technique was the best bet they'd had given the circumstances, she had been terrified. She didn't know how she'd commanded her body to move and cut and do the right thing when there'd been a voice inside her head screaming at her the whole time.

"Why dinna ye go in, lass?" Aulay said gently.

This man...she marveled at his beautiful, chiseled features. The square jaw under his short beard and the dark eyes that burned holes in her skin.

"Um..." she said. "Turn away."

"Nae."

She raised her brows. "Turn away, Aulay."

"Nae, lass. I will watch ye because I want to see ye whole. Ye will become mine tonight and there wilna be any more secrets, nae unspoken thoughts, and nae hiding. Every inch. Every crease. Every curve."

Heat scalded her cheeks. His words ignited her desire. Her muscles tightened and clenched, and she found that she didn't know what to say. That she actually wanted to undress just like he said.

Without another word, she untied the laces of her dress and let it fall onto the steps of the bath. She pushed her shoes off her feet. His chest rose and fell deeper and quicker as he slowly looked her over in her chemise. She took the edges of the chemise's skirt and pulled up and over her head, and then she stood naked before him, except for the woolen stockings, which were tied under the knee with garters.

There she was before him, all her curves, saggy breasts, and rolls of fat on her behind and on her waist. Only, there was no trace of disgust on his face. There was a sense of awe as his gaze slowly went up and down her body. It felt like he was touching her, ever so lightly, with a feather.

"Just seeing ye makes me as horny as a young bull, lass," he said.

His voice was a molten, smoky croon that made her knees weak.

He dropped to his knees before her and gently untied the garters that held the stockings in place. Then, slowly, he tugged the stockings down her legs one by one. His caress was like a kiss, sending tickles up her legs and straight into her groin. Burning and aching, she watched him as he slowly kissed her leg, going up, higher and higher, until he reached the apex of her thighs.

She was burning by that point. Tom had never done this. No one had ever done this. No one had made her feel this desire, this freedom, this all-consuming need for one single man.

Aulay.

He spread her folds and sealed her sex with his mouth. Pleasure shot through her in a lightning bolt, sharp and powerful as he touched her there. Slowly, he began exploring her folds, and moved closer to her, putting one of her legs over his shoulder. She held on to the side of the bath with her hands, frozen in place as intense bliss whirled and grew inside her.

"Do ye like that?" he murmured as he planted a kiss right there.

"Yes," she whispered.

"And this?" He plunged his tongue and circled it right around her clit. She jerked as exquisite pleasure spilled through her.

"God, yes..."

He kept working her, asking from time to time what she liked and doing exactly that. Every stroke, every touch, every caress was hotter, and when he inserted a finger inside her, she gasped. The invasion was sweet and wonderful. He stretched her with his fingers, moving in and out, and around and around. She hadn't had sex with a man since Tom—not for three years. And it had never, even in the happiest moments of their marriage, been this good. Her head spun. She lost all sense of where she was. She knew only he was here, with her, and she was his. Totally and utterly his. She wanted him to invade her...to claim her.

An orgasm slammed through her body, the waves intense and sweet. She felt like she was flying, but he held her tightly, and she was clenching all around him.

When she sagged against him, he stood up and caught her in his arms. "My sweet lass," he said. "Ye taste better than honeyed fruit."

She bit her lip and hid her face against his shoulder. "Come now," he said. "Get into the bath."

"But what about you?"

"We have all the time in the world. Ye need to enjoy yer bath first."

She nodded and he helped her get in. As she lowered herself slowly into the hot water, it prickled her skin pleasantly.

"It smells so nice," she said as she leaned back against the wall. "What is it?"

"Rose, rosemary, meadowsweet, and lavender oil soap," he said as he handed her a cake of white soap with embedded petals and leaves. "I traded for it when I was in the Kingdom of Galicia a few years ago. Though 'tis made in Naples, I believe."

"Hmmm..." she murmured as she inhaled the scent. She foamed the soap against her hands and handed it back to him. She first washed her hands thoroughly, the foam turning brown from the residue of blood on her fingers. To her surprise, Aulay took a cup and poured hot water over her hair. Then he foamed his hands and started washing her hair. She melted as his deft fingers massaged her scalp, lifted her hair, and smoothed the soap suds through it.

"Oh, Aulay...this is almost as good as sex..."

He chuckled and kissed her shoulder. "Ye deserve to be treated this way every day, lass."

Something stabbed her in the chest. No one had ever told her that. Sineag may be exactly right. Aulay may be the one man meant for her. A man born in another time.

~

JENNY WOKE UP IN THE MIDDLE OF THE NIGHT, PRESSED UP against Aulay's hot, hard back, his firm butt against her crotch. She had fallen asleep after the bath, exhausted from the eventful day.

Aulay's back was like a warm rock, his skin under her palms smooth and silky, save for the wound she had stitched a couple of days ago. He slept, his ribs rising and falling evenly as he breathed. Jenny felt clean and calm and cared for. She took a deep breath, inhaling Aulay's masculine scent. The room was quiet and dark, the night sky visible through the slit window. The air still smelled like soap and herbs from the bath. The linen sheets were smooth against her skin.

She ran her palm down Aulay's broad, muscular chest and over his stomach. He had such a nice, hard stomach. She reached the apex of his thighs and the hair surrounding his cock. Her nipples hardened as she thought of his length and his size that she'd seen last night before going to bed. Biting her lip, her breath accelerating, she lowered her hand and laid it on his cock. It was thick and velvety, and as she circled it with her palm, it twitched and hardened.

"Lass..." came Aulay's rumbling voice. "What are ye playing at?"

She chuckled and planted a kiss against his back. She didn't recognize herself. Who was this horny woman initiating sex with a man who wasn't her husband or boyfriend...who was her captor?

"Sorry I woke you up," she murmured. "I don't know what I'm playing at. Do you like it?"

She started moving her hand up and down his erection, and the growl that came out of his chest reverberated through her whole body.

"Ye can wake me up for this anytime," he said, his voice husky. "Och, lass..."

She loved hearing the sound of pleasure in his voice. She wanted to give him more of it, like he had given her last night. He was getting harder and harder in her palm, his cock a smooth, velvety rock. He sucked in air as she sped up and started kissing his back. Such a big back, an ocean of corded muscles moving and straining as he arched his spine.

Then he spun around and pushed her onto her back and towered over her, his arms on the mattress on either side of her head.

"Vixen..." he murmured, looking her over like she was a delicious snack, setting her insides on fire. "God's blood, I'm aching for ye. I must have ye."

Her breath came out raggedly... This would be the first man she'd sleep with after Tom.

"'Tis the first time for me since Leitis..." he said, echoing her thoughts.

Something squeezed in her chest, and she was lost for words. Instead, as an answer, she pulled him closer to her. "I'm aching all over for you, too," she managed.

He positioned himself against her entrance and massaged her sex with his hard cock. She arched her back, her fingers curling around the sheets as sweet pleasure spilled through her. How would he fit into her? She hoped she hadn't grown back together like a virgin.

Then he pushed into her, invading her space like a conqueror, like a king claiming new land. The deep, primal part of her rejoiced at the invasion, and as he stretched her to the limit, she gasped. He was on top of her, his weight pleasant. He pulled her undertunic up and exposed her breasts.

"Hmm," he murmured, cupping one and circling his thumb around her nipple. "So full. So bonnie."

He took one nipple into his mouth and sucked as he began moving in and out of her.

"Ah!" she cried out at the intense sweetness that burst through her body, and all thoughts evaporated from her head.

"Look at me, lass," he said, and she opened her eyes, meeting his dark, intense gaze. "I want to see yer face as ye come around my cock."

But it was more than that. As his thrusts grew stronger and faster, she couldn't look away. There was more than just lust that connected them. Something intense and wonderful and deep. A shared pain, she knew. A part of her soul was, perhaps, in him.

Her pleasure intensified as he angled himself so that his thrusts massaged her clitoris, and she shuddered, opening up to him. Never before had she felt this with anyone.

And then he sent her over the edge, and she was falling, falling, falling apart into a million pieces. He bucked and grunted like a pained wolf, and he was coming, too. She felt the jerks of his erection inside her.

And as she melted away in his arms like wax, she knew there was one problem. She didn't belong to this time. She wanted a baby, and the only way to have that baby was back in her time. Eight days.

And yet, for the first time, she didn't want to think about that appointment, about her ten eggs that were left, about her clinic and her empty apartment.

For the first time in her adult life, in Aulay's arms, she didn't feel the ache in her chest because she didn't have a child of her own.

It was new and beautiful...

And terrifying.

Because she would still need to leave one day. And what would be left of her if all this happiness was taken away?

CHAPTER 22

As HE WOKE up the next morning with Jenny in his arms, Aulay felt like he'd found treasure. He'd been looking for a treasure ship—but instead, he'd found this woman.

She understood him and challenged him. She fit him. She was perfect.

She was insatiable. They had made love four times last night, like a pair of horny adolescents. Feeling her tightness around his erection, thrusting into her over and over again, made him feel like they were both in the presence of the divine.

Jenny stirred in his arms and opened her eyes. "Good morning," she said and stretched, pressing herself tightly to him. He kissed her, morning breath and all.

"Good morning," he murmured. "My sweet, soft, beautiful lass."

She had told him that faerie, Sìneag, had sent her through time to him because they were meant for each other. And he'd started to think that may be true. It was still hard to believe he got two great loves in his life. How happy and lucky and blessed he was.

She nuzzled against his shoulder. "I need to go and check on Mhairi and the baby."

"Nae." He tugged her to him. "Nae yet, lass."

"I must, Aulay."

"What about checking on me first?"

"Right, I do need to look at your wound..."

"Nae that." He pulled her on top of him, and when his erection brushed against her, she giggled.

"That must wait, I'm afraid."

Despite his protests, she got out of bed and dressed. She tied her long hair in a simple tail that hung down her back and grinned at him. "I'll see you later."

Aulay stood up and began dressing, too. Yesterday, Colum had come back from another sea expedition with no signs of the shipwreck. It might have sunk after all. They'd search again today, and if they didn't find anything, they'd need to go to the Isle of Man, which had been claimed by the English, tomorrow. If the shipwreck was there, Aulay was ready to fight for the treasure.

As he pulled on his braies, he realized he didn't want to be apart from Jenny. She had him wrapped around her finger.

When he was dressed, he went to Seoras's room. Jenny was there, holding wee Sìomon and talking to Mhairi. Both the new mother and the beautiful bairn were well. Bhatair was there, too, and he was looking at the wound on Mhairi's stomach.

Bhatair wasn't complaining or starting a fight with Jenny. It seemed his attitude had changed completely towards her since last night.

"How are ye, lass?" Aulay asked Mhairi.

"I'm all right," she said as she winced.

"She's in pain," said Jenny. "But the wound looks good."

"I'll give ye more willow bark," said Bhatair as he covered Mhairi's stomach. "It does surprise me how good it looks."

Jenny smiled, and Bhatair nodded to her. For a proud man like him, this was a big acknowledgment of respect. A wet nurse came into the room together with the woman Aulay had asked to take care of Mhairi. Jenny gently passed the lad to the wet nurse.

Peace covered Aulay like a warm blanket. Sìomon's birth and Mhairi's survival had healed something within him. It gave him hope and joy and blurred the memories of the terrible loss and heartache he'd felt with every failed birth and Leitis's death.

"We will feast tonight," said Aulay. "In honor of Sìomon. And in yer honor, Mhairi."

Jenny frowned at him. "She can't move or stand up."

"Aye, I understand. The best food will be brought to ye, Mhairi, but I feel like this is a great blessing, and God kens we all need a blessing in our lives these days. May I show the lad to the clan tonight, Mhairi?"

"I like the idea," said Seoras. "I'll make sure he's all right, Mhairi."

Mhairi smiled. "Aye, ye're right, Uncle. Sìomon is a blessing. A blessing that wouldna have happened without Jennifer."

Everyone looked at her, and pride for his woman glowed in Aulay's chest.

"Let it be so," Aulay said.

While Jenny and Bhatair went to check on Una and Ailis, Aulay went to order the feast for tonight. Mayhap he was mad. Despite not having found the treasure, despite the possible English attack that could happen at any moment, despite the sick and the wounded in the village, Aulay felt like happiness was finally within his reach.

Sìomon had been born. And Jenny...she made everything better.

Later that night, the great hall was lit with many candles and braziers. They illuminated the MacDonald heraldry hanging on the walls. The embroidery that Aulay's mother had made of a great fleet of birlinns coming to a new shore. On white table covers, silver and gold dishes of roasted game and fish, fruit and breads, cheese, pies, and pastries glistened. The clan musicians were positioned on a small stage and played jolly music, the room full of the sounds of flute and tambourine and bagpipe. Clansmen and women put on their best clothes and sat laughing, eating, drinking, and singing. Aulay didn't stint on drinks. The most valuable casks of French wine were opened, and the best ale, normally reserved for important guests, was offered to everyone.

Next to Aulay, at his table of honor, sat Jenny. The firelight made her red hair shine like polished copper. Her skin was alabaster and smooth. Her lips, full and delicious, smiled at him. God almighty, how he loved it when she smiled. Mhairi had lent Jenny her best dress for feasts and celebrations, and she looked beautiful in the rich gown the color of the deep ocean on a sunny day.

Seoras sat at his other hand, the bairn in his arms. Colum was by Seoras's side, uncharacteristically for him, cooing at his new nephew. This was a glimpse of the Colum that Aulay had known before he had been kidnapped. The golden lad who everyone loved. The lad who could befriend a stone and lift a miser's mood, full of optimism, charm, and confidence.

Mayhap there was hope for him. Aulay knew that once Colum proved his loyalty to the clan, he would no longer be plagued by the doubt and rejection of his people.

Aulay stood up and, even though he didn't say anything, a hush fell over the great hall.

He raised his goblet. "Today we have a great miracle to celebrate. My first nephew was born, Sìomon MacDonald, the son of Seoras." The people raised their cups and goblets, too, and gave a roar of approval. "But it may have been very different if nae for Jennifer and for Bhatair. Jennifer showed courage and skill, and Bhatair was open to new methods. Thanks to Jennifer, Sìomon and Mhairi are alive. Ye all ken how I wish someone like Jennifer could have done the same thing for Leitis and my bairns."

His voice shook as he said the last few words, and the clan

was silent. He saw women wipe at their eyes and men stare into their cups with sadness.

"To Sìomon and Mhairi! And to a good woman who saved their lives," he cheered, and everybody echoed him.

After they all drank, the music resumed, and Aulay turned to Jennifer and offered her his open palm. She raised her eyebrows. "Would ye dance with me, my lady?"

She blinked. "I don't know how to dance a medieval dance."

"Ye will be fine. Come."

She sighed out and placed her hand into his. "I'm afraid I'll embarrass you, Aulay."

"Never."

The music was cheerful and fast. He led her, and soon she caught up with the steps and the jumps and the turning and spinning. A bright smile bloomed on her face from ear to ear. Her eyes glistened with excitement and joy. His chest lightened and delight spread through him like sunlight.

At that moment, that was all he wanted. At that moment, he was happy.

He wanted to never let her go. He wanted her with him forever.

Because he knew in his heart that he loved her. That what he felt for Jennifer wasn't an infatuation or pure lust. It was something deeper—deeper even than what he had had with Leitis. It was as though Jennifer had been made for him.

And he had been placed on this earth to love her.

He felt his own smile fall as she made the next jump. Unease washed over him like the fin of a shark passing near a swimmer. She was bound to go back. He wanted her to stay, but she still had that egg thing she needed to do. She wanted a bairn of her own.

He needed to talk to her and make sure he knew what she was feeling and if she still wanted to return to her time.

If that was her wish, he'd help her. He'd make sure she got

what she wanted and needed in life. Even if it meant giving up his own happiness.

He stopped and pulled her to him. "Come with me, Jenny. I must have a word with ye."

CHAPTER 23

THE SEA BREEZE flapping her skirt and playing with her hair, Jenny felt like she was flying as she walked by Aulay's side on the cliffs outside the castle. The western sky was ablaze with the setting sun, oranges and pinks and reds spilling into the sea. The rugged cliffs and the shore of Islay that stretched to the west were dark.

The scent of the sea, the whisper of the waves against the shore were lovely and lulling.

But not as lovely as the man she was walking next to.

Her skin prickled pleasantly in his hand. And her chest... Her chest felt so tight it might burst. Or she might float over the sea and drift off into space.

She knew what it was.

She was falling for him. Hard. Falling for the man who held her prisoner. Falling for the man from the wrong time.

All those feelings were good. And right. The man was, too.

But the epoch was completely wrong.

They stopped at a high point overlooking the sea, and Aulay stood behind her and wrapped his arms around her shoulders. He was so warm. Warm and hard and masculine. But her thoughts kept going back to what she'd left behind.

Her friends. Her family. God, did her parents and her sisters think she was dead? They must all be so worried. And what about Amanda and the clinic? Her poor friend would have needed to take on all of Jenny's patients and seek temporary help.

And her goddamn appointment. One week left. One week, and that would be it. Only, she didn't feel such a driving need to go home anymore. It was as though the hole in her chest that had been left by the absence of a baby was healing.

Filling up.

Why was that? Was it just that her feelings for Aulay were distracting her? Was she hiding some truth she didn't want to see?

"Why do you want a child, Aulay?" she asked.

He kissed the top of her head, his short beard briefly scratching her scalp.

"I havna given that much thought recently," he replied. "I want someone to care for and to raise and to teach. Besides, I always kent 'tis my duty to my people and God to leave a legacy. Having an heir is my obligation to my clan and the generations to come. And to Scotland in a way."

"Obligation..." she murmured. "A child is not a debt to be paid, Aulay. It's a person, a human being. A child should be born out of love."

"Aye, ye're right." He was quiet for a while, then he said, "Something must be wrong with me, Jenny. And I canna even believe I'm saying this out loud, and to a woman I very much care for... But I wonder if there's a curse upon me which didna allow poor Leitis to birth a bairn...and to survive. When I lie in bed and try to fall asleep, sometimes my mind wonders all these terrible things... Like, what if in my selfish pursuit of heirs, because of this obligation that I felt, 'twas I that had killed Leitis?"

It was as though his pain had slashed across her own chest. She turned to him and took his dear face in both of her hands.

His eyes were teary, his thick brows drawn in a pained expression.

"No," she said firmly. "It wasn't your fault. It was no one's. How many women die in childbirth because of how underdeveloped medicine is in these times?"

He swallowed and kissed her hand. "Ye may be the best physician in the world during this time. My clan is very fortunate to have ye."

She kissed him gently. "Thank you for saying that. You have no idea what it means."

The sky was getting darker now. The sun had just set, and the golden-orange light made him look even more godlike.

"Tell me about her. About Leitis. The woman whose dresses I wear. The woman you loved..."

The woman he'd loved. Yes, he'd loved her. Or he wouldn't have kept her dresses, wouldn't still be so grief-stricken about her. Good God, Jenny was jealous of a dead woman. It was petty of her. She shouldn't feel that way.

"Leitis was an amazing woman. She was bonnie. She was kind and intelligent. She was confident and kent her own worth. Our marriage was arranged by our clans, and she told me right at our wedding that she wouldna let me in her bed until she kent I was a good, worthy man." He chuckled. "So, I had to win her over at first. And right then, I kent this was the woman for me. I thought that Leitis had been my one true love. Until I met ye."

Until he met her... Her heart thundered in her chest. She was melting, evaporating. Happiness filled her to the core. But despite this feeling like she was on a cloud made of pink cotton candy, flying around with MacZeus, a godlike Highlander—despite the fact that she was falling hard for him—she belonged to another time. And he belonged here. And she could never give him the heirs that he wanted so much.

"Why didn't you try to marry a younger woman to have heirs?" she asked.

He chuckled softly, watching the sky. Purple light reflected in his dark eyes, and they were glistening. "I didna think I'd be able to keep living if I was hurt again when another woman died because of me." He looked at her. "Why didna ye marry after yer husband?"

She looked down at the ground. Her shoes were dark against hard yellowish moss. "I couldn't imagine being betrayed and hurt again. When my husband told me he wanted a divorce because he was in love with someone else, I...felt like I was cut in two. I know a child would never do that. I saw that in my own family, growing up. My parents love us. My sisters have their own families. They all look happy. I thought I'd be happy, too. I've always wanted that perfect image of a happy family—a mother, a father, and a child or two...or three. And he took that away from me. But a child would never do that. So, I thought even though I'd be without a husband, I would still like to have a baby."

He chuckled. "A child will leave one day. Marry their husband or wife. They will choose someone over ye one day."

She bit her lip. "I never thought about it that way. You're wise beyond your years, Aulay."

He glared at her. "As long as 'wise' dinna mean 'old.'"

She giggled. "But what about you? Can't Colum be the next laird? He'll be a great leader. No, he isn't your own son, but he's your nephew, so he's still your blood. And Seoras. And Sìomon after them."

"Aye. 'Tis exactly what I have thought. But just like ye, I've always wanted my own. Wanted to bounce my own bairn on my knee and come home to my own wee family. To ken I had given them all they needed, and that even when I'm gone, they'd be taken care of."

She hugged him around the neck and looked up at him. He was so tall, she almost had to tilt her head all the way back. "Here we are. Two old people complaining of what can never be."

He growled and his gaze darkened. "Call me old one more time... I'll show you old."

He kissed her, his lips warm and hungry and demanding, and she forgot everything.

~

HER LIPS WERE LIKE VELVET, AND AULAY COULDN'T GET enough. He tasted them over and over again, feeling himself harden, feeling himself burn for her. One touch from her, and he was on fire.

This woman was everything. He loved talking to her, he loved making love to her, he loved just being in her presence.

He was breathing her in, trying to make him hers, a part of his bloodstream. Her tongue was hot and sweet, and she tasted of raspberries and wine.

He had a strange sense that she was disappearing from him when she looked out at the sea. She had come to him like a vision from another world on that island. Called to him like a siren called a seaman to his demise. And he'd come to her, taken her to his home.

And now he wanted to make her his. But she wasn't. She had given him her body, but her heart...he wasn't sure she could give him her heart.

And he wanted all of her, or he'd need to let her go.

He caressed her back, running his hands up and down her beautiful body, her full arse. He fondled her breast right through her dress and played with her nipple until it hardened and she was moaning and arching against him.

Then he brought his arms around her and picked her up, letting her legs wrap around his waist. His shoulder complained with pain, but he ignored it. What was a wee bit of pain when he could have her?

"I'll show ye old," he growled into her mouth. "Ye think an old man can do this?"

With one arm holding her, he undid the girdle that held his braies, lifted her skirts up, and was inside her in one swift movement. Her tight, sleek heat took him in, and they both gasped.

"Aulay..." she murmured. "Anyone can see us..."

"Let them," he growled. "Let them all ken ye are mine."

He began moving inside her. God's blood, she held him like a fist. They both moved in one rhythm. Her plump breasts bounced against his chest through her dress. He leaned down and sucked her nipple through the fabric. She was so soft and beautiful and so perfect against him. He was all heat, tight and tense and burning.

She was holding on to his shoulders. Behind her, the last sunrays of the day were dying, the pink and orange turning purple, the sea and the sky black in the east. He was claiming her before the whole world. In front of God, and sky and sea and his own land, he claimed her.

And she was loving it. Like a glove and a hand, they fit. She was moaning those throaty moans he loved hearing from her. Those moans that made him even harder. She was tighter and tighter around him, and as he kept holding her with one arm, with his other hand, he found her sleek folds and gently rubbed the center of her pleasure.

"Oh, Aulay," she groaned out, and he knew she wouldn't last long.

"Tell me a young pup can make love to ye like that. Ken yer body like that. Make ye sing like that."

"No one..." she said. "Fuck it, Aulay... Oh God..."

She cried out loudly from pleasure. And she was over the edge tightening and clenching around him in her sweet release, milking him. That was his own undoing, and in a moment, he felt himself buck and tighten, and release and spill into her.

"Mine, Jenny, ye're mine," he growled.

As he held her in his arms, quivering and sagging against him, Aulay realized this may be one of the last times they would do that. She wanted to leave and return to her time. And if he loved her, he couldn't hold her here any longer against her will. The thought of losing her was like a knife in his soul.

But there was so much he could offer her. He could make her happy, give her everything she'd ever wanted.

Mayhap a bairn.

She had said something about eggs and needing modern medicine to have a child, but mayhap there was a chance. He kent well enough how to make a child...

And so, breaking the decision he had made after Leitis's death, he looked at her and said, "Jenny, marry me, lass."

She gaped at him speechless, then slowly slid from his embrace and stood on the ground. Her eyes became sad and teary. And then she said one word that shattered his entire world into pieces. "No."

CHAPTER 24

AULAY'S HEART was wrenching and aching as Jenny stood before him, hastily straightening her skirts.

"Nae?" he asked.

He supposed he should not be surprised. Or feel this hurt. She had not told him she'd stay with him. She hadn't promised anything. She'd asked to leave, tried to leave, and he had not let her.

"I can't, Aulay," she said, still without looking at him. "I never told you I'd even consider staying."

He turned away. The sky was dark now. In the west, a thin line of orange and pink glowed on the horizon, the last light of the day about to disappear. To the east, the castle and the village were a small gathering of fires flickering against the vast darkness of the night. Like his last hope of finding happiness.

If he couldn't be with Jenny, he would never be with anyone else. This was it for him.

"I ken ye didna. I suppose I hoped. I told ye I can give ye everything ye want."

"What do you know about what I want?" she asked as she straightened her disheveled hair. "What I want is to go back. You're not giving me that."

He caught her hands and pressed them against his chest. "Look at me, Jenny." When she finally met his gaze, her eyes were deep and wide, and searching. "Here's me, a man of flesh and blood. Feel this? My heart is beating for ye. I want to be with ye for the rest of my days. To love ye and worship ye and make ye happy. Tell me whatever lies behind that time traveling rock is better. Tell me that the world of carriages that move by themselves and a house where ye live alone and sleep in an empty bed will make ye happier than I will."

She was breathing hard. He saw tears moistening her eyes.

"No, it won't. But there's more to consider. No matter how much you and I both want to, you can never give me a baby. And I can't give you one, either."

She gently pulled her hands from under his and stepped back.

"What is more important, Jenny? An heir I may never have? Or being with the woman who will brighten the rest of my days? I ken what is right for me. Are ye sure ye ken what is right for ye?"

She stood and watched him silently for a while. Her throat moved with unspoken words. It seemed she wanted to say something, but she shut her mouth. She bent down to tug her heel deeper into her shoe, and an object fell from her dress. Something metallic pinged against the rock and rolled into Aulay's foot. He bent down and picked it up. It was hard to see in the dim light, but he could tell that it was round and covered in grime. He scrubbed the dirt off with his thumb and gold glistened from under it. He rubbed it against his tunic until the image shone through—a king sitting on the throne with an orb and a scepter in his hands.

He knew that coin. It was a gold penny issued by King Henry III. But where would Jenny have gotten such a coin?

The English treasure ship.

His world turned icy cold and dark. The small coin in his hand weighed like a boulder and burned his fingers like nettle.

He looked at her. All innocence, rejecting him because she was bound to another time. And yet, this had been in her clothes all along.

"Where did ye find this, lass?" he asked. His own voice sounded dead to him.

"The coin?" she said. "On the Isle of Achleith."

On the Isle of Achleith? He and his men had searched for the treasure every single day for over two sennights now. Had the shipwreck been at Achleith this whole time?

"Did ye see a shipwreck there?" he asked.

She frowned and looked at the coin. "No."

"Why did ye hide this from me?" he roared, shaking his fist with the coin.

His heart was torn to pieces. Part of him realized she'd hurt him with her rejection, and perhaps he didn't know where that hurt ended and the surprise of the coin in her dress began. He had suspected she was on the English side all this time. He had suspected she'd been a charlatan. She had rejected both suggestions and told him an insane story about time travel.

Could all of that be a lie? How could he have believed her at all?

It all made sense now. If she was for the English this whole time, she had successfully seduced him and gained his trust. Of course she wasn't a time traveler. She was a woman from his time, brave and courageous enough to invent a story to cover her true mission. Besides, the idea of an enemy from his time was better than a time traveler who didn't belong here at all.

Because even if she were an enemy, he could breathe easier knowing she was somewhere in the same world as he was.

She took a step back, and the distance between them felt like a chasm miles deep, impossible to cross.

"I didn't hide it from you," she said. "I didn't think anything of it at first. Then I kept it to possibly buy me a passage back to Achleith."

"Ye kent I was looking for the shipwreck this whole time."

"How would I know the shipwreck had anything to do with the coin?"

He scoffed and shook his head. "Lies."

One word, and the chasm between them just got wider.

"I had suspected all this time if I fell in love again, I'd be hurt. Never did I imagine someone would nae just hurt me, but first gain my trust and then betray me."

He felt himself pulling away, closing his heart off to her and anyone else.

"I congratulate ye on fooling me and making me fall in love with ye, break my resolve for ye. Making me open up and hope, imagine finding happiness once again. My people warned me about ye all this time. They were right."

CHAPTER 25

"THE INCISION IS LOOKING WELL," said Jenny as she covered Mhairi's belly with the dressing the next morning. Then pulled down Mhairi's undertunic and pulled up the blanket over her. "How's the pain?"

A faint frown crossed Mhairi's face. "It hurts a wee bit, I wilna lie. But Bhatair's mixture is helping. The pain is like a shadow."

As Jenny had asked, the servants had cleaned the bedchamber and changed the bedsheets. The room now smelled faintly of vinegar because that's what Jenny had asked them to wash the floors and the surfaces with. Seoras stood with Sìomon by the slit window and gently rocked him from side to side.

Jenny squeezed Mhairi's hand. "You're a hero. You've gone through an enormous ordeal."

"Anything for that bairn." She threw a loving look at her husband and her baby.

"Here's more of willow bark and mandrake root mixture." Bhatair poured a liquid from a dull glass bottle and put it on the chest next to Mhairi's bed. "Take this at noon."

"Aye," Mhairi said.

Jenny and Bhatair looked at Sìomon. His cord stump had

started to darken and wasn't infected. He looked a little bit yellow but not to an alarming degree. Slight jaundice was normal in newborns and would likely clear up on its own. He was getting enough milk based on his quantity of urine and stool. Jenny was happy with his condition.

Soon they left Mhairi's bedchamber to let her rest and went down the stairs of the main keep. When they were walking down the slope of the inner bailey, Bhatair asked her, "Is anything the matter, Lady Jennifer?"

Last night, Aulay had proposed to her, and she had rejected him. He had found the gold coin. And now he thought she was an enemy and a liar.

And her heart was shattered into pieces.

Losing him, his trust, his affection felt worse than her divorce. Felt even worse than the day she'd found out she may never have a child of her own.

Jenny looked up at Bhatair, realizing distantly he'd asked her a question.

"Everything is fine."

Except that her heart was a goddamn wreck, and how could that be when around her in the bailey it was business as usual? Warriors trained, children ran around, servants cleaned, and farmers brought produce to the castle. Horses neighed, metal banged against metal, there were cries and shouts as people worked. The breeze coming from the sea was cool on her cheeks, but Leitis's dress protected her from the chill. Thinking of the woman, and how Aulay had mourned her, reminded Jenny that she'd rejected a great man. She hadn't seen Aulay yet today, but she hadn't been able to stop thinking about him even as she examined Mhairi.

"Ye dinna look fine, lass," Bhatair said.

She frowned and studied him. His blue eyes were on her, carefully looking her over. Did he care about her? What had happened to him that he wondered about her well-being? Had she really won him over?

Even him...but not Aulay.

The goddamn coin. She'd had no idea it was connected to the shipwreck he was after. And he didn't believe her. Was it because she'd rejected his marriage proposal?

Had that been the right thing to do? In a perfect world, she would be able to have a baby the old-fashioned way, so she would have said yes to him. She would have wanted to stay and be happy with him. She would do good in this community. She would even be willing to stop dyeing her hair and become gray.

"I appreciate you caring, Bhatair," she said. "I'm just tired, that's all. A lot on my mind. Thank you for asking, though. Nice of you."

"Aye..." Bhatair said. "Do tell me if ye're getting sick. I still have leeches."

Jenny wondered if she would ever allow leeches to be placed on her body. She supposed if it was ever a matter of death or leeches, she'd chose leeches. But otherwise...

The sound of a baby wailing came from Ailis's house when Bhatair and Jenny were ten feet away. They exchanged a glance and ran towards the house. Bhatair went in first, and as he opened the door, Jenny's ears hurt from Una's desperate, desolate cry. She lay in her crib on her back, feet and hands moving jerkily up and down. Her blanket had fallen off, and she was in her soiled baby gown, the scent of excrement thick in the room. Her face was red, her mouth wide open, and her eyes closed to slits as she cried.

Without looking at the bed, Jenny hurried to the crib, swaddled the baby, and picked her up. "Ailis, what happened?" She turned to the bed and froze, icy cold.

Bhatair was leaning over the unmoving Ailis lying among dirty sheets. He held a mirror over her mouth and waited. Her eyes were closed, and she was pale...so, so pale...

As Jenny forced herself out of her stupor and bounced Una on her hip, she became quieter and leaned to Jenny, laying her little head against Jenny's chest and making a movement with her head and with her little hand, searching for a breast.

"You're hungry, you poor thing..." murmured Jenny. "Bhatair—"

He straightened and looked at her. His eyes were so incredibly sad.

It didn't register in her mind until she heard him say it. "She's dead."

Dead.

The evidence was there. Smudges of bloody mucus around her mouth. Pasty skin. Unmoving chest.

She must have coughed blood. Her flu must have turned to pneumonia that had gotten worse without proper treatment.

Her and Bhatair's patient was dead. She saw the guilt and sadness corrode his features like they had twisted her own. She shook her head mournfully. "I'm sorry I failed you, Ailis," she whispered and pressed Una's little body to her.

What would happen now to this baby? She would need a wet nurse and a lot of care. She needed a mother. Tears blurred Jenny's vision. What wouldn't she have given to change things for Ailis? To fight harder for her? To try to convince her to let Jenny treat her properly?

"'Tis my fault," said Bhatair.

It was Jenny's, too. However, she needed to be professional and support her colleague. He had done everything he knew to be right in this medieval world and with the limited resources available.

"No, Bhatair," she said, bouncing Una. "It's not. It happens. We cannot save every one of them."

Bhatair nodded thoughtfully. "I'll go and fetch the priest."

"Thank you. I'll clean Una and try to find a wet nurse for her. She's wet and hungry."

She took Una to the same wet nurse that nursed Sìomon and asked her if she could feed Una. The woman said of course.

Jenny was amazed at the sense of community and help in the village. But she couldn't stay and watch the little orphan nurse.

Her heart was breaking, shattering into million pieces for Una. For herself. She couldn't stop the tears. Grief poured out of her in dark, uncontrollable heaves. She gave out one loud, bark-like sob, startling Una and the nurse, both of whom looked at her in surprise.

"Sorry," she muttered and hurried outside as though she was about to vomit, searching for a safe place to empty the insides of her soul.

She ran around the corner and sat on the ground, leaning against the wall of the house. She pulled her knees up to her forehead and sobbed. For the mother who had left too early. For the child who needed one.

For herself and for Aulay.

For a love that was so sweet and that it seemed she had already lost.

"Jenny," his voice came, and she jerked upright, hastily wiping her wet face. Aulay stood around the corner, looking at her with his eyebrows drawn together. His eyes scanned her up and down quickly, searching for signs of injury, no doubt. "What is the matter?"

She cleared her throat. She wiped her nose with her sleeve. "It's Ailis," she said, her voice raspy and tight. "She's dead."

"Nae..." Aulay took five large steps to her. The next moment, she was in his arms, in the confinement of hard muscle and the masculine scent of sea and leather and his own tang. "I'm sorry," he whispered against the top of her head. "I'm so sorry."

She let go and sobbed into his chest, shaking, convulsing as hot grief poured out of her. He held her the whole time, and she clung to him like her life depended on it, like he was the whole world. And somehow, she knew that he'd always hold her like this if she needed him to.

Then she was spent and just stood pressed against him, surrounded by him, feeling empty.

"Can you do something for Una?" she asked finally and stepped out of his embrace.

As he let go of her, cold, empty air wrapped around her instead of his arms. It felt wrong. So wrong.

"Aye. Of course, I'll take care of her. The orphanage is there for her, I'll ask them to build one more bed when she's old enough. Until then, I'll find her a foster family. Dinna fash, Jenny. She'll be well taken care of."

"That's good," she said as she wiped her still-wet eyes. "Thank you."

Their eyes met, and he opened his mouth to say something. There was that distance, that awkwardness between them. Did he still believe she was an enemy? She wanted to tell him again that he was wrong, that she wasn't his enemy and never would be. That she regretted their argument last night.

But Colum appeared behind Aulay, his dark hair plastered against his forehead. He looked between them and cleared his throat.

"The ship is ready, Uncle," Colum said.

Aulay nodded. "Aye. Good. We're sailing right away."

He nodded to her, so polite, so distant, and turned around to walk down to the gate with Colum.

"Wait!" Jenny cried, and he turned. "Take me with you. Please."

Aulay scoffed and shook his head. "I am sorry Ailis died, lass. But I wilna be manipulated again. Ye showed me yer true self last night. I wilna make the same mistake twice. I'll send word about ye to England. Ye'll nae leave this island until a ransom arrives for ye."

Shock slammed through her as though she'd just run into a concrete wall at maximum speed. Then came anger, a red-hot wall of fire. He was holding her hostage now. For what? For finding a stupid coin?

"This is bullshit!" she yelled at his back. "You're insane!"

But he kept going, completely ignoring her.

She ran after him. "What happened to your beautiful speeches yesterday? Did they mean nothing to you? What about believing and trusting me? Haven't I proved to you I'm a good healer? Didn't I save Sìomon?"

His lips were a thin line. "I am grateful for what ye've done for my people, but I wilna let ye fool me again."

They were coming close to the entrance gate, and Jenny's heart was pounding. If they left now and discovered the ship on that island, that would be the last time they'd be going there. The last time she could escape.

"Laird! Laird!" called one of the guards, and Aulay and Colum went to the side. "Come, look at this."

Six men, two guards among them, stood in a circle and looked at something. Jenny didn't even notice what it was. At the same time, a cart with sheep's wool was being drawn down the slope from the castle to the village. With her legs weak, she slowed down until the cart shielded her from the view of Aulay and his warriors. She walked at the same speed as the cart, and to her surprise, they passed the gates, and she was walking down the slope.

She was expecting a call, an angry uproar because she had left the castle, but none came, and everything was quiet. When she was a good distance away, she sped up and hurried through the village and down to the jetty. She spotted *Tagradh*, Aulay's ship. Several men sat at the front of it, but no one sat in the rear. While they were talking and looking in the direction of the village, she tiptoed over the rampart onto the ship and hid between some sacks at the back.

She could be discovered at any moment, but if she wasn't, she may finally be on her way back home.

Only, she wasn't sure if home meant the same to her now as it had a few days ago.

CHAPTER 26

THE SHIP ROCKED as one of the last Highlanders got out. Jenny peered from behind the sack, watching twenty or so MacDonald warriors climb the hill of the island that would finally take her home. The Isle of Achleith was the same huge mass of rocks and moss that she remembered. The cliffs and rocks bulging like the distorted face of a giant.

As she watched the last of the men climb to the top of the island and then disappear behind the curve of the slope, she made her way to the side of the ship. It was anchored close enough for the men to disembark and walk through the waves to the shore, and far enough for the hull not to scratch the ground.

She had no choice but to jump into the water, as well. As she did, the icy cold of the Irish Sea stole her breath. She hurried through the water, freezing and soaked from the waist down. Well, it would all be worth it, as long as she could get back to her own time. She had only six days till her appointment.

As she stood on the gravelly beach, and began climbing the hill, an ache pierced her chest. She thought of Amanda, Kyla, and Natalie, and of her parents and her sisters and her nephews and nieces and her two brothers-in-law.

She wondered if they were still looking for her or if they

thought she must have fallen into the sea and drowned. Did they have a funeral for her? If she got back to her time, how in the world would she explain her disappearance? If she told them about time travel, they'd put her in a psychiatric ward, no doubt.

As she climbed higher and higher, small pebbles skittering down the slope from under her shoes, she thought about the good things in her life she'd go back to. Her pediatric practice. Her family. Her friends. Her apartment in New York with heating and electricity and a fridge. Antibiotics and other medicine that could save people's lives.

There would be no Una, and there would be no Aulay.

She'd be one of many doctors who could help patients in the twenty-first century. But then the people here wouldn't have anyone who understood the importance of antiseptics, cleaning tables and instruments, and keeping good hygiene.

Like Aulay had said, there was no one like her in this time.

The thought about how much good she could do for the people of this time made her stop. Her legs just wouldn't move and walk her up the hill. And Una...poor girl...she needed a mother, and Jenny wanted a baby.

But what about her own baby?

Yes, her own baby. She wouldn't abandon the thing that mattered most to her for Aulay. A man who, just as she had feared and suspected all along, would easily betray her given a chance. He'd believed in her for a time. Then suddenly he didn't. How could she trust him not to hurt her again?

She couldn't.

That gave her the strength to keep walking. She looked back at the ship, and the view from here was spectacular. The vast Irish Sea was dark because of the gray clouds in the sky. The wind brought the scent of the sea and algae. It flapped her wet skirt, piercing her legs with cold needles. She shivered. There was no other land in sight. Of course, that would be problematic once she returned to her own time. How would she be able to call someone to come for her from an uninhabited island?

Well, she'd think about that once she got back. Maybe she could flag down a passing ship. She'd done it in this time.

Finally, she was on top of the island, its surface covered in grass and moss. Occasional clover blossoms showed white among the grass. Seagulls flew high in the sky, squawking.

She needed to hurry. She had no idea where the Highlanders were. Only, as she moved towards the place where the lighthouse used to stand, where she knew the rock was, it became hard to walk. Surely because she was cold. Not because the thought of leaving Aulay, of living in a world without him, filled her chest with dread.

There it was, the rock, dark against the moss and the grass. Maybe twenty steps away.

Something dark moved at the periphery of her vision, and she heard the thumps of many feet against the ground and the rhythmical clunk of metal against wood. From behind the curve of the other side of the island, the Highlanders appeared. They ran up the hill, first a couple, then all of them. They carried chests, swords, and armor in their hands and ran, quietly, efficiently.

When their eyes landed on her, they frowned and slowed down, breathing heavily. "What are ye doing here, lass?" asked one of them, beads of sweat gathering on his forehead.

"Get the hell out, lass," said another.

She gaped at them, surprised they weren't grabbing her and taking her with them.

Until one particular giant figure stopped before her, shielding the sun, which was barely protruding from behind the leaden clouds. Aulay's face was furious, his nostrils flaring, eyebrows drawn together. There must have been a dozen swords in his arms.

They had found their treasure ship.

"What, God's arse, are ye doing here?" he thundered.

She gaped, words escaping her. She felt rooted to the spot, unable to move, unable to say anything.

His gaze dropped to the rock behind her, and his face lost all expression. Then she saw something behind him, from the south —three ships were coming, their red sails bearing three golden lions.

They were so much bigger than Aulay's ship.

She looked at him again. The threat in his eyes made her want to recoil. He was a predator on a hunt, and she was his prey. The anger in his eyes, the readiness to get what he wanted, made her feet feel cemented to the ground. He was not going to let her slip away.

But she wouldn't give in so easily.

She ran to the rock. Just one touch of her hand to the palm print and she'd travel back in time. She wouldn't let him catch her again. She wouldn't let him imprison her, not when she was only twenty feet away from home.

The clatter of metal against rocks told her he'd dropped the swords on the ground. Quick, heavy steps sounded behind her.

But she pumped her legs harder, the sodden dress cold and heavy around them. Ten feet to the rock.

"Stop!" Aulay cried somewhere close behind her. "Ye wilna escape!"

Five feet. Almost there.

Her foot slipped on a smooth rock. Her ankle twisted in an unnatural angle, and there was a painful snap in her muscle. She cried in pain as she fell, the hit against the hard ground knocking all the air out of her. She could almost touch the stone. She reached out to it, ignoring the pain and the discomfort.

Strong arms picked her up and pressed her against a hard chest. "We must run, lass," he said as he moved. "There's nae time. Ye're hurt, and I wilna leave ye behind."

"Let me go, damn you!" She wriggled and beat against his chest, but he held her so tight, it was like fighting against a tree. "Let me go! I was almost home!"

"Nae."

He ran down the slope like a madman. Jenny bounced and

rocked as he moved. When they reached the beach, *Tagradh* was ready to go. The sail was unfurled, and the anchors were pulled up. The men were at the oars and signaled with their arms for Aulay to hurry to the ship. "Come on, Laird! Make haste!"

But the English were already coming from behind the cliff. Arrows flew from their ships, hitting one of Aulay's men. He cried out as he broke the arrow that pierced his shoulder. Another man replaced him at the oar.

"Go!" Aulay yelled. "Leave! Hurry!"

His men started moving the oars and Colum yelled quick commands as he steered the ship.

"They wilna survive if the English catch up with them," Aulay muttered. "Now we must go and hide before the enemy sees us."

As Aulay climbed up the slope, Jenny thanked the lord for small mercies. Even though she was in his captivity again, she was still on the island and still had a chance to return home.

CHAPTER 27

THE CAVE SMELLED like algae and fish. The carcass of the English ship was like a beached whale, dark and disemboweled. The torn sail hung flapping in the wind. There were still English coins glistening in the sand, as well as swords and armor dug into the ground like stones.

A large cliff shielded the cave from the sea, and somehow, the ship had gotten through the opening between the cliff and the island. All this time, both the English and Aulay had sailed around searching for the ship, never realizing there was a hidden cave here.

Aulay didn't care about the remnants of the English treasure for a moment. Jenny sat on a large boulder before him as he kneeled in wet sand. Her injured leg lay on his knee. There was a gash along her ankle that needed treatment, probably from when she'd fallen. He was barely able to keep his fury down. No, that wasn't even right. He was beyond furious.

She'd defied him once again. She'd sneaked out and fooled him. And he hadn't even known how close he was to losing her forever and never seeing her again. Having held her in his arms, and now holding her ankle in his hands, he felt like she was an extension of him, the second half of him, the lost part of his soul.

"How could ye have put yerself in such danger, Jenny?" he murmured a restrained beratement as he slowly moved her foot in a circle. "Ye betrayed me once again."

"How did I betray you exactly? I told you right from the beginning I wanted to leave and asked you to take me with you. You forbade me, and I never agreed to obey you."

She pulled her leg away from his touch. "I'll look after my own ankle, thank you very much."

He sat and looked at her, furious and beautiful in the semi-darkness of the cave. Waves rustled gently against the sand, and the sea was loud on the other side of the cliff.

"Ye probably sprained it a wee bit," said Aulay, looking at her ankle. Not long ago, he'd kissed it as he made his way with his tongue and mouth up her inner leg and thigh and right to her sex. Back then, she'd craved his touch, begged him for more, all hot and wet and his. Now, she was pulling away. "But yer cut is what worries me. I dinna have a thing to stitch it."

He pulled his tunic up and over his shoulders and handed it to her. His wound hurt as he moved. "Use it to stop the bleeding," he said.

Even if they were angry at each other, her eyes grazed over his naked torso, and he knew she liked what she saw. Mayhap, just like he, she thought of the moments when they were united and connected, moving as one, breathing as one. He didn't remember sex being so good ever before.

"I don't need the whole tunic," she said. "If you tear a little bit, that would be enough."

He nodded and tore a rag from the lower part and handed it to her. She pressed it tightly against the cut.

He put his tunic back on and gave her the pouch of drinking water that he always had on his belt.

"We canna make a fire yet. I dinna want to attract their attention." He looked around. "There's some dry driftwood from the shipwreck, though. We can light it once the English are far enough off. I always have my fire-steel with me. Even if we're stranded," he said, "we will survive."

She rolled her eyes. "Great. I don't need to survive. No fire or driftwood. I need to get up that hill and touch that rock and go back home."

He swallowed hard. He knew the moment he'd seen her face and that rock that she was telling the truth. And then she was reaching out, trying to touch it...

"So 'tis true?" he asked, not recognizing his own voice. The chill from the sand seeped into his blood and traveled to his soul. "Did ye really travel in time? Was I wrong to have accused ye of being the enemy?"

She looked under the cloth. The bleeding had stopped. She wrapped the rag around her ankle and tied it well. "I did travel in time, Aulay."

He swallowed and nodded. That was worse than her being an English enemy.

"Show it to me then. I want to see for myself. I dinna want any doubt left."

She looked at him. "If you try to stop me—"

"Ye're part of my very soul, Jenny. And if ye really belong to another time, I will let ye go. I want to be certain first."

She looked at him for a long time. "Okay."

He nodded, picked her up, and carried her up the hill to the rock.

CHAPTER 28

JENNY WAS IN AGONY—AND not just from her ankle. The feel of
Aulay's hard body against her, his arms holding her like she was a
treasure, made her heart ache. Because he was taking her to her
way out. To a future where he did not exist.

"How's yer ankle?" he murmured.

His eyes left hers only for a few moments, to find his way up
the hill. Otherwise, she felt the weight of them, the warmth that
spread through her body like intoxication.

When they reached the top of the hill, she could see the
English ships almost at the horizon, heading north.

"They're going to Islay," Aulay said through clenched teeth.
She felt his heart beating faster. His jaw was set, and he was
clearly worried. So was she. Somehow, in only eight days, she'd
started thinking of Islay as her second home.

"Oh, my goodness," she whispered. "Mhairi and Sìomon...and
Artur...and all the other orphan kids! Una..."

"Colum will ken what to do."

But she knew he was still worried.

"It's out of your hands now, Aulay," she whispered. "You can't
do anything to help. You have to trust Colum and the prepara-
tions you've made."

He nodded, though his jaw muscles tensed. "Aye. Ye're right, lass."

He looked at her and then somewhere behind her, his dark eyes filling with sadness. Then, without saying another word, he walked to the rock.

When he gently placed her onto the ground next to the rock, Jenny could feel the strength of the magic. The carvings started glowing, and she had a sudden urge to pull away, to grab on to Aulay, and never let go of him. When she met his eyes, they were as round as she'd ever seen them.

"'Tis true..." he murmured.

"Yes, it's true. If I touch it, I'll be gone."

Aulay's face was ashen. His Adam's apple bobbed. "I believe ye."

She stared at the rock. There, just a touch away, was her world. She could make it to the appointment. She could return to her patients. She could live in a world of convenience with light just a flick of the finger away, food perfectly packed and sold at a nearby grocery store, her warm and clean apartment. A world where she wouldn't be told not to treat a patient because she was a woman and didn't know anything.

A world where medical technology could help her have a baby of her own, to hold and love.

"Ye can leave," Aulay said. "And I will never see ye again. And my heart will be gone with ye forever."

She imagined her life without him. Same as before. Long hours working at the clinic. Empty apartment. Hopefully, she'd have a baby, but that may not happen even with medical intervention. And in that scenario, the emptiness right in the middle of her soul would still be there.

And with Aulay, it wasn't. Sìneag was right. He was the love of her life.

"You didn't believe me," she said. "You thought I betrayed you. How can I ever trust you again?"

"I am sorry I didna trust ye, lass. I love ye. Whatever years I have left, I want to spend with ye. I shouldna have mistrusted ye. Part of me kent ye couldna be an enemy. But it was easier to push ye away because I didna want to be hurt again by losing ye. Like I am in danger of losing ye now."

She realized she was shaking. It could be because she was sitting on the cold ground, and her skirt was still soaked, and the wind was cold. Or maybe it was because he'd said he loved her. As much as he was afraid she'd hurt him, she was afraid he'd hurt her. He already had when he'd turned against her and suddenly decided she was an enemy. But she knew her rejection had hurt him, too.

He dropped to his knees in front of her, a gorgeous giant with wind playing in the strands of his long, silvery hair. His eyes were dark and gleaming under his thick eyebrows. "I ken I have nae right, but I am asking ye. Dinna go. Be my wife. I love ye, and I give ye the word of a Highlander, I would rather die than betray ye like yer husband did. Ye're a healer. I never thought my soul could be healed, but ye healed me. Be my wife and be with me for the rest of our lives."

Her vision blurred, and her eyes burned with tears. A chasm tore at her, a split between her greatest hope and greatest fear. "I want to believe you."

He shifted closer to her. The wind brought the scent of the sea and freedom and hope...and him. "Do ye love me, lass? Please tell me, do ye love me like I love ye?"

She nodded, unable to say anything.

"Then give me one more day. Let me show ye how our lives would be. And tell me at the end of this if ye think yer life back in yer time is worth the loneliness ye will feel without me."

Maybe she was insane. After so many days and so many obstacles, she was finally right here, at the rock. And yet, she was not ready to leave him. The thought of separating from him was like cutting her own flesh.

And what was one more day compared to the rest of her life

without him? Like a junkie, she needed one more fix of him, one more dose of Aulay.

Then she'd live the rest of her life remembering how good it was.

"Okay," she said. "One more day."

~

THE REST OF THE DAY WAS GLORIOUS, JENNY THOUGHT. THEY drank from Aulay's water flask and ate the bannocks he'd packed for the journey. He made a fire in the hidden cave from driftwood and the dry wood of the ship.

They talked and cuddled and kissed... There was so much making out, it was as though they were both teenagers.

In the evening, he carried her up to a pretty spot that faced west. They sat at the edge of the cliff, watched the ocean, and talked more. They talked about everything. About their families, friends, and relationships. She found out there was not much difference between the relationships in the fourteenth and twenty-first centuries. If anything, it seemed this life was simpler.

Aulay asked her more about her clinic, and after she told him in detail what she did, he said she could have the same clinic here. He could build her the same pediatric practice.

"Mayhap ye could even teach healers and physicians from all over Scotland. Do ye realize what a positive impact ye could make here, lass?"

She smiled as she watched the sea. The wind was gentle, and it was warm now, the sea almost smooth. The sun was low, and its orange-yellow-red reflection blazed through the water. The ground under her hands was cool and the moss prickled her skin a little through the fabric of her dress. She loved the scent here, the sea and moss, and earth. The waves rustled softly down below.

"You're right. That would be amazing. I'd stir history a little bit, I suppose... Not sure if I should do so much to change the course of events globally... But I could definitely do some good."

"Aye." He rubbed her shoulder. "Ye could."

"How easily can you get some rare things from the Mediterranean and the Middle East?"

"For ye, anything, lass. What do ye need?"

"Well, opium poppy... I'd use it to make laudanum, which would be the best anesthetic available in this time. Also, bulb garlic from the Mediterranean, ginger, and other herbs and medicinal plants."

"Aye, lass, of course. Anything ye want."

Jenny smiled. She could see herself planting and cultivating them.

Anything she wanted... She knew he was for real. She saw it in his eyes, heard it in his voice, felt it. He felt like a part of her now, the formerly lost part.

"What about never being able to have children with me?"

"I've been living with the idea of accepting that I will have nae heir for a long time. I'd rather have a life with ye. I may never have a blood heir, but I also like knowing that ye wouldna die of childbirth. Colum will be heir. If the clan accepts him and forgives him."

"That's good." She smiled.

She liked that, too. Only, could she really give up the possibility of having her own baby, something she'd have dreamed of her whole life? The thought of not having a baby of her own was no longer so painful when she imagined the life she could have with him.

"Ye're everything to me," he said. "My happiness. My love. My soul. Ye're the love of my life and my destiny."

Jenny's eyes burned with tears. She felt the same way about him.

She could be a mother to Una. Actually, the thought of that buzzed through her soul with as much excitement as the thought of staying with Aulay.

"Okay, Aulay," she said. "I'll be your wife. I'll stay with you forever."

He beamed, seeming about twenty years younger in the blink of an eye. He kissed her, and as he pulled her closer and her blood set on fire, only a small part of her wondered if she had really thought this through.

But that rock wasn't going anywhere.

CHAPTER 29

A SCREAM WOKE AULAY UP. He raised his head and looked around the cave, his hand tightened around the handle of his sword, which lay next to his head. But the waves barely moved in the shielded bay of the Isle of Achleith. The cave around them was dark; the sky was visible between the wall of cliffs that shielded the cave from the sea. The carcass of the English ship still lay there, half sunken into the water, dark and dead.

He didn't hear screams anymore. Instead, he pulled warm, soft Jenny tighter towards him. She was nestled against him, her back to his chest, her soft, incredible arse pressing into his groin. He moved his pelvis to nestle against her arse and was hard right away. Last night, they had made love on his léine-chròich, which he'd laid on the sand, and they'd covered themselves with his cloak.

His future wife... He buried his face in her red hair and inhaled her scent. Her own sweet, delicious scent mixed with the odor of wet sand and sun.

He'd claimed her, and she'd claimed him. She was staying with him. The wee precious fox was going to be his wife. She was going to make him the happiest man alive. His chest was so full and light, it was about to burst like an inflated waterskin.

The only worry he had now was Islay and the three English ships that headed there.

As though echoing his thoughts, another scream reached his ears. This time he knew he hadn't imagined it. It was weak and far, but it was real. Another scream-grunt followed the first one.

He took his claymore in his hand and sat up. Jenny woke up and sat next to him. "What is it?" she asked, rubbing her eyes.

"Ahh!" came a groan from somewhere above and closer. "Ahh!"

"Someone's on the island," he said. "Stay here."

He stood up and hastily put on his léine-chròich.

He looked at her and took her shoulder. "Promise ye'll stay here and hide, lass. There, in the depths of the cave. Aye?"

"But, Aulay, if someone's injured—"

He squeezed her shoulder tighter. Anguish stabbed his chest. "Promise me!"

"I promise..."

"Actually..." He swallowed hard. "Ye have permission to leave the cave for one reason only. To go through yer stone again if that means saving yer life. Aye?"

Her beautiful eyes were so big and glistening and full of fear. "Aulay, you're frightening me..."

"Lass, just promise me."

She pressed her lips together. "I promise."

He exhaled a relieved breath and kissed her. It was a hard kiss, not a tender one. A kiss that said, *I love you, and I would rather die than let something happen to you.*

Then he left and climbed the steep slope up the hill. When he was high enough to peer over the curve of the slope, his stomach sank to his heels. His Highlanders were fighting. He saw Colum and Seoras and twenty more men fighting the English. Swords and Lochaber axes swung and clashed.

The English were in chain mail and chain coifs, the Scots only in their léintean-cròich. There were twice as many English as there were Highlanders. Why had they come back here? What happened?

With a roar, he launched right into the next fight. Colum swung his sword against two English knights, both in long chain mail and red surcoats with three golden lions. With a groan, Colum slashed diagonally across, but his taller opponent brought his sword up and blocked Colum's while the second man slashed his sword, aiming for Colum's side.

Aulay managed to reach them before that blade could cut through his nephew's léine-chròich and open up Colum's kidney. Aulay's claymore met the Englishman's sword and pressed against him.

Colum threw a quick glance at Aulay before he was pulled back into the fight. Aulay's blood sang the song of spilled blood and too-quick death. The island was full of battling warriors. Aulay hit the man's shield and knocked it out of his hands. He brought his sword up and over his head for another attack. Aulay saw the fear in the man's eyes. He stood too awkwardly, the hand holding his sword was too far back, and he didn't have time to protect himself from what was coming from Aulay.

Aulay swung his sword down, cutting through the side of the man's helmet and right into the bone of the forehead. The man grunted, his eyes rolled back, and he fell. Aulay pulled his sword free.

Colum's opponent lay dead, too, and Aulay grabbed his nephew's shoulder. Panting, Aulay asked, "Are ye all right, lad?"

"Aye, Uncle. Are ye?"

"I am. How did ye come here?"

"The Sassenachs attacked us, but we managed to stand strong, and we sank one of their ships. They left. Then we waited but they were nowhere to be seen. I decided we should come back for ye, but once we neared Achleith and left the ship, they ambushed us."

"God's arse..." Aulay said through gritted teeth. "They ken

they have a better chance to beat us here than on Islay. Bastarts need more than three ships to storm Dunyvaig."

Colum frowned. "Where's Jenny?"

"She's—" Aulay turned to where the slope led down and went completely still.

Two hundred feet away, three English warriors were going down the slope to the hidden beach.

Jenny...

In his periphery vision, Aulay saw the dark form of another English warrior attacking Colum with a sword. But Aulay couldn't pay attention to the clash of metal.

His whole being became alert; the hair on his arms rose like a wolf's hackles. All he could think of was Jenny... With his heart stuck in his throat, he darted behind the warriors. When he reached the top of the path, two of them were already down below, on the beach, looking around. The third one still climbed down the slope.

"Stop, ye bastarts!" he roared as he flew down the slope.

Pebbles and earth rolled out from under his feet. He almost lost his balance and tumbled down a three-hundred-foot cliff into the now-angry sea that crashed against rugged rocks. The three men looked up at him. The one who was still on the path turned around and ran up the hill towards Aulay.

Every step Aulay took reverberated in his chest as he ran. He roared for Jenny. She should hear him nearby and hide better. His claymore clashed with the enemy's sword like lightning. He struck with his sword, over and over again, meeting steel. The man's feet slid down, spraying dust and sand and pebbles. Aulay glanced down at the crashing waves. Then one push and the enemy plummeted to his death; only a scream followed.

As he hurried down the slope, one of the men waited for him on the beach.

A female scream pierced the air, and Aulay's blood froze. The second enemy dragged Jenny, who was struggling and pushing against him.

"Let her go!" Aulay made a movement toward her, but the first man thrust his sword at him, and he had to deflect. He was too distracted and in an awkward position, exposing his side.

Red-hot pain ripped through him as the blade cut through the léine-chròich and his own flesh. He grunted and staggered, losing his balance as he breathed through the shock of the wound.

It was bad. He knew it was bad, far worse than his shoulder wound.

And the man had an advantage now. He slashed his sword across and Aulay grunted as he lifted his sword high against the attack. The two blades clashed. The man forced his sword down until Aulay's own claymore dug into his cheekbone.

Pain ripped through Aulay's body as he kept pushing back. His side felt hot, so incredibly hot and wet.

Aulay stole a glance at Jennifer, and his skin crawled. She had a chunk of wood in her hands, and she swung to hit the English warrior. The man slapped it away like a fly, then whacked her hard across the cheek.

Protect her...

He couldn't do a single thing when Leitis had been dying in his arms.

But he could protect this woman from his enemy.

He roared and, ignoring the pain, pushed back the Englishman's sword. Then, while he staggered back, in a single strike he thrust the sword into the man's face.

The enemy grunted, fell on his knees, and slid to his side on the beach, the sand darkening with his blood.

Feeling dizzy and tired, Aulay strode across the beach towards his last enemy. He had Jenny in his grip, his sword at her throat. Her eyes were big and worried as she looked at his side.

"Let her go, ye pig," Aulay grunted out. "Ye will be sorry ye touched a hair on her head."

The man's teeth were bared, his eyes glinting in contempt. "This Scottish whore is not worth spit."

Aulay raised his claymore, but it felt like his own arms dragged him towards the ground. He felt a lot of liquid squelching in his left shoe, the side where his wound ached as though an invisible beast was gnashing its teeth against his flesh. Everything became blurry and swam.

But Jenny's face was so worried and so scared, that it hurt him even more than his wound. Nae. He could not have that. He had to save her.

"Clann Domnhnaill!" he roared as he sprinted towards the man, his bloodied claymore glistening.

The man pushed Jenny to the side and slashed low, aiming to cut Aulay's gut open, and he barely managed to deflect the blow. But he was too weak. The man knew it, too, and he grinned.

Then he changed his grip and hammered the blunt end of the hilt into Aulay's face. Bone cracked under his eye, and the world exploded in pain. He was struck dumb for a moment, then another hit came to his stomach, knocking all the air out of him. And then his back collapsed, struck with something cold and hard, and he knew he'd fallen.

When the tip of the sword glistened over his head, he knew this was the end. But he didn't want it to end, not when he'd just found Jenny. Not when she'd said she'd stay with him and marry him.

Nae, God, please, dinna take me yet...

Through his blurry vision, he saw Jenny's figure come behind his enemy and knock something against his head. The enemy turned to her, swinging the sword.

Then came another figure... He thought he heard Jenny cry out, "Colum, careful!"

There was the clunk of metal hitting metal, and pained grunts and the shuffle of wet sand.

And then there was nothing but hot, clammy darkness.

CHAPTER 30

AULAY'S FOREHEAD was still burning when Jenny laid her hand on it. Three days he'd been getting worse. Today, on the fourth day, he was as hot as a furnace, red-cheeked, delirious. She sat by his bed day and night, sick with worry.

She wiped a clean, wet linen cloth along his forehead, and he jerked and gave a small moan. It killed her to see him like this. Her MacZeus, almighty and powerful... He was now human. Vulnerable. Sick.

Dying.

Aulay blurred in front of her as tears filled her eyes. She slowly drew the cloth along his forehead again. Back on the island, she had let Colum cut her dress and had used the rag to stop Aulay's bleeding. On the ship, there was a sort of first aid kit with somewhat clean cloth, and she'd used that, although it was not sterile.

Back on Islay, she and Bhatair had sterilized the wound, and she'd stitched it. It was quite deep, and it was a miracle the blade hadn't penetrated a kidney, or he would have been dead from blood loss by now.

Still, he had lost a lot of blood. For a large man like him, it was bad. Back in her time, he'd have already gotten a blood transfusion, not to mention IV antibiotics, which would already have killed the infection.

The wound in Aulay's side was the color of cherries, and pus oozed from it.

And there was not a damn thing she could do to help him except for sitting and praying and feeding him willow bark tea.

A knock at the door had her raising her head, which felt like it weighed a ton. "Come in," she said.

Bhatair entered with Colum and Seoras. Behind them, Artur and other orphans lingered, trying to see past the three men. Bhatair walked towards Aulay with a glass jar in his hand. The dull, muddy liquid swayed as he walked, and black leeches wriggled.

"Any changes?" asked Bhatair as he placed the jar onto the chest that stood by the bed.

"You are not putting them on him," she said.

"But, my lady—"

Bhatair's shoulders rose. He'd looked shrunken and small ever since Aulay had gotten worse.

"He's lost enough blood," she hissed. "Any more and you will rob him of his last reserves."

She knew she must sound like a cornered wild animal. And she had been unnecessarily harsh with him.

"I'm sorry," she said, rubbing her eyes. "You don't deserve me lashing out at you like this."

Bhatair nodded. "Aye. 'Tis all right. Ye love him. Ye're afraid for him. We all are."

Colum and Seoras were two giant statues. She'd seen both fight, and they were relentless. Highland warriors in their prime, unstoppable and terrifying.

And yet, now they were rooted to the spot and helpless.

"Can I bring ye some raspberries, my lady?" asked Artur, peering from behind Colum.

"Can I bring something for the laird?" asked Ceana, one of the orphan girls.

Jenny realized how strangely quiet it was outside. The usual sounds of a living and breathing medieval castle didn't come through the slit window of Aulay's bedchamber. There was no hammering of metal against metal. No laughter and talking. Dogs didn't bark. Even the usual squawking of birds and bleating of animals didn't reach her ears. Since they'd brought Aulay home, the clan, like the laird, had been quiet.

Distantly, the church bell tolled in the village, and Jenny shuddered. In the complete silence, the sound lashed against her nerves. "Why are the bells tolling?"

"Everyone's in the church, praying for the laird," Colum said.

She nodded and brushed the cloth down Aulay's ashen face. His long, black eyelashes fluttered as though a ripple went over his handsome face. How she wished his eyes would open. His beard had grown over the past three days, and she let her fingers smooth over it.

"Oh...right."

Colum moved to her and dropped to his knees before her. He took her free hand in his. She'd never seen him like this... Desperate, small. His dark eyebrows crawled up, and his mouth twitched. "Ye will save him, Jenny, aye?"

She blinked. "I—"

"Ye saved my nephew, Sìomon, and my sister-in-law. Ye worked a miracle there... Please, make another one with him."

Something tiny and hot crawled down her cheek and a wet droplet fell on her wrist. "I don't know if I can this time, Colum... He needs antibiotics..."

"Anti— Dinna matter. Anything he needs. Where can we get them?"

"We're already giving them. Bhatair and I have been putting the antibacterial mixture with garlic and honey on his wound, but it hasn't done enough to help. He needs proper medicine, something very strong."

Colum squeezed her hand tighter. "Tell me where to get it and I'll go."

Another tear crawled down her cheek, leaving a burning trail behind it. She began shaking. *It's in the future*, was the answer to his question. But she couldn't say that.

"Lad," said Bhatair.

Colum and she both looked at the physician. Bhatair locked eyes with her. They both knew what this meant. Infections like this...

"There's nothing that can help him, lad," Bhatair said. "Unless 'tis a miracle from God. But it looks like God is calling for him."

No, no, no. This cannot be happening.

Colum dropped his head and stood up, helplessly clenching and unclenching his fists.

"Leave..." Aulay's voice was weak.

Jenny's gaze shot at him, and she quickly wiped the tears from her eyes. He had his eyes open and was looking at the people in the room.

"What did you say?" she asked him.

His eyes found hers and he managed a shadow of a smile. "I told them all to leave. I want to spend my last hours with the woman I love."

Her chest exploded in pain. His last hours... Everyone else stopped existing.

She thought she heard Colum say, "Aye, Uncle."

Then there was the shuffle of shoes against the floor, the soft click of the door, and then silence. She moved to sit on his bed and cupped his face. His skin scalded her.

"These aren't your last hours!" she said firmly, pressing out a smile for him. "I won't let you die."

He shook his head and gave her a weak grin. "Lass. I lived a good life. It was worth it. Most men never get to love a woman and find their mate that God had intended for them. I have been fortunate. I have had two. So, if I have to die, 'tis a happy death doing my duty—protecting my people and the woman I love."

She shook her head stubbornly. "No. I forbid you to die. I

just found you. I just agreed to a life with you. Don't die, Aulay. Please, don't die."

"Ye should leave, Jenny. Go to yer time. I lied to ye. Well..." He let out a short, shaky breath. "Rather, I didna tell ye something. The rock on Achleith isna the only one. There's a stone like that on this island."

She froze. "What?"

"I didna tell ye because I was afraid it would be easier for ye to leave me. I'm sorry, Jenny."

She swallowed. She was angry with him, but not because he'd kept her prisoner. Because if there was a rock nearby, she may have hope...a hope to go to her time for antibiotics and bring them here. If she'd known this earlier, she could have gone sooner. Now it may be too late whatever she did. But she wouldn't give up. Not yet.

"Where is it?" she asked, her hands shaking with hope.

"On a hill at the base of an ancient ruin. Ye ken it. Ye must have seen it on yer way to the woods."

She jumped to her feet. "It's only a ten-minute walk! If I run, maybe five..." Her throat convulsed in a high-pitched whimper. "You goddamn idiot! Why didn't you tell me this sooner!"

"I'm sorry—I didna want to lose ye. Go now, love. Ye're free."

"There's no time to waste." She leaned down and kissed him. "Hold on, you hear me! Don't you dare die!"

She ran to the door, her chest filling and exploding with hope. But as she opened the door and ran out onto the landing, she thought she heard him say something.

"Goodbye, my love." His soft words hung in the air behind her.

CHAPTER 31

JENNY WAS out of breath when she climbed the hill. She panted as she looked around the crumbled walls and rough rock. There it was, at the base of one of the pieces of the ruin, the rock with the hand carving and the symbols. Her heart was drumming as if ready to break her bones and jump out of her chest.

She hurried to the rock, every step feeling as though boulders were tied to her feet. She sank to her knees in front of the rock. Like the one on Achleith, this one buzzed and vibrated and called to her. The carvings glowed as though lit up with neon lights. She was going back to her time. Finally, she was.

The scent of lavender and grass hit her, and a shadow fell over her. She looked up. Sìneag. In her hooded green cloak, her face round and freckled, her eyes bright. Only, her face wasn't smiling anymore. There was real worry written over it. "I just came to tell ye, Jenny, ye only have two passes left. After that, the tunnel of time will forever be closed for ye. So do choose wisely now."

It meant once Jenny brought the antibiotics to Aulay, she wouldn't be able to return to the twenty-first century again. There was no guarantee the antibiotics would work. What if she got the wrong one? What if she was too late?

And if he survived this time, he would surely be in another battle. Some other illness may take him from her, and she would be alone and stuck in the Middle Ages.

There were still two days left till her appointment in New York. She could still make it.

And abandon Aulay to his sure death?

Despite these sacrifices and possibilities, she needed to make a decision.

No, never. Love was worth the risk. Her life would be complete with Aulay. Love filled that void in her soul.

So, there it was, her choice made. She'd chosen the man she loved over a child she may never have.

"Thanks for the warning," she said. "I don't have any time to waste."

She put her hand into the handprint. Cold stone disappeared from under her palm, and she was falling and falling into oblivion.

An eternity later, she sat up. She was still near the ruin. Her head felt heavy and empty, and for a moment she didn't know where she was and why she was here. She was just perceiving. This was the ground. It was wet and smelled like soil after the rain. Grass, moss, and wild plants were all covered in droplets of water. Here were the remnants of some crumbled, thick, ancient walls, all wet, as well. The air was cool and humid. The sun shone through a gap between steely clouds.

She scrambled to her feet. She had the feeling there was an important reason she was here and that she needed to hurry. Why was she dressed like a medieval woman? A long dress tied at her waist with a belt. She looked around again and her gaze dropped to the rock Somehow, through a brain like molasses, it hit her.

Aulay. Antibiotics.

There was no one in sight. There, where Dunyvaig Castle used to be, was a ruin. And around it, a town. A modern town.

With roofs made of tiles and roads made of asphalt. She felt cold.

Frantically, still in her medieval shoes, she ran like a crazy woman through the wet, empty land. The ground was soft and muddy, and it was like in a nightmare: no matter how much she tried to speed up, she was still slow. Her side ached, the ankle she'd twisted a few days ago started to hurt, and she began limping.

Finally, she got to the nearest house that she saw at the edge of the town. Cars were parked on the narrow street, but no one was outside. Power poles lined the edge of the street, lines hanging from house to house. Gulping for air through her aching chest, she reached the cottage and banged on the door. It was a simple, rectangular house with beige walls and a dark tile roof. Next to it was a large hill with bushes and grass.

She banged once again, struggling to catch her breath. The door clicked and an old lady opened it.

"Please help!" Jenny blurted out. "I need to get to the nearest hospital."

The woman looked her over, nodded, and shut the door in her face.

Jenny gaped at the closed door before her for a moment, then knocked more frantically. "It's a matter of life and death! Please!"

Behind her, across the street, a door opened, and another old lady looked her over. She had a white bob and a thin face with a white mouth. Large glasses perched on a sharp, pointy nose. She wore a thick, brown, woolen sweater. "What is the matter?"

"I need to get to the nearest hospital, now, please!"

"Are ye hurt?"

"Yes. No. It's for someone else. They're dying."

She nodded and disappeared for a moment behind her door. Then she appeared again, putting on a raincoat. She slid her feet into rubber boots and said, "Gail will not help a soul if someone is dying in front of her."

As Jenny hurried towards her, she walked down her stairs, unlocked her ancient Land Rover and climbed up with surprising agility. Jenny got into the passenger seat. As the woman struggled to start the car, Jenny's heart drummed. With every beat, she knew Aulay's time was coming to an end.

"What's yer name, dear?" said the woman.

"Jenny. Jennifer Foster."

"Ah, nice to meet ye. Philippa MacDonald."

Philippa turned the key over and over, each time the engine whirred but died. "Is there another film being made somewhere on the island?" Philippa asked, looking over Jenny's dress.

Jenny started to shake. She didn't have a plan for how to explain her dress. So, she simply nodded.

The engine revved and the car moved. Finally! As though something had been unplugged in her, Jenny opened her mouth to say something about a film...

But instead, she said, "Actually, not a film, Philippa. I traveled in time..."

While the houses passed the car window, Jenny kept talking. The Isle of Achleith. Aulay MacDonald kidnapping her. How she fell in love with him. How he was dying now back in time and needed antibiotics.

They drove for a few minutes, and Philippa didn't say a word, just listened and nodded. She stopped the car in front of an old house that looked like her own cottage. There was a sign there: "Port Ellen Health Centre."

"Can you please wait for me here?" asked Jenny, "and drive me back to the ruin?"

Philippa shrugged. "I have nothing else to do. Maybe ye'll entertain me some more with yer interesting stories. In fact"— Philippa laid her hand on the door handle—"I'll come with ye."

Jenny ran into the practice. It must be a GP's and a dentist's office. Inside, two people sat in the waiting area. Behind the reception desk, there was no one.

"Follow me, dear," said Philippa and marched down the corridor to her left. "I'll show ye where the GP is."

Philippa stopped before a white door. Unceremoniously, Jenny opened it. The GP was a man in his forties with a good mane of dark hair and a handsome face. He was leaning over a patient and examining his throat. He turned to Jenny. Something about him reminded her of Bhatair, and her heart squeezed. How was Aulay? *Please, let him live...*

"Antibiotics!" she yelled. "Now!"

This was no way to come into a doctor's office and demand medicine. Fear must be turning her into a crazy person. She must look insane to the doctor.

The GP's face reddened, and he pointed at the door. "Out! Who the hell do you think you are?"

"Please, my fiancé will die—"

"Out, I said!"

Philippa tugged at her elbow. When the door closed, the people in the waiting area peered from behind the corner at them. Philippa winked and tugged Jenny to the door on the opposite side of the corridor.

"Forgive my son," she said and opened the door. "He won't mind. I know where the good stuff is."

It was the supply closet behind that door, and Philippa went in. Shelves with medicine lined the small room. Philippa took a plastic bag and scooped in half of what was on the shelves. Bandages, syringes, pills—some stuff would be useful, some less so. There were several antibiotics that Jenny knew worked with wound infections, and Philippa took a few packages.

"No, Philippa, please," Jenny said. "I don't want to rob the poor GP of medicine."

Philippa waved her hand at her. "I worked my whole life as a receptionist in this practice. My late husband, his dad, was a GP before Aaron. I'm sure he can buy more medical supplies, but it looks like 'whenever' ye're going, ye need them more. Especially if ye need to save Aulay MacDonald, who left a huge legacy for Islay."

Jenny watched her swipe more of the medicine into the bag. "Did he?"

"Aye. On Islay, we appreciate our ancestors. And if the stories of faeries are true, I better get on their good side."

She handed the full plastic bag to Jenny. As she closed the door and they headed back through the corridor under the astonished gazes of the two patients in the waiting room, Philippa glanced at one of them and said, "Dinna stare, Peggie, ye might pop yer eyes."

The woman averted her gaze, and Jenny suppressed a snort. Relief warmed her whole body as she carried the bag. Once they were out of the clinic and briskly walking towards the car, Philippa said, "I remember a story of Aulay MacDonald. He was gravely injured and almost died of infection. But he didn't. Some say he was always loved by the faeries." They climbed back into the car, and Philippa started it swiftly this time. The engine revved and whirred. "One of them couldn't stand it if he died and brought him a cure. So, he survived. If I remember it well, he did marry an Irish lass later named Guinevere. Today the name is commonly known as Jennifer."

Jenny cried, making the houses passing by into blurry spots. "I'm so grateful to you, Philippa," she said, her throat tight. "What would I have done without you?"

"Ah," Philippa said. "I'm just an old lady. I lived my life, and it's a blessing to help others live theirs."

Jenny sniffed and wiped her eyes. "Would you please do me a huge favor?"

"Yes, lass, anything."

"Would you please call my family...my friends...and tell them..." She stopped, thinking. What should Philippa tell them? That Jenny was alive? That she'd traveled back in time? Philippa might get in trouble with the police if they were searching for Jenny.

"You know what, nothing," she said. "Don't worry about it."

It was probably better they assumed she was dead. That was what they must have thought, that she'd fallen off one of the cliffs.

"As ye wish, lass. Though I could call them if ye like..."

"No. They won't believe about time travel, anyway. I'm still stunned you believe me!"

They drove off the asphalt road and up a small, packed-dirt road leading to the ruin.

The woman chuckled. "There are many strange things in this world, lass, that we don't understand. I always put out milk for the brownies and never disrespect a lonely black dog jogging along the road, as it may be a Black Angus. If it jumps in front of me and bares its teeth, I know I'll be dead within a week. There's a rowan tree at my house. And once or twice, I've been at the old ruin and could smell lavender where there was none."

She stopped the car at the bottom of the hill leading to the ruin. When she pulled up the hand brake, she turned to Jenny. "Are ye sure ye want to go, lass? Ye can still stay here. Ye can still choose this time."

Jenny stared at the ruin up the hill. It looked like the broken crown of a sleeping giant.

"I'm sure. Love is worth the risk. All I hope is that I'm not too late."

Philippa was grinning, a sweet, cheeky smile from ear to ear. "Aye, lass, ye go and save him. Be happy."

Jenny reached out and pulled Philippa into a big hug. "Thank you, dear Philippa," she said, and as she threw a last glance at her, she opened the door and hurried up the hill.

CHAPTER 32

AULAY OPENED HIS EYES. Above him was the wooden board of his canopy bed, drapes hanging from the four corners.

I am alive...

How? He wasn't burning in the fires of hell. His head wasn't filled with tar. The pain in his side wasn't an agonizing, spreading incineration that conquered his body like a despotic king.

Instead, he felt tired. His eyelids were heavy, his body as weak as a kitten.

A tiny stab in his shoulder, like a bee sting, had him slap it with his other hand...only to find a warm arm blocking his palm. He looked up and stopped breathing.

"Don't you dare move, Aulay," Jenny said.

Her eyebrows were drawn together, her eyes focused on his shoulder. That was the look of concentration she had when she was healing.

When he looked at his shoulder, there was a thin, transparent object in her hand like a long stick, with black, even lines along its length. She was pushing another stick that went inside the cylinder with her thumb, and a transparent liquid moved down. The whole thing was attached to his shoulder, and that was what stung.

"What the hell are ye doing to me?" he growled.

He meant for it to sound threatening, but his voice was weak.

She removed the object, pressed a white ball of something like cloth against the wee wound, and put a small square of another thin cloth that stuck to his skin on top of it. When he looked at the cylinder, it had a small, thin needle at its edge.

She put a long, thin cap over it and beamed at him, the focused, bossy physician gone. "It's an antibiotic."

Before he could ask what was an antibiotic, she leaned down and kissed him, her lips lush and soft and delicious. He'd just raised his weak arms to wrap her in his embrace when she pulled back and pressed the back of her hand against his forehead.

She nodded and rewarded him with another smile that melted his heart. "Much better."

Questions bumped in his head. What had happened? What was an antibiotic? Why was he alive? But the most important one was... "Why are ye still here, lass? I told ye to leave..."

"I'm here because this is where I belong, silly." She gently cupped his jaw, and he leaned into her soft palm. "With you."

His heart pumped against his rib cage. "Keep saying those words, lass, and I'll get back to life better than with any miraculous treatment."

She giggled and sat at the edge of his bed and laid her hand on his chest. He covered it with his palm. "I'll keep saying them every day. But it was the antibiotic that saved your life. Your wound got infected. You were dying. When you told me about the rock on Islay that I could use, I went there right away and traveled to the future. A nice lady helped me to find medicine and return here. The antibiotic did the rest. It killed the bacteria that caused your infection, and your wound is now healing nicely." She gave him a broad smile. "You'll live, Aulay. A long and happy life. With me."

A long and happy life with her...

Everything became very still and quiet. The chirping of birds from behind the slit window stopped, the sound of shuffling feet from somewhere behind the castle door silenced. His breath halted. The only sound that was left was the deafening drumming of his aching, hoping, bursting heart.

He moved his elbows to try to sit upright, but there was not enough strength in his muscles, and he sagged back into the bed.

"God's blood, I hate feeling weak like this," he muttered.

"Stay put, MacZeus. I know you're almighty and powerful, and it's hard for you to be weak. But your body needs to heal. You lost enough blood to fill the Irish Sea. I'm ordering you to lie back and rest."

He couldn't help but chuckle. "I like it when ye command me like that... I do prefer it in bed, though."

She licked her lips, and a bonnie blush covered her cheeks. Her eyelashes cast shadows over her skin. "Easy, tiger. I'll command you in bed all you want. But that'll have to wait."

He looked her over. She was in the blue dress he remembered her wearing the day she sneaked onto his ship. She hadn't changed, hadn't rested. Dark circles were prominent under her eyes. She looked paler and thinner.

"Did ye eat at all, lass?" he asked.

"Oh yes, of course. Mhairi is sending Laoghaire regularly with food and water. Mhairi can't walk yet, but both she and Sìomon are doing very well."

"'Tis good. I'm glad to hear Mhairi and the bairn are well. But Laoghaire?" He frowned. "She was never yer best friend."

"No, but she was very thankful and impressed with Mhairi and Sìomon. I think she's a sweet girl, actually, underneath her sharp tongue."

Aulay let a long sigh out. "Lass. Ye'd be better off in the future. When ye were there, didna ye change yer mind? Dinna ye want, still, to have yer own bairn?"

She chuckled. "The thought crossed my mind—I'm not going to lie. But I love you, Aulay. And I chose you."

Warmth spilled through his veins. She was in love with him... They stared at each other. Something beautiful blossomed between them, an understanding, a feeling that bound them and connected them in a cocoon of warmth and acceptance.

"And I realized I want to be a mother to a child, and it doesn't matter if it's a child of my own body or not."

"Ye're right, lass. And there's a wee bonnie bairn ye ken who lost both her ma and her da and needs a family to love her. Ye can be her mother and give her all the love ye've always wanted to give to yer own bairn. And I can raise her and teach her, and bounce her on my knee."

"Una." Tears filled Jenny's eyes. She blinked and smiled and nodded enthusiastically. "Beathan told me, 'Sometimes 'tis the family God lets ye find that matters the most.' It was as though he was giving me his blessing to adopt Una, even though he never knew it back then. You and Una will be mine...if you still want that."

A warm, light emotion rose up through his chest and tightened his throat.

"If I still want that..." he muttered. "Aye, of course I still want that. 'Tis what I live for, lass. For ye...for a life with ye and with a wee daughter."

Her smile broadened, but her eyes watered. "But Aulay...I would never be able to give you your own children. Do you really understand that?"

"I do, lass. I've done my duty as the laird of this clan. I can be proud of the legacy that I leave behind."

"You can. You know, in Islay, even seven hundred years from now, people know who you were and honor your memory. Philippa MacDonald, the lady who helped me, knew about you. Your legacy is so much more than you can imagine. It'll stay for centuries after you."

He couldn't breathe. "Ye dinna ken what this means to me, lass. Ye brought me peace. Ye brought me love. Ye brought me back to life."

She gave him a cheeky gaze that melted his heart. "So... You still want to marry me, then?"

Surprising himself with the strength in his arms, he grasped her by the shoulders and pulled her to him. His wound complained, but he didn't care. Jenny giggled as she settled comfortably on his chest.

"Aye, lass. I love ye. Ye gave back life to my very soul. Ye filled the emptiness in me. I want to give an oath to the whole world that ye're mine and I'm yers."

She smiled. "I'm already yours, silly. And I will always be."

EPILOGUE

Two months later...

"The itsy, bitsy spider climbed up the waterspout..." Jenny sang over Una, joining the thumb and index finger on each of her hands, then making a twisting motion as she raised them.

Una, who was now eight months old, giggled, sitting in the high chair next to her at the great table. Jenny had ordered the chair from the village carpenter based on the design of twenty-first-century high chairs.

Through the hum and the music of their wedding feast around them, Aulay joined Jenny's song.

"Down came the rain and washed the spider out..." he boomed with his gorgeous Gaelic accent.

He had such a deep, masculine voice, like the drone of a jazz singer. As if hypnotized, Una stopped giggling and gave him the broadest one-tooth smile from ear to ear. She reached out with her little hand and brushed her tiny fingers through his short beard.

"Out came the sun and dried up all the rain..." continued Jenny, giggling. She loved seeing them like this. The love and tenderness Aulay showed Una made Jenny tear up every single time. And now, at their wedding feast, she and Una wore matching pale blue gowns with golden embroidered fronts.

"And the itsy-bitsy spider climbed up the spout again!" concluded Aulay loudly, and Una waved her arms in excitement. "Whatever 'spout' means..." he sang in the same melody.

Jenny giggled. "I told you, it's a tube or a channel for water. Every house has them to let rainwater down from the roof."

"Aye." He kissed her cheek. "I ken. Hard to imagine every house having that."

"Having what?" asked Colum, who approached the great table from the other side. He wriggled his fingers and winked at little Una, who squealed in delight.

Behind him, the great hall swarmed with people. Along five rows of long tables, dozens of guests ate, drank, talked, and laughed. The whole of clan MacDonald was here, including warriors, but also simple people, like farmers, tradespeople, and villagers.

A music platform had been erected at the end of the hall, and musicians played a cheerful medieval tune.

The hall was decorated for the feast. Jenny had insisted on fresh flowers, so only those that still bloomed in September decorated the walls and the tables: bluebells, heather, thistle, and some white wildflowers Jenny didn't know the name of.

Tables burst with dishes. Roasted swans, grilled boars, salmon, and partridge. Pastries, pies—both sweet and savory—cheeses, fresh bread, and so much wine, ale, and beer. Cup bearers ran around, pouring the drinks freely. Dogs sniffed about, hoping for some table scraps. Children played between the rows. Laughter, squeals, and singing were all a loud hum.

Jenny didn't feel like a stranger here anymore. People weren't trying to burn her at the stake. They'd completely changed their minds about her after what she had done for Mhairi and Sìomon and after she had saved their laird's life.

Mhairi and Sìomon were thriving. Jenny watched Mhairi and

Seoras sitting next to each other at the long table, cooing over their swaddled son. While Mhairi was recovering, Laoghaire had volunteered to watch over the orphans and surprised everyone with her kind but disciplined ruling over them. Somehow, even boys adored her lessons about manners and dancing. Girls learned from her how to run a household and sew clothes. But also, Laoghaire blossomed with them and smiled broadly and often.

Jenny could hardly imagine that she'd wished she and her girlfriends had gone to Hawaii instead. She loved Scotland—the rugged, dramatic landscape of Islay, the murmur of the sea, the loyalty of the people. She'd always miss her family and friends in the twenty-first century, but she'd found an even bigger family here.

Esteemed allied clans were also present—the Mackenzies, Cambels, Ruaidhrís, and others. With astonishment, Jenny had learned that she was not the only time traveler when she'd met Amy, Amber, and Kate of clan Cambel and Rogene Mackenzie and her brother, David, as well as James, who'd married Catrìona Mackenzie.

"Spouts," said Jenny to Colum, before explaining their use.

"Ah, Aunt," said Colum and winked. "It astonishes me what things ye ken..."

It was the first time he'd called her Aunt, and Jenny frowned. "I'm like eight years older than you! Please don't call me Aunt. It makes me feel old. Call Aulay Uncle all you like. He's the old man here."

"Ye ken what I do to ye when ye call me old," Aulay growled, and Colum blinked and look away.

Oh yes. She knew. Jenny had wanted him to wait for six weeks after his injury, the time usually advised by surgeons. But he couldn't. Against his doctor's wishes, he started making love to her. Granted, he did it gently, letting her do most of the work.

She was just as guilty—his touch had the power to make her

as horny as a cat in spring. And so, she broke her own recommendation with him...often!

"Aulay!" she said, feeling heat flushing her cheeks.

"We still need to consummate the marriage," he said. "Or someone might question its legality."

Colum cleared his throat loudly. "Ahem. I wanted to say, a ship just docked at the port—"

Before he could finish speaking, the large doors to the great hall opened, and a tall man with a group of warriors strode in. The musicians stopped playing. The hubbub of voices died out. Children froze and stared at the man in awe.

He was tall, broad-shouldered, and middle-aged. His shoulder-length hair was dark with some strands of silver. He wasn't particularly good-looking, didn't have any other distinguishing features, except for his posture. He stood with his back and broad shoulders straight, his chin lifted.

At one of the nearby tables, someone squealed and jumped up. It was Anna, Aulay's niece, who was married to David Wakeley.

Anna hurried down the aisle. She was expecting, even though her slim figure was still not showing, but everyone knew she was carrying another potential heir to Aulay's legacy.

Anna dropped to a curtsy before the man. He looked at her with warmth, then let her stand and grasped her in a bear hug—very unusual for the Middle Ages.

"'Tis our king, Jenny," said Aulay with pride as he stood from his seat. "Robert the Bruce."

Jenny raised her eyebrows. She knew Aulay and the king were great allies and friends, but they hadn't known if the Bruce would make it to their wedding with so much happening on the English border.

When the Bruce let go of Anna, his illegitimate daughter, he marched down the aisle towards the great table. Jenny stood up and curtsied as Anna had taught her. Aulay and Colum greeted their king. Robert walked around the table and took an honorable seat next to Aulay.

"I appreciate ye came, Yer Grace," said Aulay.

"Aye," said Robert the Bruce, eyeing Jenny with curiosity. "I appreciate the invitation. I couldna come earlier. We are preparing to siege the Isle of Man. I hope I can count on yer birlinns and on the English treasure, swords, and armor ye found."

"Aye," said Aulay. "Ye can always count on me, my king."

Bruce clapped Aulay on the shoulder. Jenny poured him a cup of wine and he raised it gratefully.

"And ye, too, Colum? Will ye come to fight?" Bruce asked Colum, who was still standing at the other side of the table. Jenny had the sense that Colum had no one else to talk to in the clan. The only one that he was real friends with was Aulay.

"Ye ken I always will, Yer Grace," Colum said. "Any news of Queen Elizabeth and yer daughter Marjorie?"

Bruce sighed deeply and drank the whole cup of wine in one go. "They're still kept with the English. But we must start to prepare for what's to come next year. By John the Baptist next year, the English army will come to Stirling. I heard rumors Edward already started gathering an army. Word is out all over Europe for the best knights to gather in London and go to Scotland for riches, land, and glory." Bruce scoffed. "They're already dividing our castles among each other, the pigs. But they dinna ken us. With ye, Aulay, and Colum, with my loyal clans Mackenzie and Cambel and Ruaidhrí, we will show them what Scottish steel is worth."

"Aye, Yer Grace," said Colum.

"Ye will have to gather come next spring near Stirling. There's a wee place called Bannockburn. We will set camp around there and start training men. Everyone is welcome to come. Young. Old. Warriors. Farmers. This battle will define Scotland's future for centuries to come."

Jenny had heard about the Battle of Bannockburn, but only

vaguely. Still, it was one of those legendary events in history everyone knew of. She caught Rogene's eye. She was a historian, so she knew much more about these things. It was amazing to see history unfold before her eyes, a doctor, who had nothing to do with history. It must have been ten times more thrilling for a historian like Rogene to see what she'd learned about come to life.

"Everyone will be there, Yer Grace," said Aulay.

"Me, too," Jenny said. "You'll need a good doctor... um...physician."

Bruce glanced at her with curiosity. "Are ye a physician, my lady?"

"Yes."

"Jenny saved my life from a rot-wound," said Aulay with pride. "And she saved my grandnephew, Sìomon, and his mother using something called a cesarean section. She cut the womb open to get the child, then sewed it closed."

Bruce's eyes widened. Jenny poured him more wine, and he took a sip, eyeing her.

"We will need a skilled physician, Lady MacDonald. I am impressed a woman possesses such skills for professions regularly performed by men. My respect."

She smiled. "Thank you. I'll help in any way I can."

"She even started a hospital here at Dunyvaig," said Aulay. "And already physicians and midwives from the mainland have arrived to be taught. Our own physician, Bhatair, didna trust a woman at first. But now he's her biggest advocate and invited his colleagues with whom he studied in Paris to come and learn from her."

Bruce raised his eyebrows and nodded slowly. "Most impressive. Careful, Aulay, I may call upon her to serve at my court once the war is over."

Jenny smiled. "I appreciate it, Your Grace, and I'll happily help next year in Stirling, but I can't be separated from our daughter, Una."

She let her daughter curl her little fist around Jenny's index finger. The tiny palm was warm and just a bit sweaty. And just the touch of her baby brought a warm tingling of motherly love around her palm.

"Aye," said Bruce, "I respect that."

"Ye can count on my clan," said Aulay.

"And on me, Yer Grace," said Colum. "I'll do everything to prove myself to Scotland and my clan. Nae matter what."

Bruce clunked his cup of wine with Colum's. "We need more men like ye, Colum. Ye have my highest regard and respect. For everything ye did for me and my family."

Jenny watched Colum's eyes darken, and he threw the whole cup of wine back into his throat. Aulay must have seen the glint of something in his eyes, too.

"Colum," Aulay said, "'tis good ye're trying to prove yerself. But remember there is more to life than just the war. Take it from me. I never thought I would love again or get marrit. Mayhap ye should think about finding a wife, too."

Colum scoffed.

"What woman would want to marry a man who'd turned traitor, Uncle?"

Bruce sighed deeply. "Yer uncle is nae wrong, Colum. The right woman would see past the wounds and failures of yer past."

Jenny exchanged a long, deep gaze with Aulay and kissed him briefly on the lips.

"She certainly will," she said.

She didn't know who she was saying this to. Colum, Aulay, whom she loved more than life itself, or the king.

Or perhaps she was saying it to herself. In that crazy adventure that was her summer vacation in Scotland, she'd traveled back in time to the love of her life. The Highland laird from an earlier time.

She'd seen past her own wounds and realized she could be all that she ever wanted—a wife and a mother and a doctor—

without giving up any part of herself. Thanks to that, she'd found happiness.

He'd claimed her through time.

But most importantly, she'd risen up and claimed him right back.

THANK YOU FOR READING HIGHLANDER'S CLAIM. FIND out what happens next when Aulay's nephew Colum meets Danielle, his soulmate from the future, in HIGHLANDER'S DESTINY.

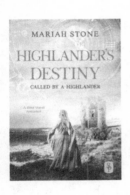

FIERY PASSION. FIERCE ENEMIES. Forbidden attraction. A modern British spy and a medieval Highlander fight for a shared destiny of love and freedom.

READ HIGHLANDER'S DESTINY NOW >

⭐⭐⭐⭐⭐ *"This is the most heart-wrenching story in all of history."*

SIGN-UP FOR MARIAH STONE'S NEWSLETTER:
http://mariahstone.com/signup

FANCY A VIKING?

And other mysterious matchmakers are sending modern-day people to the past too, also to the Viking Age. If you haven't read Holly and Einar's story yet, be sure to pick up VIKING'S DESIRE.

A captive time traveler. A Viking jarl on a mission. Will marriage be the price of her freedom?

READ VIKING'S DESIRE NOW >

⭐⭐⭐⭐⭐ *"Fabulous! What a great way to start a new series!"*

OR STAY IN THE HIGHLANDS AND KEEP READING FOR AN excerpt from HIGHLANDER'S DESTINY.

~

LANDS NEAR STIRLING, JUNE 2022

THE VAST LANDS OF BANNOCKBURN SPREAD OUT BELOW WHERE Danielle Field stood on top of a hill. It was nice to breathe in the fresh air that smelled of trees and grass and flowers. She recognized thistle, Scottish bluebells, and the small white flowers of cow parsley blanketing the grassy hill.

The town of Bannockburn, with its gray and orange roofs, extended over a large area. These days, it was part of the city of Stirling. Back in the Middle Ages, this was the site of the famous Battle of Bannockburn. The reenactment of the battle would take place in a bright green field where triangular and round canvas tents and a few pavilions had been raised. Dozens of people in medieval clothes trained on swords, shot arrows, and made formations commanded by horsemen. People lined around the perimeter, watching them rehearse for the reenactment, on June 23.

As much as Danielle loved plants, her sister, Jamie, loved history.

"You see the statue of Robert the Bruce?" Jamie asked, leaning towards Danielle and pointing at the statue close to the Bannockburn visitor center. Jamie worked in the museum at Stirling Castle, and was excited to be one of the coordinators of the reenactment for the first time.

By her side stood a medieval warrior. He wore chain mail and a chain mail coif and watched the practice with a dreamy expression. A local actor named Liam, he certainly suited the role, with his ear-length red hair and short beard.

When Danielle had arrived to visit Jamie at the visitor center, he'd volunteered to come for a walk with them. Based on the glances Jamie kept exchanging with him, there must be something going on between him and her little sister. Alarm bells rang in Danielle's head. Could she trust this bloke to treat her sister well? She scanned him for any signs of there being something off. But he seemed a regular chap who was too much into history.

"Yes, I see it," Danielle said. It was a large bronze statue of Robert the Bruce on a horse, atop a tall pedestal.

"Fun fact," said Jamie, her crystal-blue eyes sparkling. "It was built in 1964 by Pikington Jackson for the Earl of Elgin."

Liam nodded seriously. Danielle giggled and hugged her sister by the shoulders. She was as tall as Danielle and built in a similar way: narrow hips, barely any waist, flat chest. The mean girls in high school had called her a stick.

"Only you would call that a fun fact," said Danielle.

Liam looked at her, puzzled. He must have found it fun, too.

Danielle grinned. "I missed you. It's good to take my mind off work."

Jamie looked at her. "Yes. Work. You came to visit so suddenly. Don't you have some important operation or something?"

Danielle crossed arms over her chest and shifted her weight.

The best way to spoil the mood was to think about work right now. "Not anymore."

"Where do you work?" asked Liam.

"She's in MI5," Jamie told him conspiratorially.

Liam blinked at her and looked her over. "You? A spy?"

Danielle gave him a forced smile. This was why she was glad she didn't meet many new people outside of work. Because she either had to lie about what she really did, or she would get reactions like that. She had told Jamie and their parents not to tell people, but of course they did.

"I'm not a spy. I'm an investigator."

He whistled. "A real-life female James Bond."

"She really is!" Jamie said.

No, Jamie. She really must like this man if she kept trying to make sure he was impressed.

"Not James Bond, Liam," Danielle said. "I help prevent cyber-attacks and sit at the computer all day. It's quite boring, actually."

That was what did the trick to tone down the curiosity in people like Liam who asked too many questions.

"But didn't you have a special operation in Venezuela...or Colombia or something?" insisted Jamie.

Danielle tensed. Jamie shouldn't know more than she was supposed to. Not only was Danielle now under investigation at work, but she might also get fired in less than a week. Yes, she had had an operation in Venezuela. Her informant, Juan, had gone missing. He'd since been found and was now in the UK receiving psychological care. She was on suspension while her bosses led the investigation. The hearing was in five days, and she was going back to London tomorrow for the first interview. Truly, it had been her own mistake in judgment.

The mission was meant to prevent a large-scale cyberattack where hackers planned to break into UK bank security systems to steal private information and money. Juan had gone to meet with a known and highly sought-after hacker.

And hadn't come back.

And the cyberattack had happened, but they'd managed to stop any money being transferred. The hacker was still out there. After disappearing for a month, Juan had been found, suffering from PTSD. And who knew what he had told the cybercriminals?

They worked with a local gang that took care of roughing up anyone who crossed them.

"Darling," Danielle said, "you know I can't talk about details with anyone."

Liam put his hands on his waist. "Jamie Field, what other secrets do you have?" He shook his head, an admiring grin on his face.

Yes. The bloke liked Jamie. Protective instincts had Danielle clench her hands into fists.

His face fell when he looked at her. "Wait...Field..." He frowned, and Danielle's gut twisted. "Danielle Field, right?"

Danielle swallowed hard. He'd made the connection surprisingly quickly.

"You're that girl, right?" he insisted. "That girl that got kidnapped and kept in a basement by that psycho?"

Jamie's face got a worried look. "Um..." she said.

Danielle spread her hands wide. "Yes, Liam. I'm that girl."

"Oh. Bugger." He looked her over with different eyes now. Surprise. Pity. Suspicion that something may be wrong with her. Those were the typical things she'd seen on people's faces once they found out. "How are you?"

She gave a fake smile. "I'm fine, as you can see. I'm alive."

Well, that was debatable. She was alive. But she had no life. No friends. No relationships. No boyfriends.

It was better that way. Trust was what had led her into that bastard's basement. Sixteen years ago, he'd taught her a valuable lesson. To never trust anyone.

So her work was perfect, really. It was about keeping her

distance and being observant and studying patterns. And since she didn't want relationships anyway, that was just as well.

"She's fine," said Jamie with a nervous smile.

"God, I remember that story," said Liam. "It was all over the news. Your whole town went searching for you, didn't they? Not just the police. And you were right next door at your neighbor's the whole time. I remember telling my mum I wanted to go and help. She didn't let me, of course. You were down in London. I was here in Stirling. But when they found you, every newspaper wrote about you."

Danielle nodded and pursed her lips. Not everyone in Britain remembered that story, but apparently Liam did.

"Yes," she said, trying to focus on the groups of people that marched in round formations across the field. "They did. Listen, Liam—"

She was about to tell him she didn't want to talk about it, when Jamie's phone rang loudly.

"Hello?" she answered, clearly relieved not to talk about Danielle's kidnapping any longer. "Oh, yes, we'll be right back."

She hung up and looked at Liam. "We need to go back." She squeezed Danielle's hand. "Sorry, hun. But you have the key for my flat, and I'll meet you there later after work. We'll go to the pub and have dinner."

Liam looked sheepish. "I'd like to join, if that's all right?"

No, it wasn't. Her sister was her best friend, and she longed to spend time with her.

"Great," Danielle said.

Jamie beamed. Liam was important to her, Danielle could tell. Ah, well. More chances to check this man out.

"Okay," Jamie said, kissed Danielle, and the two of them were off down the slope. Danielle watched them walk into the distance, then looked around. While they had talked, the sky had become very dark. Wind picked up, and droplets of rain hit her face.

There was a grove of trees five hundred or so feet away. She picked up her purse and hurried there to hide from the weather. As she ran, the rain started pouring down, and as she gained the protection of the trees, the scent of rain reached her nostrils. Raindrops battered against the leaves above her. She didn't have an umbrella, but standing in a clearing under the thick branches wasn't that bad.

She walked to a boulder and sat down. Looking around, she saw there were several large boulders and the barely noticeable remnants of old mortar between rough rocks. Why hadn't Jamie mentioned anything about this? Usually, she'd be chatting about how this was a remnant from the ninth century or however old it was.

Danielle looked into the grayish curtain beyond the line of the tree crowns. She'd wait out the rain and then go back to Jamie's flat. She'd also try to be more understanding and trusting about Liam.

Gazing around, she noticed some sort of a carving on one of the stones. Curious, she approached it. The rock was very old and crumbled, but she could just make out a carving of a handprint. The other carvings were worn away, too, looking more like wrinkles in the stone.

She put her hand on the rock. It was cool and smooth. A vibration went through her, like a small earthquake. The carvings began to glow.

She snatched her hand back and stood up.

Glow? Stone?

Then there was a sharp scent of grass and lavender, and as though out of nowhere, a woman appeared next to the rock. Danielle stared at her, carefully watching for signs of danger.

The woman beamed at her. She had the pleasant appearance of a girl next door, with a round, strawberry-shaped face, a pointy nose, and big green eyes. She had long red hair that streamed from under a hood. And a medieval dress was visible under her green cloak.

"Did you come from the reenactment practice?" Danielle asked.

The woman giggled. "Ye can say that." She had a strong Scottish accent and a melodic voice.

Was that a yes or a no? Maybe she was Liam's friend, or maybe she knew Jamie. "Right," she said. "Well. Looks like we're stuck here for a while."

"We dinna need to be. My name is Sìneag. I just opened the tunnel through time for ye. Ye should go through it."

Danielle laughed. "What?"

"Did ye see the stone glow?"

"Yes."

"It means the tunnel is open for ye. If ye put yer hand on that rock, ye will go into the tunnel through the river of time. At the other end, there's a person that's destined for ye."

Danielle couldn't believe her ears. She'd heard a lot of interesting stories and explanations through the years, but never anything as ludicrous as time travel and tunnels through time and fated mates.

She crossed her arms over her chest. "Right. Humor me. Who's that person?"

"Colum MacDonald. A Highland warrior. A man of honor. A man ye can trust."

Danielle raised an eyebrow.

"Because ye dinna trust anyone, do ye?" Sìneag said, narrowing her eyes at her. "Even yerself. 'Tis why ye let that man take ye and hold ye captive."

Danielle felt her face fall. "How do you know? Did Liam tell you? Jamie couldn't have done this to me..."

Sìneag smiled. "I can see into yer heart, love. Ye're lonely. Colum is lonely, too. Together, ye are two parts of a whole. Ye can help each other heal."

Danielle shook her head and scoffed. "Look...it's an interesting story and all, but come on. We're both adults."

"Ye dinna believe me?" Sineag's eyes glistened with mischief. "Ye dinna trust me."

"No, of course not."

"So what's the harm in trying, then? Prove me wrong. Prove 'tis all children's stories. Touch the stone."

Danielle froze. Her gut told her not to do it. It twisted and turned and churned. Like back when she was sixteen and Sebastian, the new, young neighbor she'd had a crush on, had invited her to play chess with him and prove she could beat him.

The next time she'd leave that house would be about a month later, under the protection of the police, rolled out on a gurney towards a waiting ambulance.

But her logical mind kept telling her this was impossible. Some woman she'd never met before came and told her about a soulmate who was back through time?

"Nonsense," Danielle said. "Sure. But once I touch the stone, would you please not talk about soulmates and time travel and so on?"

Sineag smiled, and Danielle didn't like the glint in her eyes at all. "Aye, lass."

Danielle sank to her knees by the rock, and there it was, that strange pull again. *Don't do it!* her gut yelled. But what did her gut know when there were no signs of anything being the matter? She didn't trust herself. The strange woman was right about that.

She placed her hand into the handprint. But she found no stone under her palm. Instead, there was cool air, and something sucking her in, and she was falling, tumbling down headfirst into the darkness. Panic squeezed her stomach, and shock hit her like an icy wave. Her gut was right. Whatever this was, she shouldn't have done it.

And then there was only darkness...

Keep reading HIGHLANDER'S DESTINY.

ALSO BY MARIAH STONE

MARIAH'S TIME TRAVEL ROMANCE SERIES

- CALLED BY A HIGHLANDER
- CALLED BY A VIKING
- CALLED BY A PIRATE
- FATED

~

MARIAH'S REGENCY ROMANCE SERIES

- DUKES AND SECRETS

~

VIEW ALL OF MARIAH'S BOOKS IN READING ORDER

Scan the QR code for the complete list of Mariah's ebooks, paperbacks, and audiobooks in reading order.

GET A FREE MARIAH STONE BOOK!

Join Mariah's mailing list to be the first to know of new releases, free books, special prices, and other author giveaways.

freehistoricalromancebooks.com

ENJOY THE BOOK? YOU CAN MAKE A DIFFERENCE!

Please, leave your honest review for the book.
As much as I'd love to, I don't have financial capacity like New York publishers to run ads in the newspaper or put posters in subway.

But I have something much, much more powerful!

Committed and loyal readers

If you enjoyed the book, I'd be so grateful if you could spend five minutes leaving a review on the book's Amazon page.

Thank you very much!

SCOTTISH SLANG

aye – yes
> **bairn** - baby
> **bastart** - bastard
> **bonnie** - pretty, beautiful.
> **canna**- can not
> **couldna** – couldn't
> **didna**- didn't ("Ah didna do that!")
> **dinna**- don't ("Dinna do that!")
> **doesna** – doesn't
> **fash** - fuss, worry ("Dinna fash yerself.")
> **feck** - fuck
> **hasna** – has not
> **havna** - have not
> **hadna** – had not
> **innit?** - Isn't it?
> **isna**- Is not
> **ken** - to know
> **kent** - knew
> **lad** - boy
> **lass** - girl
> **marrit** – married

nae – no or not

shite - faeces

the morn - tomorrow

the morn's morn - tomorrow morning

uisge-beatha (uisge for short) – Scottish Gaelic for water or life / aquavitae, the distilled drink, predecessor of whiskey

verra – very

wasna - was not

wee - small

wilna - will not

wouldna - would not

ye - you

yer – your (also yerself)

ABOUT THE AUTHOR

When time travel romance writer Mariah Stone isn't busy writing strong modern women falling back through time into the arms of hot Vikings, Highlanders, and pirates, she chases after her toddler and spends romantic nights on North Sea with her husband.

Mariah speaks six languages, loves Outlander, sushi and Thai food, and runs a local writer's group. Subscribe to Mariah's newsletter for a free time travel book today!

- facebook.com/mariahstoneauthor
- instagram.com/mariahstoneauthor
- bookbub.com/authors/mariah-stone
- pinterest.com/mariahstoneauthor
- amazon.com/Mariah-Stone/e/B07JVW28PJ

Made in the USA
Middletown, DE
12 February 2024